The Secret of Christmas

BookSurge, LLC
5341 Dorchester Rd, Suite 16
North Charleston, SC 29418-5618

Printed in the United States of America on acid-free paper.

The Secret of Christmas

Designed by Vicent Squeglia

Publisher's Note: *This is a work of fiction. Names, characters, places, and incidents either are the product of the author's imagination or, are used fictitiously, and any resemblance to actual persons, living or dead, events, or locales is entirely coincidental.*

Library of Congress Cataloging-in-Publication Data is available upon request.

ISBN 1-58982-131-9

Reiter, Bernadette G. and Pélissié, Jean-Marie, The Secret of Christmas

---

Special Sales

These books are available at special discounts for bulk purchases. Special editions, including personalized covers, excerpts of existing books, and corporate imprints, can be created in large quantities for special needs. For more information call
866-308-6235

The Secret of Christmas

Bernadette G. Reiter
and
Jean-Marie Pélissié

Dedication

*This book is dedicated
to all little boys and girls
who have lost a parent.*

Foreword

In our time, so burdened by terrorism and war, we need stories of courage, love, and hope as never before. This is such a story. It is for children and adults of all ages, especially for those who lost a parent when they were young or even old. It involves a little girl and her mother—grieving over her husband's untimely death—and a little dog. I don't want to give away the story because that would be unkind to the reader. It would deprive him or her of an unforgettable experience.

Perhaps the best way to write the foreword for this wonderful story is to tell how I related to it myself.

When I was five years old—the age of the little girl in the story—Hitler took over my hometown, Vienna, Austria. I remember the scene like a flashlight memory: the cheering crowd was all around us as I held the hand of Lisle, my governess. I looked at Hitler passing by slowly in his Mercedes and fixed my eyes on his mustache.

"Just like Papa," I thought. My beloved father, who used to tickle the soles of my feet with his mustache as he kissed them and who had disappeared without a trace. I had been heartbroken when Papa vanished. I looked for him for weeks convinced that it was my fault that he had gone away. I promised my mother that I would never be bad again…just to have him back.

One day, I thought I saw him on the street and ran in front of an on coming car. Luckily, the driver braked just in time and I escaped with only a few bruises. "For a boy of five, you shouldn't be so careless," the doctor warned me. Nevertheless, I thought I saw Papa everywhere. The pain was like a wild animal living inside of me. Gradually its grip lessened, but never did it leave me entirely.

Papa's sudden disappearance remained a mystery. My mother, seeing that I was inconsolable in my inability to understand the situation, got me a puppy that I named Raxi. The little dog and I became inseparable and he became my greatest source of comfort. When my mother told me that we had to leave Vienna and join my grandparents in Prague, my first question was whether or not Raxi could come along with us. He remained my companion during an odyssey that took my mother and new stepfather via Siberia, Russia, all the way to Shanghai, China, where we lived under Japanese occupation until the end of World War II in 1945. I refused to part from Raxi and made my mother agree to take him along with us to what seemed the end of the world.

When the Allies came to liberate Shanghai, I became a shoeshine boy and, after six months of polishing the shoes of American soldiers, I got lucky. A kindhearted American soldier took me under his wing and promised to write to his alma mater, Grinnell College in Iowa. Three months later I received a scholarship and got myself a job as a dockhand to work my way on a converted troop transport ship. I pleaded with the crew to let me take Raxi along, but they told me it was against the rules. Raxi and I had to part after ten years of him giving me unconditional love.

When I received my Ph.D. at Harvard in 1954, my mother and stepfather were there and so was the lieutenant whose shoes I had shined. I shined them one last time in gratitude. I was able to see Raxi many more times until finally he died in his sleep.

The Secret of Christmas teaches that each one of us can find heaven. You, the reader, will discover an amazing little girl's story. I found the possibility of heaven in America. When I got off that ship under the Golden Gate Bridge in San Francisco more than half a century ago I fell to my knees and kissed the American soil. I never got over that feeling. The love and courage of good people and the unconditional love of a little dog sustained me to live through the darkness. *The Secret of Christmas* will speak to everyone and will refresh the hearts of anyone who faces grief and loss. It's bound to become a classic on a par with Oscar Wilde's *The Happy Prince* and *The Selfish Giant*.

JOHN STOESSINGER

Former Director of Political Affairs Division of the United Nations, presently professor of Global Diplomacy as the University of San Diego, and published author

Chapter One

Night settled over the little town enveloped in snow, looking much like a postcard announcing the beginning of Christmas Eve's last-minute hustle. Lights blinked from roof edges outlining houses as lazy curls of smoke drifted to the sky to merge with the laden clouds. A quiet hush cocooned the sleeping town.

Dreams drifted down in a swirl of light, fluffy snowflakes to a child who slept cuddled with her faded, rumpled bear. Nicole, little Nickie, wandered in the heavens at night in dreams spun from imagination and innocence.

In her fog-like dream it was a spring morning with never-ending rolling meadows and flowers dancing in gentle breezes. Nickie turned in slow motion. It was as if she had been dropped into a fuzzy-edged bathroom tissue commercial.

She romped through pastoral splendor. She was happy because she was with her daddy. Daddy, who made everything soft like Charmin commercials on TV. Daddy, who made everything safe and colorful like springtime.

Yet an unseen force gripped Nicole and forcefully pulled her away from her father. Desperately they reached for each other, as the very air around them seemed to darken suddenly.

"Daddy!"

Nickie woke up from the nightmare breathing hard. She felt sweaty and terrified. The once-familiar room was now a black and frightening empty space. Clutching her bear under one small arm, she jumped from her bed and ran whimpering out of her room. Little bare feet hardly touched the cold oak floor as she raced toward the safety of her mother's bedroom. She stopped in front of the door, turned the shiny brass knob, and pushed it open.

Rebecca Halstead was in a deep sleep rehearsing the preparations for the Christmas party to make it perfect. She had to make it perfect. It was her responsibility after all. It should have been her husband conducting the annual company festivities. Lately Rebecca felt like the weight of her obligations made her hundreds of years old instead of the mere thirty-three that she was, but in her dreams she didn't have time to think about herself. She had to pick up the pieces of her life and give the employees the illusion that everything was normal. It was a stability her husband could inspire by simply showing his unique genius and exercising his unwavering drive to succeed.

Nickie stepped quietly into her mother's dark room, trying to hold her breath in case it disturbed Mommy's dreams, but all the control broke down and quiet crying spilled out. As Nickie approached the bed, she saw her mommy and brightened. Eager to erase the bad dream, she pounced on her with the exuberance of a kitten ready to play.

It startled Rebecca to be awakened out of a well-orchestrated dream. She fumbled, trying to find the knob to turn on the mauve, stained glass Tiffany lamp on the night table. When the soft light illuminated the room, she pulled her frightened daughter into her arms and caressed her with comforting words.

"Nickie, honey, is that you? Come to Mommy."

She maneuvered Nickie into a more comfortable position next to her and stroked her curly, blond, chin-length hair as she whispered soothing words. "There you go…hey, hey…what are you so upset about? My little angel had a bad dream?"

Nickie nodded, determined to let her mommy know she was brave and yet scared that if she closed her eyes, the sadness would come back.

"Was it about Daddy again?" Becca—as her husband used to call her—gently coaxed the contents of the nightmare.

Nickie burst into deep sobs and buried herself in her mother's chest. Becca held her, twirling Nickie's hair and letting soft, coiled locks wrap around her fingers. She smoothed the curls off her face and kissed her little frown-creased forehead and button nose. It was hard to believe Nickie was nearly five years old, yet nestled in her arms she was still her little baby, she even smelled like baby shampoo.

"There, there. Sh, sh." As Becca rocked her, she wondered whether the consoling words were for Nickie's sake or her own. "We shouldn't worry about Daddy anymore, Nickie. Daddy's in Heaven now, and I know he's happy there. He wants us to be happy, too. Do you think you can be happy for Daddy and go to sleep now?"

Nickie nodded and dried her tears with the back of her hand. Rebecca felt her starting to go limp and arranged the bedding around her, tucking invisible security around her precious little child. She traced her round face and the outline of her heart-shaped lips. Nickie cuddled closer and poked her toes against Becca's shin.

Becca held her tight. She remembered how just last summer they both went to the park with a picnic lunch waiting for Daddy to join them. They had lain on the blanket with Nickie's head resting comfortably on Becca's stomach and played the imagination game with the clouds. She thought of those moments when everything was simple and carefree. Nickie always saw animals in the puffy clouds that drifted through the azure sky. There were ponies with wings, puppies, and fluffy kittens. They were her imaginary pets for a fleeting moment until they dissipated and transformed into a new friend with a made-up name. Nickie would point at the sky and say, "Mommy that kitten is for you. His name is William, and I'm giving him to you because I love you. And he needs a mommy just like mine."

"My precious little girl," Becca whispered. "Mommy loves you so much. Don't be scared anymore. I won't leave. Here you are, little angel. You can sleep with Mommy and dream about lots of fun things like ice cream and doggies and clowns and all kinds of things." She patted Nickie's head reassuringly and allowed herself a dreamless sleep, which took her into a place of nothingness.

***

Mommy's soft, soothing voice drifted into a mist, and Nickie started to hear the sounds of a heavenly choir. She poked her head through a cloud and looked around to see tinsel-bedecked angels in long gossamer robes flitting about in the air using their tiny flapping wings. The angels were busily engaged in licking ice cream cones and playing with dogs. During the merriment, a clown angel flew crookedly past and crashed into a cloud with a loud *kersplat*. The sight of all that fun made her laugh out loud.

Just as Nickie saw the clown angel bounce back out of the cloud as if suspended from a big rubber band, she felt a gentle hand on her head and turned to find her father caressing her hair. It was her daddy all right, and yet he was somehow different. He was tall and trim with ice blue eyes that smiled, and he had pale curly hair just like hers, but Daddy was somehow bright like the sun. Much to her surprise, he had a giant, glowing halo that framed his face and body.

She blinked hard in disbelief and opened her eyes wider just to make sure he was real. He had huge, splendid wings. She was astonished and pleased that her daddy was the most wonderful angel she had ever seen— even in books, even in her imagination! She stood on tiptoe and stretched to reach his neck to give him his usual hug and kiss.

***

Nickie, like a marionette orchestrated on heavenly strings, hit her mother's chin with an outstretched hand, awakening her. In a fog of sleep, Becca moved Nickie's hand away from her face, sighed, and drifted back into her own nighttime world.

The clock on the nightstand was the only sentinel seeing time advance, as 2:00 A.M. became 4:00 A.M. In those still, dark hours, Rebecca awakened to find Nickie flopped over her like a rag doll draped over a puffy cloud in the sky. Anxious to see when the alarm would go off, she rearranged Nickie and tried again to drift into a slumber. Soon morning would dawn, and then all the hassles would begin. It made her tired thinking about all the things that still needed to be done for the party. Her mind wandered into old, tiresome thoughts. "If I fall asleep right now, I could still get two hours."

Nickie found herself happy in the place where daddy lived. She played and jumped. She stirred, kicked, cuddled, and turned around Rebecca like a restless puppy.

With each movement Rebecca pulled Nickie close and kissed her forehead. She knew the lack of sleep was going to have an impact on her ability to complete all the unfinished tasks for the party, but her child needed her, too. It never felt like there was enough time for any of those special moments, like looking for animals in the sky. She cradled Nickie now while she slept just to feel her gentle breathing and hold on to the treasured moment. A script of chores kept intruding like a continuous loop in her head. Attempting to find sleep one last time, she shifted Nickie toward the other side of the bed just as the clock radio sprang to life.

The energetic voice of the DJ, Roger Dodger, filled the room. "Good morning, you winter sleepyheads. Wake up! Hey, you! That's right, you! Wake up! You need a shave, and so does your husband. Come on! It's the last shopping day before Christmas! And if you want any choice at all, you'd better be lined up when Hillside Mall opens up this morning."

The annoying Hillside Mall jingle played in the background of the DJ's patter. Rebecca stared at the ceiling feeling tired and irritated by the sounds of the dawning day.

***

Nickie turned and went further into the dream. She squinted at the sky. It was a blue that can only come in dreams where color is made of light and touch and sound and tastes like cotton candy, all sweet and spun with love.

She looked down from the little hill where she was playing. At the bottom stood a huge toy train looking just like the one Daddy had given her, only here it was bigger.

The reverberating loudspeaker voice of the conductor announced, "Little *Nickie* is next! A birthday ride for Christmas, sure, and a happy birthday for Nickie!"

She stared at the conductor as he climbed up the locomotive steps. He looked like Uncle Russell, Daddy and Mommy's friend. He was medium height, firm build, with salt-and-pepper colored hair, and kind brown eyes that crinkled at the corners when he smiled at her. "How does he know how to drive a train? Maybe he learned it from Daddy," she thought, "or maybe he has a remote control like the one from the trains at the toy store."

Nickie jumped with both feet onto the first step and skipped up the rest into the train, which was warm and inviting, and waved her hand out the window at Uncle Russell—but his face had changed to someone she didn't recognize anymore.

The train started to roll forward and go around a cartoon-like sun that looked like it was cut from cardboard dusted with a coating of tiny glitters that sparkled and changed brilliance the longer she stared.

Suddenly, standing in front of the toy train was a huge, bigger-than-life shaggy dog with droopy soulful eyes and a friendly face. The dog looked like a St. Bernard made out of hundreds of pieces of brightly colored cloth. It sat up and shook as if it had just had a bath and wanted her to notice him.

Nickie leaped out of the train, ran toward the St. Bernard, and gave him a big hug. She wished with all her heart that it could be hers forever. The dog wiggled around like an enormous, effervescent puppy and gave her a huge lick with his soft red cloth tongue.

Unexpectedly, the dog put his front paws around his funny, huge face and pulled his head off. It was a big costume instead of a real dog. Inside, to Nickie's surprise and delight, was David, her daddy.

"Happy birthday, Nickie!" he said in a slow motion, exaggerated dream voice.

Nickie couldn't believe her eyes. The answer to all her prayers and fervent wishes was right there, just as she had imagined so many times.

"Daddy! Daddy! Can you come to my birthday party?"

He held her and kissed her button nose. "Sh, my little sweet pea. I love you, Nickie. Now get back on the train! Quick!"

Nickie jumped back on the train just as Daddy said she should. As it rumbled away it blew a loud whistle that erupted and woke her.

Chapter Two

Morning arrived like a train pulling into Grand Central Station—on time, on demand, or maybe too demanding right now on the eve of her daughter's birthday when there were just too many things to do. How could anyone have known David would die when Nickie was only four and a half years old? It still felt like a nightmare from which she would soon awaken, and there he would be like nothing had happened.

Everything reminded her that he was gone and that her Nickie would have to learn to understand that Daddy would never come home to her hugs and kisses again. It made no sense that David could die simply taking her antique VW bug in for a tune-up. She imagined the squeal of the old brakes, as he must have tried to stop to avoid the Dodge Ram truck that raced through the intersection just as the light turned red.

Becca felt like nothing would be normal again. She was young and attractive, but inside everything felt vague, undefined, and very serious. It was as if David's absence created a void that was impossible to fill. A part of her was missing his daily presence, and it felt awkward to be around people. Even the office was now a foreign and distant place.

The whistling kettle forced her back into the moment, into her kitchen. It was something as routine as pulling the culprit pot off the stove that brought back the focus of now.

Becca, as if by rote or like a well-programmed robot, called over her shoulder, "Nickie, it's time to wake up!"

No sound came from her bedroom. Becca decided to check to see if Nickie was awake.

"Nickie, Nickie, my little angel. Time to wake up!"

"Is it my birthday yet?" a tiny sleep-encased voice responded.

Becca entered the room. "What?"

Nickie rubbed her eyes. "Daddy said it was my birthday."

"Your birthday is tomorrow, angel."

Becca playfully tousled Nickie's hair and caressed her smooth, chubby, rosy cheeks. She knew and understood that faraway look in Nickie's blue-gray eyes rimmed with long upswept lashes. "Were you dreaming about Daddy again?"

Nickie giggled and nodded, as if to acknowledge the presence of an imaginary spirit that transfixed her gaze at the wall. "Daddy licked my face. He was a big doggy and he said 'Happy birthday!'"

Still feeling emotionally fragile, all Becca could do was sit on the edge of the bed, pull Nickie to her, and hold her for a long moment that she never wanted to end. She pushed back the little bangs she had cut too short only a week ago and whispered, as if it were a conversation only they knew, "You miss Daddy a lot, don't you, Nickie?"

Nickie nodded, looking very serious. She knelt on the bed throwing her arms around Becca's neck. All of a sudden she brightened as she thought about her dream. "But he wished me happy birthday."

"Yes, in your dream, I know. Dreaming is the only way to have Daddy here right now, isn't it?"

Nickie wrinkled her brow and clutched her stuffed bear. "I wish he *could* come for my birthday—and it's Christmas, too. Right, Mommy?"

"Right! And you're the only girl I know who has her birthday on Christmas. Santa Claus knows that, too, so we've got to be good. Let's get up and get ready to go to Auntie Caroline's house to see your cousins."

Nickie started to climb out of bed, but stopped. "Hey! I know! I'll ask Santa to bring Daddy back for my birthday."

Becca hugged Nickie and tugged playfully on her earlobe. "We've really got to hurry now, angel. We're going to be late." She pulled the covers back and chanted "hi-ho" like the Seven Dwarfs in *Snow White*. "We've got to go and go and really, really *go*!"

Becca tickled Nickie, who giggled, and then boosted her out of bed and chased her into the hallway and back to her own room to get dressed.

***

Coffee dripped through the filter and filled the room with the rich smell of breakfast. The toaster popped and displayed warm, golden brown bread ready to be plucked.

Nickie sat quietly at the table, dressed in jeans with a bright red knit sweater interwoven with a big black and white cartoon Dalmatian on the front. She pulled up thick matching socks that wanted to slide inside her high-top red boots. These were her fun-time clothes, as mommy called them. She picked up her spoon and played with floating cereal flakes that bobbed in a bowl of milk, trying to squish them to the bottom of the bowl and make them stay. She looked at Becca while she swung her feet, pretending they reached the floor, and thought that maybe Mommy wouldn't be too busy to remember her birthday.

"Mommy, are you going to be busy on my birthday?"

"No, sweet pea, mommy has something special planned for your birthday."

"Really?"

"Promise."

Nickie reached into the cereal box. Somewhere there had to be a prize. The picture said so on the box. The cereal crunched as her hand sank deeper in order to explore the depths where the treasure might be hidden. There it was! She retrieved the cellophane-wrapped prize. It was a bright yellow and orange whistle. "Look, Mommy, a present for me!"

Becca snatched the toast. "Oh, lucky girl. It must be because someone knows it's going to be your birthday soon."

The phone rang. Becca grabbed it and cradled it against her shoulder. "Hey, Russell, I appreciate what you've done, you're a dear. Thanks for starting to get things organized for the office party. Now I know why David couldn't live without you at his side…. Yes, I'll make time when I get in to see the latest innovation you've been working on for so long. I'm going to be a little late. I need to drop off my little baby at my sister-in-law's."

Nickie put her spoon down. "I'm not a baby. I'm going to be five, remember? That makes me a big girl now."

Becca put her hand over the receiver and turned to see Nickie looking forlorn among cereal box skyscrapers surrounding the milk-laden pond of floating Frosted Flakes. She felt a pang of guilt for neglecting her little one in favor of office pressures. "To me you'll always be my baby."

She never thought she would inherit the day-to-day operation of David's software company. He was the inventor, and she was the one who knew how to sell his creations. They were a team, but today it felt like she was a team of one. She had never before felt so lost. It was like swimming in an ocean with no shore. David had been the captain of the company ship, a steady hand on the rudder knowing where they needed to go.

Becca returned to the telephone. "Listen, Russell, I really need to go and get ready now. I need to hang up. We'll talk when I get in."

Becca sat down at the table and slid her chair closer to Nickie. "That's a nice toy you got from the cereal. Can I see it?"

"It's whistle."

"And a very bright-colored one, too."

"Mommy, if I blow it, I bet it sounds just like the train in my dream with Daddy."

"I bet it does, too."

"Mommy, are you going to go away to Heaven like Daddy?"

"No, I'm going to stay here and wrap my big arms around you and never, never, never let you go." Becca pulled Nickie off her chair and onto her lap. "Okay, Nickie, now you remember about today? Mrs. Perhowsky went away for Christmas, so you'll be with Auntie Caroline and your cousins. Mommy's going to be working late today, so you'll eat dinner there, too. Won't that be fun?"

"But Mommy, tomorrow is Christmas and my birthday." She put her hand on Becca's cheek. "I don't want you to go."

Becca took the hand and kissed it. "Look, Mommy will be with you all day tomorrow. I promise! Now scoot, and let's get ready to go."

Nickie leaped off of Becca's lap. She snatched the whistle, tucked it into her pocket, and started to skip out of the kitchen toward the entry. She stopped and turned. "You know what, Mommy? Um, can I have a puppy for my birthday?"

Becca moved Nickie toward the entryway and pulled her red jacket from the coatrack. "Oh, Nickie, darling. We've talked about this before."

Nickie pushed her arms through the sleeves. "Okay. Then can I have a puppy for Christmas?"

Becca yanked her dark gray tweed wool coat off the hanger. "Nickie, a puppy wouldn't be happy here. We're away so much. He'd bark and howl, and he'd be very sad."

She looked at her pale complexion in the mirror of the credenza and pushed her strawberry blond shoulder-length curls behind her ears. She smoothed a cream colored silk blouse underneath the coat. Only Nickie made it worthwhile to go forward. Thankfully her little girl was okay. She always checked to make sure she wasn't getting too thin and losing the soft, comforting roundness of a child.

Nickie planted her tiny fists on her waist. "Well, I don't think it's fair."

"But the puppy wouldn't be happy here."

Nickie puffed out her lower lip. "It isn't fair! Everybody else gets stuff for Christmas and stuff for their birthday, and all I get is the same stuff."

Becca shook her head, knowing there was no way to win the conversation. She picked up the phone while talking to Nickie. "No, Nickie, you get double-the-stuff. You get more stuff than anybody on Christmas. Really!" Becca dialed Caroline's number and checked her watch.

Nickie stomped her foot and turned her back to Becca and thought about her dream. "But I *can* have a puppy. Daddy told me before he went to Heaven that he'd buy me a puppy."

"Busy!" Becca slammed the phone back on its hook. "Sweet pea, I know Daddy said you could have a puppy, but right now Mommy doesn't have time to take care of a puppy and everything else."

"But I'll take care of him."

"When you're older and can really take care of him, then we can see."

"But Mommy, I'm going to be older tomorrow."

Becca bent down and hugged Nickie. "I know, and that makes you such a big girl, but I think we still need to wait a bit."

"What about when I'm five and a half?"

"We'll talk about it then, okay?"

"'Kay. I'll be old enough then. I know it, Mommy. I can take care of him then, and I'm going to give him a special name, better than the puppies in the clouds."

"Yes, you'll name him the best of all those animals in the sky." She opened her purse, took out a light pink lipstick and traced the contour of her heart-shaped lips. She smudged the dark green eyeliner that rimmed her blue eyes flecked with amber and pinched her cheeks to give some color to her alabaster skin.

Becca knelt down to Nickie's height to help her shove tiny fists into mittens that were connected by a string threaded through the sleeves of the small jacket. "Come on, angel! We've got to get out of here right now. Auntie Caroline is waiting for us!"

Chapter Three

Caroline Hastings's kitchen was an organized accumulation of clutter. She was pretty with a tall, lithe build that betrayed she was at one time a dancer. She looked ten years younger than her true age, thirty-nine. Her red hair still sparkled under the sunlight with only a few white strands that accentuated the copper and gold and framed her face with big, unkempt curls. Some days she felt like her kitchen—disheveled—and never seemed to have enough time just for herself.

It had all happened so quickly—falling in love with Steve and then having children in what seemed like one pregnancy after another—but it all added to the tempo of endless demands that somehow made it easy to push into the past that her brother was no longer alive.

"Who wouldn't feel harried," she thought, "especially today, with four children who don't want to cooperate?"

She looked into the family room at fourteen-year-old Kathy who was enthralled by a teen cosmetics commercial and deliberately ignoring Zachary, twelve, and Jeremy, who was nine. While their older freckled-faced sister sat riveted to the TV, the two boys organized a boisterous game of "toss-the-little-sister." That was Sarah, two and a half, and the object of their raucous game.

Just then the telephone rang. Caroline picked up the receiver and pushed her long copper-colored bangs back from her eyes, they needed to be cut months ago. Through all the noise and mayhem, she tried to understand her husband Steve, who was calling from Chicago O'Hare airport. She covered the mouthpiece so the children wouldn't overhear her conversation, but with all the chaos she wondered who could possibly hear her anyway.

She turned her back to the children and whispered, "They made a big deal of it. They even wrote a special letter to Santa pleading for a SpeedoRacer. Of course, now they all want their very own private SpeedoRacer."

Steve Hastings was a handsome man in his early forties. His hair was already turning silver at the temples, giving him a wise, sophisticated look. His pilot's uniform accentuated his serious, yet caring demeanor. Fidgeting with his tie, he looked outside with dismay at white blowing snow swirling around the windows and obscuring the sight of airplanes parked on the tarmac.

It wasn't much consolation knowing he wasn't the only one stuck there. Other pilots milled around waiting their turn to call home. It always seemed like Christmas conspired to keep him from getting to his family. He knew, too, it meant extra hassles for Caroline.

In a reassuring voice he said, "Well, it took some looking, but I found one. That's the good news."

Caroline knew the all-too-familiar sound of his voice when there was more to come. "Uh-oh. And the bad news?" Hearing Sarah's frantic wails, she shouted at the kids, "Boys, put your little sister down! Kathy, get off your butt and do some crowd control. Please!"

Kathy shrugged her shoulders and rolled her eyes. She picked up the remote control, increased the volume, and went back to watching her program, muttering, "Give me a break. As if I care what they're doing."

Zak and Jeremy continued to toss their curly-headed little sister like a medicine ball. Sarah giggled and screamed with laughter as they shoved her back and forth.

Zak grinned at his mother with freckle-faced mischief. "She likes it, Mom. Look!"

Caroline cupped the mouthpiece of the telephone. "Well, just try to keep it down. I'm talking to Daddy, okay?"

She turned back to the phone. "I don't like the sound of this, Steve."

Steve replied in as calming a voice as he could conjure. "We're snowed in, honey. It's a blizzard. Doesn't look good. I don't think I'm going to make it out today."

"Oh, no! Not the day before Christmas! Steve, I still have things to do...without the kids!"

Steve looked around at all the stranded passengers. "Sorry, honey. I have no control over the weather. You know, 'safety first.'"

Caroline knew there was nothing he could do. "So, when?"

"Tomorrow, maybe."

"Tomorrow! But—" Caroline grabbed the dishtowel on the counter, popped open the oven, and retrieved a tray of nearly burnt cookies. "Oh, no!"

Steve smiled. "I've heard that same tone about 372 times so far today."

Caroline frowned and dropped the towel. She toyed with a cup of cold coffee that had been sitting on the counter for hours. "Yeah, I guess...it's just that...well, see...and I've got Nickie today, too. Well, how could I say no, Steve? Understand, David was my only brother. We just haven't seen them much since David's death, you know, and it was only for one day when you'd be home."

Steve looked out the window at the blizzard and nodded to himself. "I'm afraid all this is going to make you very crazy."

"You're right, but see, it wouldn't make me crazy if you were home." She sat down and groaned.

Steve softened his voice. "Just remember I'll be home for Christmas." He turned in time to see other pilots snickering behind his back at his attempt to placate his wife.

Caroline's shoulders sagged. "Okay, okay. You know how to make the blizzard go away? Just put your lips together and blow. Come home as soon as you can. Love you. Bye." She sighed and hung up the telephone.

From the corner of her eye she caught Sarah feeding applesauce to the teddy bear with a spoon. She jumped up and pulled a paper towel from the roll. "Oh, Sarah! Applesauce is not for the teddy bear!"

She rushed to wipe the applesauce off the stuffed animal, as Sarah teetered out of reach in peals of giggles. Caroline saw that she had applesauce in her hair and on her face. She stopped, clutched the towel to her chest, and laughed along.

***

Becca looked at the clock on the dashboard of the car. It was peculiar how it still felt like David's car and not hers. It still seemed to smell like him, but somehow that was fading. The drifting of all things familiar made her want to capture every scrap and molecule—just like holding on to the fading pain of losing him, because it felt as though if the sorrow went away, so would David's memory. But there was no time now to think about it. She knew she was late.

As if to try to catch up on lost minutes, Becca jumped out of the car and quickly opened the door, unfastened the seatbelt, lifted Nickie out of the seat, and set her down on the sidewalk. She squeezed her hand, and they hurried up the walkway to the front door, which was decorated with a big Christmas wreath. She coaxed Nickie along. "Come on, angel. We're late! Your cousins are waiting for you. You've got all your stuff?"

"'Kay, mommy." She clutched Becca's hand and hid behind the folds of her long coat.

Becca rang the doorbell and again checked her watch just as Zak opened the door. She stepped into the entryway, pulling Nickie along. She noticed Zak had grown since the last time she saw him, but he still had an impish demeanor, which was punctuated by reddish-brown hair and freckles dotting his cheeks.

She was surprised to see so many Christmas decorations. There were little reminders on every table—angels and snowmen and a beautiful wood carved crèche. It was a contrast to her own house where it had seemed like a chore to just put up a tree for Nickie.

The radio in the kitchen drifted notes of Mannheim Steamroller's version of "Silent Night" into the foyer, mingling it with the scent of sugar cookies fresh from the oven. However, the rambunctious background noise displaced the traditional sounds of the holidays. The TV in the family room blared messages about new cosmetics designed to enhance lips and endure twelve hours of wear.

Kathy sat rooted to the spot, as if hypnotized. She popped four pieces of gum into her mouth as the eye shadow infomercial started. Zak grabbed Jeremy's hand and pulled him into the hallway, while Sarah wobbled behind, unsure of her footing. Zak patted Sarah's wet head and stared down at Nickie. The two boys and little Sarah stood together unusually silent with Zak folding his arms and staring at Nickie.

Zak continued to glare down at Nickie. He hadn't seen her in over six months and wondered what she was doing in his house. He smirked and opened his lips to reveal a red gumball in his mouth. They all stood like guardians in charge of their territory and stared at Nickie as if she were an alien. She stared back in defiance to the unspoken challenge.

Becca was uncomfortable with the standoff. She put her arm around Nickie and motioned for Zak to come closer, but he stood rooted to his spot. She felt a desperate need to stay linked somehow to her husband's family. She checked her watch again. It was later than she wanted it to be. She looked toward the kitchen door wondering where Caroline was. Finally she took off her coat and focused her attention back on the trio standing vigil. "Hi, kids, is your mom home?"

They went on staring, as if it were a TV game show challenge. It made Becca feel awkward. She felt as if she were solely responsible for Caroline and her children never seeing her brother and their only uncle.

Suddenly Caroline swept into the entryway with blobs of applesauce stuck on her right cheek and forehead. Becca was taken aback by the humorous image. She thought maybe tragedy and comedy were linked like twins. It seemed that no matter how sad she felt at times, a funny incident would pop up to change the mood.

"Hi, Caroline. It's been awhile. Thanks so much for watching Nickie." Becca saw a wild look in her sister-in-law's eyes. "Uh, are you all right? Caroline?" Becca asked, wondering if this were a normal, everyday occurrence. Maybe it was a big mistake leaving Nickie in the midst of all this ruckus.

Caroline groaned and wiped her hands on the apron. "Oh, yes, just the day before Christmas. That's all. How are you, Becca? Nice seeing you."

Her eyes drifted down to her niece clinging to Becca's skirt. "Hey, little Nickie, come give a big hug to Auntie Caroline. I want a kiss."

Caroline knelt down, but Nickie pulled back, lifted her eyebrows, and stared at the applesauce starting to slide down her aunt's cheek. Oblivious to the food adorning her face, Caroline stroked Nickie's soft, rose-colored cheek. "You're so pretty and I'm so glad you came over today." She moved to kiss her cheek, but Nickie stiffened and turned her head, not wanting the sticky substance on her own face.

Becca pointed to her own cheek in an attempt to show Caroline what the problem was. She chuckled, thinking it was reminiscent of the days in high school when she had tried to signal to her best friend that she had accidentally written on her face while nervously chewing on a pen. "Sorry, uh Caroline, I'm...she's...you're..."

Becca pulled a tissue from her purse and handed it to Caroline, who looked at it puzzled and put it into the pocket of her apron. She smiled, pretending to appreciate the gesture. "Thank you."

Becca pulled out another tissue, raised her eyebrows, and wiped an imaginary blob from her own face, indicating to Caroline that a sticky glob was still stuck to her cheek. Caroline misconstrued what Becca was trying to imply and moved closer to see what was on Nickie's face. Nickie was horrified by the impending impact with the blob and pulled back further.

Becca shook her head while stifling a laugh. "No, no, Nickie. It's all right. Caroline, you have a...it...sets off your green eyes well." Becca touched Caroline's cheek.

Caroline stood up and looked in the hallway mirror. "Oh, no! Yuck! Applesauce." She laughed at herself as she finally realized how startling it must have been for Nickie. She pulled Becca's original Kleenex from her pocket and wiped her face. How silly not to understand the clues Becca had given. Wearing food was certainly more of a common occurrence since Sarah was born.

"Thanks, Sarah. Well, that's the kind of day it is already." Caroline gave Sarah, Zak, and Jeremy an exaggerated glare, then looked at Becca and shook her head. "It's already crazy today." She gave Becca a hug. "I thought I'd be getting some help from Steve in dealing with five kids, but he's stuck in Chicago in a blizzard. I'm just hoping he can make it home sometime before Christmas is over."

Becca looked at the family and kitchen in disarray. "I'm sorry to hear that. I hope it's okay for me to leave her here."

"Well, when you deal with four crazy kids, what's one more? At least Nickie is under control."

"Look, Caroline. I just came in to thank you for watching over Nickie and to remind you that I have that office party this afternoon. I'm in charge, so I'll have to be there past the end, cleaning up and everything, so you'll have Nickie for dinner, right? We agreed to that?"

Caroline stared blankly at Becca. She thought about all the things that needed to be done and now this extra work and need to attend to Nickie. She raised her eyebrows, resigned to the situation, but not knowing what to say. She took a mental inventory of what was in the refrigerator to cook for dinner. Nothing much came to mind.

Becca knew Caroline's attention was somewhere else. "Caroline? Are you okay?"

Startled, Caroline flushed with embarrassment. "No, no. Just forgot! But it's okay. Probably do the kids a lot of good to have somebody new for dinner."

Becca was relieved Caroline remembered their makeshift plans. "Okay, good! And you're still planning on the little party for Nickie's birthday tomorrow?"

Caroline rubbed her forehead trying to remember what they had agreed on. "Uh...right. Right! Now that was, um, what time?"

"Five for games and fun, and I'll fix dinner." She was relieved the burden of birthday and Christmas festivities was spread among the people who were family. She felt somehow it ensured that nothing would be overlooked and extra care would be given for Nickie's double holiday.

Becca motioned to the kitchen, indicating she wanted to talk to Caroline without the children. It always seemed that kids knew when parents wanted them out of earshot and instinctively stayed close in the event a secret about what was in those wrapped presents would sneak out.

Becca nodded toward Zak and Jeremy. "Why don't you kids show Nickie your beautiful Christmas tree?"

Caroline picked up the cue. "Yeah, kids. Show Nickie your stockings, too."

They all rushed out, except Nickie, who stayed back and reached for her mother's hand and pressed against her leg. Becca understood Nickie's hesitation. Her own life had become more tentative, and Nickie seemed more timid since David's death. Becca nudged her gently. "I'll walk you in, angel, and then I have to go, 'kay?"

They went toward the door of the other room. Nickie was curious and walked ahead, drawn into the magic of family Christmas sparkle. In Nickie's imagination, tinsel looked like magical icicles and ornaments seemed like fairyland worlds that told endless stories.

Nickie was drawn into the ambiance of the season, as Becca talked quietly to Caroline. "This is extremely important for Nickie, Caroline. Having her birthday on Christmas is really hard, especially this year with David not here, and—"

Nickie overheard with the sonar ears of a child able to discern what concerns her from any distance. She called to her mother in the kitchen. "My daddy is coming for my birthday."

This innocent and unwavering announcement startled both Becca and Caroline. Nickie walked over to inspect the Christmas tree as if to punctuate her point.

Becca whispered to Caroline, "See? She's pretty upset this time of the year, you know."

Caroline felt a tight constriction in her throat and tears threatening to spill. She took Becca by the arm and drew her to the window over the sink that overlooked the backyard covered in snow. "I've told you before, Becca, and I hate to make an issue of it, but Nickie must stop thinking in the past. She needs to understand the finality of death. The only chance I have to see my brother again is on the other side, if there is such a thing."

Becca took a tissue from the counter and dabbed at the corners of her eyes, trying not to smear her eye make up. Her voice quivered. "He gave me the most precious gift: my little girl."

Caroline interrupted, irritated that she couldn't suppress her own raw emotions, and grasped at a quick solution to a painful problem. "Becca, wake up! Nickie needs therapy!"

Becca suddenly became pensive. "You might be right, Caroline. Thanks. After Christmas we'll look at getting an appointment." She paused and blew her nose, trying to compose herself. "Well, you're busy, and I'm late! I better get out of there. Thanks. Thanks a million! Thanks for everything, Caroline. You're an angel."

Becca looked at her watch and realized she was now really late. She called Nickie, gave her a quick hug, and waved good-bye to Caroline and her children.

Once her sister-in-law was out of sight, Caroline muttered under her breath, "Yeah, an angel. I ought to be hung on a Christmas tree somewhere."

Chapter Four

Morning always demanded the maximum energy and humor from DJs, and Roger took it seriously. He couldn't admit it was an attempt to be younger than he was. This time of year was especially hard. It just didn't seem like anything special anymore since he'd gotten divorced and become estranged from his teenage daughter. He told himself all the time that children her age naturally reject their parents in favor of their independence and adolescent omniscience, but Christmas eroded his paternal confidence.

Roger Dodger's voice boomed over radio sets in the quiet little snow-coated New England town with big hills that surrounded its slumbering inhabitants. "And for those of you just getting up, the stores have already been open for half an hour, and you're still in your jammies."

Inside the radio station Roger felt cozy and secure, as though cradled in an easy chair that had molded around him over decades. Roger Ferron—or Roger Dodger, as listeners knew him—was tall and pleasant with a mischievous twinkle that betrayed a young spirit. Even the reading glasses resting at the end of his nose to help him see the copy whose font seemed to get smaller every year could not diminish the prankster who teased listeners with irreverent, one-sided banter, as he cradled the microphone like a rock star. He looked like the sixty year old that he was, including the graying hair and a soft belly straining to stay in place above a well-worn tooled belt reminiscent of the flower-power days of his rebel years. He was balding, but even so he kept his hair long and held it back with a rubber band in a thinning ponytail.

Roger sipped his morning espresso spouting an exaggerated, perky monologue. "Better get up and get goin'. Lots of gooood stuff on sale today."

Even though the studio was small, it contained Roger's mess and his one treasure, a picture of his daughter when she turned thirteen. He thought she looked so sweet in that picture taken not so long ago. He was perplexed that this child had transformed and now wore punk uniforms and acted so rebelliously, according to his ex-wife, but maybe she was like him in the sixties when he was a rebel of sorts, or maybe he was still just an aging hippy himself. He couldn't fault her for expressing herself.

Roger pulled the microphone close. He felt it was his conduit to his audience, personal and impersonal all in one. "Well, pretty good stuff. At least it's on sale before Christmas! Anyway, we've got a little rundown of bizarre things on sale today, and we're gonna give that to you just a little bit later. First, let's pay some bills."

The one thing that made his job easy was Christmas because there was an endless supply of jingled Christmas ads that could fill the space when you had to think about what song to play or when you just needed it as background to fill some silence. It was time for one of those mindless ad selection decisions. It was like a comma mid thought or a period at the end of a sentence that provided a pause in order to take a break and regroup.

Roger caught Geronimo's eye on the other side of the glass that defined his broadcast space and waved for him to enter.

Unbeknownst to Roger, Geronimo idolized him. He copied his style without knowing he was doing it. Geronimo was tall and thin with long hair that he wore in a scraggly ponytail dripping down a spiny back, not unlike Roger's hair. Somehow this counterculture twenty-year-old style worked. With a comfortable, lanky saunter he entered from the control room into Roger's domain, the broadcast booth, and said, while chewing gum, "Yeah?"

Roger was surprised not to have his normal assistant. "Where's Yvonne?"

"Took off. Day before Christmas, man."

Roger looked up and for the first time noticed Geronimo, who looked familiar and yet not familiar. Maybe he had gone through too many assistants. "Yeah, okay. You're the night guy, right? What's your name?"

Geronimo looked around the room to see if there was someone else who was being addressed. Roger, his idol, had never noticed him or the way he made sure everything went smoothly. He looked at Roger and straightened his posture. "Geronimo. Man!" Geronimo thought maybe he'd done something wrong in the past and would be filed with all the nameless faces at the studio in Roger's mind.

Something about Geronimo reminded Roger of his own path breaking into the industry and the carefree days of the peace movement when you concentrated on making love not war. He looked up and started to provide a friendly response, but caught a huge, enigmatic smile traversing Geronimo's face.

"Really? Geronimo? Right, Geronimo. Catchy! So, uh, do you know where that list of—never mind. I hardly know what I'm thinking without my producer."

Geronimo frowned. "You mean she didn't tell you?"

Roger surveyed the mountain of papers in disarray on the desk "Well, I guess she did, but I…you know, wigged out."

Geronimo picked up the top page on the stack and placed it back on the heap. He pulled up his pants with an exaggerated motion, emulating a rock star. "Bummer."

Roger noted the style and picked up the schedule sheet. "Yeah, listen. I was going to take some calls here in a minute. Do you produce?"

Geronimo looked around to see if there might be a manager eavesdropping. "I'm the night man, dude. I don't produce; I fix. But hey, you need somethin'?"

Roger looked up and forced a mock smile. "Yeah! A producer."

Geronimo snapped to attention and returned a salute. "Can be done, man. What do I do?"

Roger couldn't believe his luck at finding a live volunteer. "You mean you'd—"

Geronimo grinned proudly and widely with a puppy-like exuberance. "Sure, man. It's Christmas, right? Just say I got the spirit. Fact, I'm gonna have the spirit all day, y'know. Gave away the day for a Christmas present, get it?"

Roger looked over the rims of his glasses. He wrinkled his brow as he scrutinized his partner for the evening. "Well, we're going to get to know each other pretty well, Geronimo, 'cause I'm here for two extra shifts—this afternoon, break, and this evening from seven till Christmas morn." Roger paused. "Guess we did the same thing."

Geronimo gave a thumbs-up acknowledgement. "Dude!" He offered his hand in a conspiratorial gesture. Roger took it in the spirit of comradely fun, and Geronimo turned the sentiment into a hip handshake. Roger laughed at the comical retro sight and heartily shook Geronimo's hand. Both were caught up in the humor of the moment.

Geronimo dropped his hand. "No family, eh?"

The question took Roger by surprise. "Well, not that I see anymore."

Geronimo touched the frame of the only prominent picture on Roger's desk. "That yer friend, niece, family, or somethin'?"

"Yeah, she's special to me, but that's another story." Roger wiped a tear that started to form. He always had an emotional knot when it concerned his daughter. "I...I miss being with her."

Geronimo looked at the picture and then at Roger. "Sorry, man. I say somethin' I shouldn't?"

Roger touched the face in the photograph. "No, no. That's my daughter. You know her?"

Geronimo picked up the photo, admiring the pretty girl in the picture. "Hey, man, I don't know anybody who looks like that! On the other hand, she looks vaguely familiar. Yah, I think I do know her. That's Lexi."

Roger took the picture from Geronimo. "Well, she doesn't look like that anymore. I haven't seen her much since the divorce six years ago. I'm a bit worried about that, but from what I understand she has a gothic look. She's a punk now." He looked over his glasses. "At least it's not life threatening. I hope. Last couple of times we met it was at the precinct for a couple of misdemeanors. I keep my fingers crossed."

Geronimo looked away from the picture and picked up the list of the day's announcements, sensing he had touched on something best left alone for the time being. "Hey, dude, you're a cool cat, dad." He slapped Roger's hand. "Right! So man, like, okay, what does a producer do?"

Roger stroked his unshaven chin. "Well, dude! You report to me' cause I'm the high–tech cat and you're the low-tech cat at this station." He pointed at the phones on the other side of the booth. "Well, on the day shift you screen phone calls and sometimes place calls to find out things that I spaced out on, like things I need to announce or songs that need to be queued."

Geronimo slouched, making his tall lanky body look like a question mark as a big, affable grin spread across his face. "Shoot, man. I've been producing my spacey friends for a long time. Can't be that hard, right?"

Roger winked and gave him the two-finger peace sign. "Dude!"

Laughing, Geronimo returned the gesture and slapped Roger on the back as though they'd been friends forever.

The music came to an end. Roger went back to the microphone and pointed to the control booth. "Geronimo, go back in there, because the calls are going to start."

Geronimo gave Roger a thumbs-up and exited the booth. "Hey, man, I'm your producer for the day."

With glib, dripping charm and simulating the crooning voice of Bing Crosby, Roger spoke to the audience of invisible listeners. "For the zillionth time this season, that was 'White Christmas.'"

Geronimo busied himself as he watched Roger through the window. "So I think from that photo that that's my friend Alexis's ol' man. Cool."

Roger glanced over the list of events that needed announcing and clicked the ON AIR button. "Aaaannnnd just so you can keep your calendar straight, don't forget the children's Christmas pageant tonight at eight o'clock at the Grace Community Baptist Church. Reverend Woods always gets a terrific performance out of these kids. You oughta see them. They're soooo cute."

Even though it was just a routine ordinary-sounding announcement, something about its upbeat delivery touched Geronimo. He looked through the window at Roger, who was repositioning the photograph to its usual spot. He felt close, almost like family, since they were together by themselves. Geronimo started scribbling on a piece of paper.

Roger put his feet on the desk and twirled a pencil like a baton through his fingers. "And don't forget the Grace Community Choir. That, I guarantee, will knock you right out of your chair."

Geronimo held a piece of paper against the glass with the words RANDALL BUSBY FISK scrawled in large block letters written with a thick black magic marker.

Roger looked up over his glasses to read the note and shrugged his shoulders. "What?" He wondered if it were a riddle of some kind. Geronimo saw the perplexed expression and quickly took it back down.

Roger hesitated slightly delivering the next radio announcement while trying to decipher what the three nonsensical words could mean. He verbally stroked the microphone. "It's always a terrific show, and the money goes to a needy family in our local area. A great charity. Better get there early, too. Parking is tight. Let's see…and, by the way, talking about religious events, later tonight we'll have the traditional midnight Christmas mass at the Catholic Church of the Madeleine."

Geronimo held up the paper again, which now read, THIS IS MY REAL NAME: RANDALL BUSBY FISK.

Roger burst into laughter when he finally comprehended the message and fumbled to hit the COUGH button in order to disguise that he'd lost what he was going to say.

Chapter Five

The Kirschbaums' delicatessen was like a symphony of delicious smells as Christmas baking filled the air with a sweet confection of yeast, sugar, toasted nuts, poppy seeds, marzipan, cookies, and honey. At holidays everything was a temptation taunting the senses. It was all too hard to resist, especially the sweets that took center stage over the array of marinated salads, pickled herrings in sour cream, cold cuts, cheeses, and the seemingly endless smorgasbord of options to tease the palate. All was delightfully calorific and sinful for any diet, but the Kirschbaums made everyone feel that holidays were exempt from watching the waistline.

Christmas Eve was especially busy. The bells hanging from the door jingled every few minutes as a steady stream of last-minute shoppers looking to grab a quick nosh or special treat for the holiday entered. Some came for the friendly hellos from the owners, like a last special trimming on the day. It was warm inside the deli, even when the door opened and let in a burst of cold snow flurries, but it was the atmosphere of delightful smells and tastes more than the ovens that contributed a steady, radiant heat.

Father McCurdy was in a hurry as he entered the delicatessen. He pushed his way past the customers that pointed at items in the glass display trying to decide what to pick. He fidgeted with a scrap of notepaper in his pocket that listed what he needed to pick up until it became his turn to collect and pay for the Christmas fruitcake he had ordered. This was the second year since the Kirschbaums opened for business that he had bought a cake from them.

The commotion of other customers' demands faded as Father McCurdy heard the botched radio announcement about his midnight mass. Fuming, he yanked out his wallet, slapped it on the counter, and drummed his fingers on the glass. Why couldn't those radio announcers show some modicum of respect? After all, he was now in his early seventies and had overseen the details of these annual rituals forever, or at least for what felt like all of his life. It irritated him to hear what sounded like a trivialization of his last midnight mass. How dare the DJ punctuate the announcement with rolling laughter! And, as further insult to the importance of this hallowed event, he didn't even apologize. Instead, the announcement immediately rolled over to Christmas carols.

Mrs. Kirschbaum was oblivious to the radio, which for her was background noise filling in the gaps between strings of conversations from the steady flow of customers who came in the moment she flipped the sign to OPEN. She was in her early sixties, but would never admit it, even on those days when the deli demanded all of her perpetual charisma and made her feel a hundred years old by the time they closed. She always had the energy to spread her Jewish mother wings around everyone who passed through the door. She made a point of knowing everyone one-on-one, like a brood of children that she added to her own.

Mrs. Kirschbaum moved to the cash register and slid Father McCurdy's well-worn wallet toward him, looking at the fingerprints he was making on the glass. She thought he was clearly peeved about something and needed extra attention. He looked at the radio and frowned. She followed his gaze, trying to remember what had just played because that appeared to be the source of his irritation.

Mrs. Kirschbaum didn't care what the problem was, just as long as everyone felt better by the time they left. She always embellished her tales and liberally seasoned her conversation with Old World Yiddish, emphasizing things in phrases borrowed from German, with an extra dose of mumbling for good measure. This linguistic melting pot came from her fear that maybe her English was not good enough. Since leaving Poland, she held on to her Polish traditions, always wearing her starched white cotton blouses under a fitted dress accented with a colorful apron.

Mrs. Kirschbaum never talked much about her past or her heritage. It was as if it held sadness that should remain closed in a box of memories never shared with anyone, but somewhere in those memories there was love saved up and stored that was meant to be shared with anyone who crossed her threshold.

Mrs. Kirschbaum smiled at Father McCurdy as she gave him back his change. "Thank you, Father McCurdy, and may the blessink of this Christian holiday brinkink you joy." She mumbled, "You're a good *mensch*."

Father McCurdy looked into brown eyes rimmed in gray and was caught off guard by the friendly Christmas overture. "Thank you, Mrs. Kirschbaum. Your Christmas fruitcakes brighten many hearts."

She patted his hand. "Vell, and mine is vun of them. Buy some more soon, Father. Buy all ve got! Hey, ve making you a special deal, eh?" She laughed when Father McCurdy rolled his eyes. She reached into the case and took a cellophane-wrapped cookie with a bright red ribbon and slid it toward Father McCurdy. "Here, Father, for later. My treat."

He slipped it into his pocket. "Thank you. I'll save it for after mass." Father McCurdy smiled and then glared at the speaker as the intrusion of the radio reminded him of the DJ's blunder. He took his packages to a small table in the front of the shop by the window and took a cellular phone out of his jacket pocket and a small black notebook out of his bag. He quickly looked in his book, willing the right page to appear on demand, punched the number into the phone, and waited for someone to answer.

Father McCurdy listened to the phone ring. He saw his reflection in the window and straightened his collar. He looked at the cell phone in his hand and remembered when he thought there wasn't any way he was going to use this new contraption, particularly at his age. Now he couldn't live without it. He was too intent on connecting his call to notice an elderly couple passing him on the way out. He nearly didn't see their attempt to communicate with him, but the elderly man seemed familiar as a faint recognition came to Father McCurdy.

The man tipped his derby hat. "Merry Christmas, Father McCurdy."

As the Rolodex of his mind flipped through all the parishioners he had met in twenty years, he now remembered who they were with instant clarity and cupped his hand over the receiver of the cell phone, which was still ringing. "Oh, yes, and Merry Christmas to you and Beth."

The phone stopped ringing as the station answered. Father McCurdy nodded a quick good-bye and took his hand off the mouthpiece of the cell phone. "Yes, I must talk to the disk jockey who's on right now. Father McCurdy, from the Church of the Madeleine. Yes, I'll wait." He tapped his foot, annoyed.

Chapter Six

Nickie watched Zak and Jeremy play video games. Little warriors jumped up stone stairs and clashed swords making metal clanking sounds accompanied by *dings* to emphasize that a win was soon to be awarded. She stood at a distance trying to feel invisible.

Kathy leaned over the back of the couch and yelled, "Turn off the sound. I can't hear my show." She flipped straight auburn hair back over her shoulder.

Zak stuck out his tongue. "Like you can make me. It's just stupid girl stuff you're watching."

"I'll come make you if I have to. I'll take that stupid joystick and throw it in the trash."

Zak took the remote control from the table and turned off the TV. "Then I'll take your eye shadow and flush it down the toilet."

"Give me that control."

Zak tossed it on the table. "Okay, here, take it! Like I want to watch your stupid show."

Caroline emerged from the kitchen. "Now what, guys? It's nearly Christmas. If you keep this up, I'll personally tell Santa Claus to leave all your presents at the North Pole. Get my drift?"

Kathy picked up the remote and turned back to her program. "Mom, Zak started it."

Zak picked up the joystick. "Did not!"

Kathy glared at him over the back of the couch. "Did, too!"

Caroline wiped her hands on the apron. "I don't care who started what. You're both going to be nice." She turned to go back into the kitchen and pull the last batch of cookies out of the oven.

Suddenly, Sarah stumbled by and grabbed Nickie's pants to keep from toppling over. Nickie held out her hand to let Sarah grab her index finger for support and steadied Sarah's wobbling. She turned to the table where Caroline had pictures in brightly colored frames. "See, Sarah, that's my daddy in this picture, and he's going to come to my birthday party."

Sarah stuck two fingers in her mouth, sucking on them, and stared at the photograph. She looked at Nickie and pulled them out to point at the pictures while saliva hung off her fingers and dripped onto the photos. She touched the image of a man framed in carved walnut. She giggled and drooled. "Daddy, daddy!"

"No, that's *my* daddy." Nickie sat down on the floor with Sarah who had just fallen onto her well-padded diapers.

Sarah pointed to the top of the table. "Daddy?"

Nickie stood up and cleaned the photograph with her sleeve. "That's my daddy in the picture. Mommy said he's in Heaven. I saw him with angels and dressed like a big puppy. Maybe on my birthday he'll come visit you, too."

Nickie sat down holding the picture. Sarah pulled on Nickie's golden soft curls and tried to stick her fingers in Nickie's nose. "Bebben, Daddy in Bebben."

"I don't think your daddy is in heaven. Mommy said *my* daddy's in Heaven, and that's where I'm going to find him."

"Daddy Bebben?"

***

Becca inched her way through the traffic that was being slowed by pedestrians trying to make their way around the cars in order to get to the stores. She stopped as the light turned red. She pulled her purse closer, took out the mascara, and looked at her face in the rearview mirror. Her gray-blue eyes looked red and tired, and her reddish-blond, wavy hair seemed limp. She fluffed the curls with her hand and put on the mascara, hoping to diminish the veins. It was important to look her best for the party. David would have wanted it to be festive for Christmas. Unexpectedly, the cell phone rang.

"Hi, this is Becca."

The voice on the other end was warm and comforting, like David's had been. "Hey, Becca, this is Russell. Just thought I'd let you know everything is under control. And, for the really exciting news, we have a potentially big client interested in MacroScope."

"Interested in what?"

"I'll show you when you get here. It's what I've been working on. It was David's idea last year. It's a new programming language that can be used by anyone who can type. We code-named the project MacroScope. I can't wait to have you figure out how to sell it."

"I vaguely remember David saying something about it."

"I think he was going to surprise you and officially unveil it at the Christmas party, but I guess I'm going to have to do it for him. When do you think you're going to be here?"

She looked in the side mirror at the line of traffic behind her and then at the truck stopped in front blocking all visibility. "At this rate it looks like eternity. I have no idea why we're stalled, and I can't see around the truck in front of me."

"Come find me as soon as you get to the office. I just got the last bugs out of the system, and I can't wait to show it to you."

"I'll do that. By the way, on a different subject, did you check to see if the caterer has the right time for tonight? And did anyone get glasses, plates, and napkins?"

"Not to worry. Everything's taken care of. In fact, I put everything on the table, including the tablecloth, thanks to Gloria, who was a big help."

"Thanks, Russell. It looks like traffic is finally moving. See you in a few minutes. And thank you for all you've done to help."

"Wouldn't have it any other way."

She turned off the cell phone. "What a sweetheart! So dependable." She pulled around the truck. "Finally I can get to the office."

Chapter Seven

Christmas carols floated in the background like elevator music filling space. Geronimo braced the phone between his shoulder and ear, picked up a magic marker, and wrote on a scrap of paper. He quickly took the paper, readjusting the phone against his shoulder, and held it up against the window, trying to get Roger's attention.

It was a brief note that read FATHER MCCURDY (MAD)! Geronimo emphasized the sentiment of the caller by sticking out his tongue and dragging his finger across his neck as if he were cutting his throat. He pointed at the handset and motioned for Roger to pick up his phone.

Roger hesitantly picked up the phone. He was still trying to wake up with his second cup of coffee and get into the routine of the day. He drank a long gulp and took control of the conversation. "Father McCurdy, what a pleasure. Merry Christmas. Did you want to say something on the air?"

Father McCurdy fumbled with the keys in his pocket and turned his back to the customers that might be listening. "Certainly not! I'm calling to ask you to please, *please* treat our Christmas mass with more respect. The purpose of a midnight mass is spiritual renewal! A holy sacrament! This is an important time of the year and nothing to be scoffing at!" He adjusted his collar like a stiff wayward necklace that irritated his neck and waited patiently for an apology.

Roger looked over the list of announcements, not noticing that Father McCurdy's silence demanded a response. He ran his finger down the items and found the advertisement for midnight mass. "Right, well, I…"

Father McCurdy clenched his fist. How dare he trivialize Christmas and its special significance! He sat down and put his glasses on the table, suddenly tired of dealing with what seemed to be innumerable problems complicating his last significant mass. He rubbed his eyes and looked at Mrs. Kirschbaum.

"And, furthermore, our mass is a great deal more profound and meaningful than that short little promotion you did after spouting off about the little kiddies in the Baptist pageant." He slammed his fist on the table, making the silverware jump. He blushed and looked around the deli to make sure nobody noticed, but only Mrs. Kirschbaum looked up from the counter and wagged her finger.

Startled by the sound, Roger jerked the phone away from his ear and looked at the receiver as if it were a foreign object. "I realize that you—"

Father McCurdy cleared his throat and poked the table with his index finger to emphasize every word. "Didn't you get my press release? It was very carefully worded and has a Christmas message even for those who are unable to attend."

Roger looked up at Geronimo. He pulled up his ponytail as if to hang himself and stuck out his tongue. He cradled the phone against his shoulder while he reached over and selected the next CD. "Right! We'll give you equal time in our next segment. I promise. You sure you don't want to go on the air, Father?"

Father McCurdy was startled at the thought of being "live" on the air and let out a nervous cough. "Please, see to it that you handle these things with dignity." With a scowl he snapped shut the cell phone.

Mrs. Kirschbaum wiped the crumbs off the table. She couldn't resist adding her own salve to sooth the indignation she imagined he must have felt from the one-sided conversation she heard. She moved closer to him. "Oy!" She raised her hand to the ceiling and lifted one eyebrow. "Father, nobody respectink religion anymore. A terrible thing, no?"

Father McCurdy nodded to Mrs. Kirschbaum and cleaned his glasses with a napkin. "It's a tragedy. You'd think that a radio station would be more sensitive to getting the message right about midnight mass. It only happens once a year!" He stuck the cell phone in his pocket and looked outside. Small flakes of snow were lightly drifting down.

Mrs. Kirschbaum patted his shoulder. "Very bad. Vell, you sit an' I brink you vun nice piece of strudel *mit Schlag.*"

"*Schlag?*"

"Vat, you don't vant vip kreme?"

"Okay." He smiled and looked at the flurries, thinking, "It's rude the offhanded way the DJ treated me. This is the last midnight mass of my career. It's important. I have to concentrate on the sermon. After all, this is a unique celebration."

Mrs. Kirschbaum went to the display and pulled out the biggest slice of apple strudel, took a fine sifter, dusted the top with powdered sugar, topped it with two heaping spoonfuls of whipped cream, and then brought it back to Father McCurdy along with a fork.

"Here ve go, Father. Maria, get a cup of coffee for Father McCurdy. He likes it mit kreme."

The waitress took the pot from the burner and grabbed a handful of plastic containers of cream. She poured the steaming coffee. "Here you go, Father. It's on the house. Merry Christmas."

"Thank you, Maria, and a blessed merry Christmas to you, too." Father McCurdy reached into his pocket and retrieved several folded papers and a pencil. He watched the snow dusting the window of the car parked next to the deli. Maybe it was time to review his notes and finalize his sermon for tonight. He read his first sentences to himself in a whisper. "Christmas is the time when there are no differences. In the spirit of celebration, everything is possible, and we can rise to be bigger than ourselves."

He thought about a story his father told him. Maybe he would use that in the sermon. He picked up his pencil and wrote: "My father told me this story, and it's a story I want to tell tonight."

He looked at the rumpled pages, took a bite of the pastry, and started again in small handwriting. "A cold heavy rain was falling, and the battlefield was a sea of mud. It was December 24, 1917, and Europe was in its third year of war. Separated by no more than forty yards were the French and German infantries. As usual, the fighting had raged all day, and casualties were heavy on both sides. The men were cold and tired. It had been days since they'd rested or had dry clothing or hot food. The only thing in steady supply was the endless thunder of cannons, the vicious crackle of machine gun fire, the anguished screams of the wounded, and the aching void left by fallen comrades. In the midst of this blood-soaked nightmare, no one remembered it was Christmas Eve."

Father McCurdy rubbed his eyes, smoothed the paper, and continued to write. "As night descended, the temperature dropped, and the rain turned to snow. Within a few hours, everything was wrapped in a blanket of white. A hush fell over the war-scarred landscape. Occasionally, gunfire shattered the eerie silence. It was one minute before midnight when Jacques Desmoulin, a corporal in the French army, heard something in the distance. He strained to catch the familiar, faraway sound carried by the night wind. It was a church bell. Someone was ringing a church bell. 'But who,' he wondered, 'and why?'"

Father McCurdy turned over the page. "And then, the young soldier remembered. It was Christmas Eve, and the bell was pealing its message of joy and celebration of the birth of Christ. Yes, he now remembered. Then he started to sing. First it was a hum, and then the words spilled out. '*Douce nuit. Sainte nuit. Tout au loin, dort sans bruit.*' Then he remembered his own village church, the choir, the incense. He started climbing the pile of mud, exposing himself to the enemy. His comrades looked on in amazement. Some were thinking he was a madman, but the young man was not afraid and he sang."

Father McCurdy took a bite of the strudel and a sip of coffee as he read what he'd written. Then he placed a new piece of paper on top. "From the other side, Hans Schmidt, a young German soldier, watched and heard the commotion. Instinctively, he raised his rifle and took aim in the direction of the sound. He was about to the squeeze the trigger, when the words, the melody, and the sound of Jacques Desmoulin's voice reached the German line. Hans recognized the song immediately, for he had sung it himself as a boy. As he listened, his eyes filled with tears. 'We call each other enemies,' he thought, 'but we are not so very different. We even have the same Christmas carols.' He laid his gun aside and reached for a flare, and then climbing from the safety of his trench, he shot it into the air and began to sing, '*Stille Nacht! Heilige Nacht! Alles schläft; einsam wacht.*' The flare soared and shattered the bleak darkness with its brilliant light and shone overhead like a star of hope in a night of lonely despair. Soon, one by one, all the men, French and German, stood out of the trenches facing each other and added their voices with Jacques Desmoulin's and Hans Schmidt's. Peace on Earth. Where there had been silence, there was a song and hope; where there had been darkness, there was light. On a snowy Christmas Eve in 1917, there was the true expression of love and what is possible."

He put down his pencil and rubbed his eyes. Yes, this was a good beginning for his last Christmas sermon. He ate the rest of his strudel and drank the last of the coffee before putting the creased pages back in his pocket. Now he had to think about all the last-minute chores that still needed to be done.

Mrs. Kirschbaum came to the table with more coffee. "Vell, another cup?"

"No, thanks. I've got to go get a tree—among other things—before tonight, but at least I know what I'm going to say for my sermon. Maybe your sweets were the inspiration."

She patted his shoulder. "Anytime you need inspiration, come here and sit for a vile. Harry says I alvays inspire him to cook new recipes. If my strudel give you goot tinkin, oy, the strudel I give you. Now go, go. The vetter is lookink like it vill turn bad. I don't vant to be vorry about you."

He placed a tip on the table and gathered his packages. He went to the door and waved at Mrs. Kirschbaum. "Bye. And happy Hanukkah."

"And a goot Christmas to you."

Just as he reached for the door, it was held open by Officer Santiago Moreno. A blast of cold air spilled into the deli.

Santiago was Latino, a gruff, fiery policeman in his mid-fifties with thick, unruly salt-and-pepper hair. Santiago touched the brim of his hat.

"Happy holidays, Father."

***

Santiago took off his hat and slid into his usual booth next to the window where he could watch people go by.

As if on cue, Maria immediately plopped a cup of coffee in front of him. Maria loved Santiago. She always hoped that maybe he would notice her—or maybe he would want someone younger. Maria was in her early forties, with silky black hair framing a beautiful Hispanic face. She was tall and voluptuous with curves that filled out her white blouse and straight black skirt.

At times she felt empty after leaving her family behind in Mexico to follow her dreams of romanticized possibilities in America. America held such promise. Where did the years go that had dissolved into a fuzzy memory of hopes and dreams? But nothing mattered when Santiago dropped by for a quick coffee. When he sat at her station, time stopped.

Maria gazed down at Santiago. She felt as though they were both alone and longed to ask him to spend Christmas with her, but she felt embarrassed and the words froze in her throat.

Santiago stared at the cup of coffee and once again realized he was working on a holiday. He looked at his reflection in the window and let the memories come. Without looking up, he mumbled, "I think I'll switch to a hot chocolate today."

"Wow! That's a change from your mega-caffeine fix, Officer. What's up?" She straightened her apron and tried to steady the hand holding the coffeepot. She always seemed to tremble whenever he was near.

"Usual stuff." He smiled at Maria.

"Well, sit for a while. I'll have that right up for you." She went back to the counter and poured hot chocolate in a cup. She opened the refrigerator and took out a container filled with a concoction Mrs. Kirschbaum whipped up every morning, a mixture of heavy cream, vanilla, and sugar. She scooped up a big spoonful and floated it on top of the steaming liquid.

Santiago smiled. "Thanks, Maria. When I'm through with the chocolate, a Reuben to go, please."

Maria winked. "My pleasure." She dusted the top of the cream with powdered chocolate.

Santiago leaned over the back of the booth. "With extra mustard. You know how I like it."

Maria saluted him with a spoon. "No problem, Officer! I'll give you an extra portion spread really thick."

"My name is Santiago, Maria."

"Okay, Officer Santiago."

Mrs. Kirschbaum noticed Maria spending more time going to Santiago's table than to the other customers'. She frowned and worried about Maria being the only waitress for the day. She wiped her hands on her apron and mumbled to herself. "Vy is it so hard to ask each uzzer on a date?"

She took the coffee pot from the burner and walked to the table. "Santiago Moreno! I miss you this mornink. Vat is it? You not likink my coffee any more?"

She playfully pulled the cup away from him as Maria replaced it with a steaming mug of hot chocolate with cream starting to ooze over the top.

Santiago smiled warmly. It felt nice to be around Mrs. Kirschbaum. It reminded him of what it was like to be with his mother or when she took him to his grandmother's house. They always found themselves in the kitchen where she would busy herself making cakes and encourage him to have another helping. "*Mi chiquito*," she would say. "Have some more. You look too skinny. Didn't you like it?" He saw himself pulling another plate of food toward him, wanting her to feel happy.

"Hey, Mrs. Kirschbaum. Aw, Christmas, y'know. You oughta see the stuff they got us doin' today. You'd think we was kindergarten teachers. I hate Christmas."

Mrs. Kirschbaum loved him like she loved all her children, as she called her customers; and, like a mother, she wanted Santiago to be happy. She pointed her finger at him with her other hand on her hips. "Schtop already mit the hating Christmas. Vat's not to like? Lights, presents, happy people, ve sellink lots of cheesecake, blintzes, and rolls. It's a good time of the year. Even *I* like. Be happy!"

Like his mother and grandmother, Mrs. Kirschbaum squeezed his cheeks hoping to raise a smile, but today he wasn't buying it. It was a day filled with work to cover the empty holes of past Christmases that no longer could be recaptured. He was absorbed in his own thoughts. How he wished Christmas didn't exist. It held so many bittersweet memories, like the memory of knowing his parents used what little resources they had to make Christmas magical for him. Images unfurled of saving his own money to finally buy a special gift for his mother and father. But his parents were dead now and Christmas had lost its meaning. His sister lived in California with her husband and two girls, and his brother had moved to Albuquerque with his wife and three boys. All the family close to him was somewhere else. It was now just a long night of work and watching everyone else treasure the magic.

Mrs. Kirschbaum knew she was filling some lonely spaces. She always knew that about people who needed to be comforted. Sometimes the comfort came in chicken soup; sometimes it came in words and wishes where the primary ingredient was love from the heart. "Look at me! I'm convincink this boy to be happy at Christmas." She poked her finger on his shoulder. "Tell me, vat are you doink tomorrow?"

Santiago looked into his half-filled cup. "Nothing. Resting, why?"

"Because Maria is restink, too, so you can rest together. She like you. You like her. Vat's the problem mit you people. You vant to talk or not?"

Santiago blushed. He had always wanted to invite Maria for a cup of coffee or something, but she worked in a coffee shop so what was the point of asking her out for coffee? Besides, would she even want to be with an older man? She looked so young and attractive. Could Mrs. Kirschbaum be right? He stared at her in disbelief and thought, "What a lovely, pushy woman you are."

Mrs. Kirschbaum put her hand on her hip and leaned forward. "So! Vat they got my Santiago de Chile doink today?"

Santiago smiled and pulled out his wallet. "Patrolling for pushy *yenta* deli owners. Are you one?"

Mrs. Kirschbaum wrinkled her nose and wagged her finger like his grandmother would do. "That's right!" She yelled into the kitchen. "Harry! Santiago de Chile vants to know if I'm 'pushy *yenta* deli owner!'"

A small, wire-thin sixty-year-old man with thick glasses came out from the kitchen as if summoned by invisible stage instructions that had been learned over decades. Harry Kirschbaum looked like one of Santa's helper elves. He had a spring to his walk, and yet he was stooped like someone hundreds of years old. He wiped his hands on an apron like a master chef cooking for hours, wanting to show the labors of his love and life. He stood next to his wife. "Santiago, listen! For vorty-zree years—"

Mrs. Kirschbaum glared. "Vorty-vun."

Harry looked at her and tapped his finger on the counter. "Vorty-zree years I'm sayink, 'Vat a pushy voman,' but who is belivink me? She vants the whole planet to get married. You know vy? So they come to her deli and buy cheesecake and gefilte fish and chopped liver. But vu is believink me? Zay al sayink 'she is a vonderful cook!' So vat am I doink in the kitchen cookin vile she is out here mit customers talkink and being a *yenta?* Vu am I?"

Harry and Mrs. Kirschbaum argued like two old souls that had intertwined their life stories in a tapestry of love worn through the years of life's trials.

Santiago mused over their mock feud as Maria delivered his sandwich. The smell of dark rye mingled with pastrami and sauerkraut stimulated his appetite. It made him hungry to taste the hot treat attempting to burst out of the wax paper wrapping. The feel of the wax paper made him think of his mother and the sandwiches she used to make for his school lunch.

Santiago picked up the check Maria had left on the table. Smiling to himself at the image of his mother taking fresh bread she had baked the night before and covering it with sweet gooey jams, he opened his wallet and pulled out several crisp bills. "Here, Maria. I gave you an extra tip for Christmas." Santiago beamed as if delivering a special gift.

"I'd rather you keep it and let's do something together with the money, like a movie or maybe lunch…" Maria felt the blood rush to her face. She avoided looking into his deep doe-like brown eyes and fumbled with her order book.

Santiago winked at her and tugged her apron. "Oh my, oh my. Both the deli owner and the waitress are pushy. I'm weakening. I'm weakening. Let's talk when I know more about my schedule." He turned to Mrs. Kirschbaum, "Say, Mrs. Kirschbaum. I thought you said you were going back to your people for the season."

She rolled her eyes and put a clean pot under the brewer. "Dreamink! Too much business to miss. All these Christmas shoppers spending avay their money, may they spend it in our direction! Next year in Jerusalem. But my son vu vent, he vent to Gdansk, the old country, to see the other side of the family. Then he go to Israel. He is brinkink me back a…a…a HVC."

"A what? HVC?"

Mrs. Kirschbaum shouted toward the kitchen. "Harry, vat is das zing, that HVC Jacob is brinkink me back from Tel Aviv?"

Harry opened the swinging aluminum door from the kitchen. "A movie vatcher on der TV."

Santiago scratched the top of his head and lifted his eyelids. "Oh! A VCR...I see...that's nice."

Mrs. Kirschbaum fished a pickle out of a big glazed jar. "Oy! VCR, NBC, CBS, ABC, CIA, FBI! Vat's the matter mit you people here? Not usink real vords, speaks all time mit letter! It's so confusink!"

Santiago turned to leave. His eyes searched for Maria, but she was busy with a new customer. He watched Mrs. Kirschbaum brush the wrinkles from her apron like his grandmother.

She winked at Santiago, plopped another pickle onto a piece of foil, and handed it to him. She slapped her forehead. "*Oy veh*, it should have been a cookie. Nothink sour like a pickle."

Santiago took the foil package and dropped it into the paper bag with his sandwich.

Mrs. Kirschbaum touched his arm and took a wrapped box from the counter. "Vait, here is something sweet for you. Since you alone, ven my son comes back, ve invitink you over for vatching the...vat is it? The VCB, eh?" She leaned closer and lowered her voice. "Maybe mit Maria, eh?"

Santiago smiled and chuckled. "Thanks, Mrs. Kirschbaum. Merry...uh...Happy Hanukkah!" He put his hand on the door and turned. "And merry Christmas, Maria." He looked at her for a moment, wanting to say more.

She blushed. "And Merry Christmas to you, too, Santiago."

Santiago raised his thumb up and smiled.

Mrs. Kirschbaum looked back and forth between Santiago and Maria. She waved a towel at him and laughed. "Oy! Come beck soon."

He waved behind his back and opened the door. The string of bells clinked against the glass, accentuating the chilly wind that tried to pry open the entrance. His thoughts were elsewhere as he stepped off the curb to cross the street, and he nearly collided with an old VW van as it came down the street.

The loud rock music escaping from the partially open windows ripped him into the present. Just as the VW swerved, a female hand appeared out the window with black painted fingernails. It was as if the hand didn't really belong to anyone. It merely was there to throw a wad of wrapping papers at him.

Santiago muttered and dug his fists deep in his pocket. "What the heck? Man, it's going to be a long day."

Chapter Eight

Jerry tried to scrape off the frost that was accumulating on his front windshield. He pulled off his glove and put his hand on the vent of his old VW van.

"Alexis, will you quit breathing and close that window? I can't see out the front, and the defroster is working overtime. All I've got here is a peephole."

She narrowed her eyes in a glare and rolled down the window further. She crossed her arms, looked at him, and stuck out her tongue. "Gotta throw something out."

Jerry took a tissue and wiped at the fog that was now forming. "Just throw it in the back."

She grinned and stretched her hand outside. "Too late."

Jerry was twenty-two this month even though he felt like he still belonged with the high school generation. Maybe that's why he hung out with Alexis and her friends instead of thinking about going to college. College was where his parents thought he should be, but his interests were in maintaining the carefree life and noncommittal style of his youth. Anyway, he knew his grades had suffered based on his attitude, and there wasn't a chance of getting accepted into the schools he wanted to go to; junior college seemed to him as boring as all the classes he sat through in high school, daydreaming of getting out. Well, now he was out, and he was still daydreaming about getting out. It just wasn't clear anymore out of what, so he decided to be a punk and pretend he was still living in his past. It was easier to stay with what was familiar.

Jerry yanked Alexis's coat sleeve. "Quit it! Hey, cut it out, Alexis!"

Alexis threw him a look of a defiant seventeen year old. Alexis was angry—angry at the inconsistency of her life since her parents divorced. Jerry wasn't ideal in her mind, but somehow he provided the stability she needed. It wasn't a deep relationship, but he was always there. She didn't see much of her father since the divorce, except for a couple of times at the police station when she needed him to bail her out. Jerry filled the void, though maybe not perfectly. Her mother disapproved of Alexis dating someone so much older and—in her mind—so irresponsible. That made Jerry even more just the thing.

Alexis had other forms of rebelling and showing her parents, primarily her mother, that she could do whatever she wanted. Sometimes she dyed her hair jet black and made her face look alabaster white. Now she had decided that a vibrant eggplant shade colored over her natural light brown hair with jet-black lipstick and matching fingernails was the statement to make.

Suddenly Jerry saw Santiago. He turned the steering wheel as Alexis slid against him.

She looked out the window. "What the—"

"I nearly hit someone."

"Who?"

"I think a cop."

"Yeah, right."

"Look, I don't need any trouble, least of all from a cop. For all I know the wrapper you threw out the window landed on his face."

Alexis giggled. "Now that would be funny. Imagine a cop with a gum wrapper stuck to his hat all day!"

"Alexis, just cool it!"

Jerry looked in the rearview mirror and only saw fog. He swerved around the corner. "If your dad wasn't such a cool DJ, I'd dump you off on the next street corner."

"Yeah right. And what about my *father*?"

"Man, I'd give anything to have a job where you can play really cool music all day long."

Alexis rolled her eyes. "Whatever!"

Jerry turned the music up louder. "I'm not kiddin', Alexis," he shouted. "One more stop, for anything, and I lose my license, get it? Besides, they might search us and find somethin'. You tuned in? No more fun, no more chargin' around almost hitting a cop and throwin' anything out the window. It's my van, so don't get me in trouble, okay?"

Alexis punched him on the arm and laughed. "Oh, Jerry, you are such a dweeb! People drive without licenses all the time."

Jerry gripped the wheel and glanced over at Alexis. "So? It's my license, okay, and I'm gonna decide if I lose it or not, right? Oh, man!"

They sat in silence for a minute. Jerry looked at his watch, then reached over to the radio volume knob and turned it to the right. He moved his head in time with the heavy metal music that blasted through the speakers and drummed his hand against the steering wheel in time with the music. "Time to go get Geronimo."

Alexis took the sleeve of her coat and rubbed her window to make a small hole in the frost. "He's sleepin'."

"No, he ain't. He's workin' all day today."

Jerry turned toward Alexis with a broad smile. "He's working with your ol' man."

Alexis pushed herself further into the seat and curled her upper lip. "You gotta be kidding, right?"

Jerry laughed and shrugged his shoulders. "So what's the big deal? Let's just go pick him up."

"Look, I don't want to have anything to do with my dad. He was the one that split up the family."

"Says who?"

"Says me. Mom said they changed, and they couldn't live with each other anymore. And then he left." She breathed on the window, waiting for it to frost, and etched a heart. She whispered, "Besides I'm probably why he left anyway."

"You don't know that. It doesn't mean you can't go in and see him."

Alexis stuffed her hands in her black leather jacket pockets and stared at her frosty reflection. "You gotta be joking. I don't even wanna go near that place."

Jerry touched her shoulder and felt her pull away. "You don't have to go in. I'll get 'im. Geez, woman. For such a tough chick, you sure are really a fainter' bout your dad."

Alexis yanked her shoulder from under his hand and turned her back to him. "Gives me the creeps!" She reached over and cranked up the stereo even louder. She closed her eyes, synchronized her hands with the rhythm of the song, and mouthed the lyrics.

***

Nickie walked toward the crèche and stood up on her tiptoes to get a better look. She removed the sheep from the back, kissed it, and put it in front of the figurines. "I love you, little lamb." Then she picked up the camel. "What's wrong with you, little cow?" She placed it next to the lamb. "But I love you, too!" She then took Joseph and Mary and placed them at the entrance of the wooden little door on the back. "You're the daddy and the mommy like mine...and...then..."

Caroline came out of the kitchen drying her hands. "What are you doing, Nickie?"

"I'm playing with the animals on the farm."

"This is not a farm, sweetheart. This is where Jesus was born."

"Then why are there animals in his house?"

"Nickie, that's a manger and that's where the animals live."

"Oh!" Nickie looked curiously at Caroline. "Do people live in an animal house, too?"

Caroline shook her head. "Never mind. Keep playing. Just don't break anything."

***

Music softly filled the space in the radio station broadcast booth, mingling with streams of sunlight. Geronimo sat on a small table in the corner of the room. Everything seemed mellow and calm. He watched

Roger Dodger leaning back in his chair like a big, lazy cat, monitoring the staging of his music and ads. This was what he wanted to do, he thought as he watched his mentor. Just sit back and orchestrate a symphony of sound.

Geronimo broke in like a caller. "So, wow, man! You were actually in San Francisco when it was, like, totally all happenin'?"

Roger grinned as he looked at a photograph of himself wearing a bright-colored shirt and a big necklace with a brass peace symbol. "Better than that, I was one of 'em!"

"Yer kiddin' me, man! Too much! So you had the hair and everything?" Geronimo looked at him with admiration.

"Down to here." Roger Dodger put his hand down to the small of his back.

"Wow. That's just too rad, dude."

Roger grinned broadly. "And my name, my age-of-Aquarius, flower-power name was Durphy Sparkle!"

Geronimo hooted. "Too awesome! Who else knows?"

"Only the old gang, so keep it to yourself."

"My lips are sealed." He pantomimed pulling a zipper across his mouth. "Durphy Sparkle? That is such a cool name, dude. Durphy Sparkle! Man! Unbelievable! I mean, y'know, I really envy you, Rog—I mean, Durphy." He hooted again and picked up an old album that was part of the library that stood on dusty shelves in the control room. "Y'know, I really...I mean, I missed the Beatles. I missed 'Nam and Nixon. I missed the sit-ins and love-ins and be-ins and flower power. Woodstock, man, the whole thing! I was born too late, y'know!"

Roger went to stage the next CD and smiled up at Geronimo. "Yeah, yeah, yeah. It was pretty exciting all right. We were going to change the world."

Geronimo grinned and pressed a faded record jacket of the Moody Blues' *Days of Future Passed* against the window. "Yeah, man? So, well, like, man, what happened to you? I mean you look so...so...y'know, so straight, man, when yer like, y'know, a brother?"

Roger looked at the album and shook his head. "Are you trying to tell me something?"

At that moment the doorbell rang. "Better see who wants something."

"Got it, boss." Geronimo put the album back in its designated place. "Hey, can we talk more about those old days later?"

Roger looked at the photo from Woodstock. He opened the drawer and touched the peace symbol necklace. "Sure, why not? They're interesting memories—and what do you mean old?"

Geronimo grinned and flashed him the peace sign. "I get it. It's cool, man; it's cool!"

Roger looked over the top of his glasses, picked up a CD of Cat Stevens, and muttered, "So, yeah, so like, what did happen, man?" So where did all the years go? And what of the ideologies? Nothing seemed to have gotten much better in his life. He was estranged from his wife. With every year since his divorce, his daughter seemed to slip further away. It was as if those he loved were leaving his universe. It was harder to hold on to normality as he knew it or had taken as a given over the years. Everything had slipped through a kind of gradual mist, and nothing was certain anymore. The only certainty was that his life only contained himself.

Geronimo entered the broadcast booth with Jerry. "Hey, dude, this is the man." He pointed to Roger and beamed. "You gotta meet him, bro'! This here, dude, is like the man who saw it all, did it all, and lived through it *all*." He looked down at Roger. "This is my bud, Jerry, and I wanted him to meet you."

Roger teased Geronimo. "I didn't think we had anyone on the list to come to the station today."

"Well, he isn't officially on your list, but I wanted him to meet you."

Roger extended his hand. "Pleased to meet you, Jerry." He turned up his hand, and they slapped their palms in the air in a high five.

Jerry looked around the booth. "Outta sight!"

Geronimo leaned on the desk. "Say, man, I mean, Roger. I'm goin' out on a break. You want some fresh coffee or something?"

Roger looked over the top of his glasses. "Sure, but don't be long. Lot's goin' on today."

"You got it!"

Geronimo went to the door and then turned back holding up both hands in a two-fingered V. "Peace."

Roger laughed at the throwback to the past. That was where his happy memories lived, when Alexis was conceived and everything was more straightforward. Geronimo left with Jerry, and there was only the need to get the next task done and the one after that. Maybe life wasn't so complicated when you broke it down into what had to be done now and only now. He picked up the picture of Alexis. "Life was simple back then."

***

Geronimo looked back and saw Roger reading a CD label. He motioned Jerry to follow him to the side door and let it close behind him. He pulled the front of his coat tight against the cold. He talked through the steam that escaped from his mouth and made frozen crystals on his cheeks and nose. "I mean, man, he's like the sultan of the sixties, y'know?"

Jerry opened the door of the van. "Yeah! He's awesome. Did you see all those cool pictures and that rack of CDs?"

Alexis pressed herself against the seat of the van. "Hey, it's just CDs. No big deal."

Geronimo pulled the windshield scraper out from underneath the back seat. "I mean, you oughta hear the stuff he says, man. Alex, you didn't tell me your ol' man was so cool. I mean, he is a shoot-'em-up, straight, highflyin', mainlinin' dude brother of the first order." Jerry brushed the snow with his hands. "This guy is like a god, man."

"Like you would know. You think he's so cool!" Alexis snapped back.

Geronimo scraped the ice from the window. "Yeah! You should hear his stories. They're amazing!"

"Yeah, well, I bet they're not about me. I bet he doesn't even remember I exist." She crossed her arms and scowled at them both. "Knock it off, Jerry! And you, too, Geronimo!"

Geronimo made a snowball and threw it at her window. "Hey, you never told me yer dad was a hippie and stuff."

Alexis furrowed her brow and glared. "Just shut up about my old man."

Geronimo shrugged his shoulders and put his hand against Alexis's window. "He's pretty cool, babe. Used to have hair down to—"

Alex rolled down the window. "Shut up, Geronimo! We don't get along, okay? So just forget it!"

Chapter Nine

Christmas was hectic at the police station. For Sergeant Kim it was always a day filled with unexpected problems. He felt like the director of a play dealing with a lot of temperamental people at the same time. Each task was important to the overall operation. There was the phone— which rang constantly—to answer and officers to dispatch.

Sergeant Kim looked over the desk heaped with stacks of papers in what seemed like jumbled disarray. An officer walked over and handed him a clipboard with several pages on it.

"Sir, I need your signature on the last three pages."

"What's with Christmas? I spend all my time signing things. Right now I'd give anything to be out there on the street."

"Sorry, sir. You missed one."

Sergeant Kim looked at the plaque on the wall naming him officer of the year. He flipped the page and signed. "Like I said, I'd give anything to be out on the street tonight. I've signed more times today than when I pay the bills—and the phone just won't stop ringing." He handed back the clipboard. "You're not going to give me more paperwork, are you?"

"Not at the moment, sir, but you know how Christmas is."

"Yeah, a royal pain. I just want a nice, quiet day, go home to the wife and have dinner with a frosty glass of beer." He dismissed the officer and went back to the pages needing attention on his desk Sergeant Kim was in his early sixties. He was short, round, and balding. They always teased him about looking like the dispatcher on the old TV show, *Taxi*.

Just then the phone rang. One of the officers picked it up. "Hey, Sarge. It's for you."

"Yeah, well, do tell." He punched the button on the handset. "Sergeant Kim here…I don't care what he says. That's the way we handle it, and we ain't changing for him!" He slammed down the receiver and looked up to see Santiago with two handcuffed prisoners standing in front of his desk. One prisoner was a little, unassuming, grandmotherly old lady, and the other was a man dressed as Santa Claus. "What's this? You arrest a little old lady wearing support hose and Santa Claus on Christmas Eve?"

Cliff, a uniformed officer, passed by the scene. "Nice catch there, Moreno." He slapped Santiago on the back and grinned.

"Hey, Santiago, I can see you're bucking for lieutenant."

"Certainly before you'll ever see it."

"Hey, I'm out there doing real work while you're out arresting dangerous criminals like grandmothers with assault purses."

Santiago glowered. "Get lost, Al Pacino!" He shoved his prisoners closer toward the sergeant's desk.

Sergeant Kim stared in disbelief. "This is a joke, right, Santiago? I'm going home tonight and tell the grandkids that I booked a little old lady and Santa Claus the day before Christmas, right?"

Santiago handed him a candy cane. "Ho! Ho! Ho!"

Sergeant Kim rolled his eyes and crossed his arms on top of the desk. He then noticed a small crowd of curious bystanders had assembled. "Hey, don't you have some work to do, like paperwork or something?" He leaned forward. "All right, I suppose I've got to hear this. What have public enemies number one and two done to terrorize the city already this morning?"

Santiago, with a wry smile, reached over and readjusted the little old lady's wig centering it on top of a frowning face.

Sergeant Kim noticed the heavy caked-on make up that became very apparent under the fluorescent lights. "Charley, what are you doing here?"

Charley was a little unassuming man with weathered skin who was dressed as a woman. He gave Sergeant Kim an indignant look. "I want to call my lawyer."

"Heard that a million times. Everyone wants to talk to their lawyer, like nobody every does anything wrong. It's all one big innocent mistake."

"Well, I didn't do anything, and if I did, I can explain. In any case, I'm entitled to one phone call."

Several lines lit up on his telephone and rang insistently.

"All in good time, Chucky, my boy, all in good time. You'd look better in a suit than that frumpy dress."

"Call me crazy, but I like dresses."

Sergeant Kim pushed the first, second, and third buttons. "Sergeant Kim, please hold. Sergeant Kim, please hold. Sergeant Kim, please hold." He looked up to see that Santiago had put Santa on center stage in what seemed like an unfolding scene in a play.

Santiago plopped Santa's bag in front of the sergeant, untied the sack, and opened the top. "Hey, Sarge, guess what's inside."

Sergeant Kim played with the pen his father gave him when he graduated from the police academy. He could easily be the one standing where Charley was. He remembered when he was young and how he skated very close to breaking the law. At the time he felt rebellious and hung out with the wrong crowd. He put down the pen and peered over his desk at Santa Claus, and then looked back at Santiago. "Enlighten me. I haven't got all day."

Santiago made a sweeping theatrical motion as several officers gathered around. "As you will recall from our morning briefing, Charley here never keeps a wallet after lifting it. He always passes off to one or more of his highly trained associates."

Santiago lifted Santa's sack and dumped the contents on the desk. An assortment of wallets, money clips, and purses tumbled onto the table.

The bystanders who had assembled to see the story unfold were amused and amazed. Several shook their head in disbelief, and one whispered to her partner, "Do you believe it? A Santa pickpocket—and on Christmas Eve!"

Sergeant Kim was impressed with the array of products that tumbled out before him. He picked up a wallet and examined the contents. "My, oh my! Have you been busy little elves? Let's put 'em on our little Christmas list—the 'naughty' list. Shall we?"

Several cops stifled a laugh and went back to their duties. Cliff passed Santiago. "And who are you going to go after next, the Easter Bunny?"

"Pacino, just shut up."

Sergeant Kim picked up the duty roster. "Oh, and Santiago?"

"Yes, Sarge?"

"As a reward for outstanding service to the community, you're assigned overtime tonight. The churches need traffic control." He slid it toward Santiago.

Santiago picked it up, read the details, and tossed it back. "You gotta be kiddin' me."

Sergeant Kim stood up and put his fists on the desk. "That's after backing up the parking assistance at the mall. They've got a real mess down there."

Santiago opened his mouth to protest, but the phone rang.

Sergeant Kim picked it up. "Police department, please hold." He pushed the MUTE button.

"Sarge, give me a break!"

Sergeant Kim put the receiver down. "Sorry. Look, you're single, and I have a lot a guys with families off today."

Santiago stuffed his gloves into his coat pocket. "Yeah, yeah, yeah. Sheesh!"

Sergeant Kim picked up the phone and pointed at the two prisoners. "Look, the brass tells me, I tell you, and you get to take it out on little old ladies and Santa." He punched one of the buttons on the phone. "Thank you for holding. May I help you?"

Santiago made a sweeping gesture toward the back corner of the room and escorted both prisoners to his desk. "Come on. We've got paperwork to do." He stared down at the long blank form. "I hate Christmas!"

Chapter Ten

Zak looked toward the kitchen to see if his mom was watching him. He unwrapped a miniature candy bar and threw the wrapper on top of the handful of others lying next to Sarah, whose face was painted with chocolate. She reached into the stack, grabbed a fistful of wrappers, threw them in the air, and giggled.

Zak snatched another chocolate, ready to toss the paper toward Sarah. "You look disgusting. You've got chocolate all over your face. Mom will be mad. Jeremy, give me back that brochure on the SpeedoRacer. You can't have it."

"Can, too!"

"Cannot! It's my SpeedoRacer!"

"Oh, yes, I can. It's not only yours."

Zak tried to pull the paper out of his hands. "Cannot! I thought of it first!"

"Did not! I wrote the letter to Santa Claus!"

Kathy stopped painting her toenails. "Shut up, you guys! I wrote the letter for mom and dad to find, and it's not even Christmas yet. And if you don't quit arguing, maybe you won't even get it." She looked at Sarah and Nickie to make sure they hadn't heard.

Jeremy threw down the paper. "Will, too! I asked for it first and I should get it no matter what 'cause it's Christmas."

Zak's face turned red, which accentuated his freckles. "Did not! You little boogerhead!"

"I am not a boogerhead! Mom! Zak's calling me names!"

Caroline had had enough of the fighting and yelled from the kitchen. "I've told you kids I have things to do, and I—" She stormed into the room and took in the panorama of chocolate chaos. Everyone looked guilty, with the exception of Sarah, who beamed beneath chocolate lips that betrayed their collective mischief.

Caroline picked up the open bag of chocolates that was almost empty. "Where did you get these?"

All except Nickie pointed immediately at Sarah.

"Sarah?" Caroline raised one eyebrow.

Sarah smiled, giggled, and clapped her hands. "Mommy, more caddy."

Caroline laughed and knelt to pick her up. "Oh, sweetie, you get blamed for everything, don't you? You couldn't be the instigator." She looked over at the other kids.

Kathy went back to painting her toenails. "Wasn't me, Mom."

Caroline sighed. "All right, you kids. Pick up the wrappers."

Resignedly, as if banished to a penal colony, Zak and Jeremy started to pick up candy wrappers.

For the first time Caroline noticed Nickie standing quietly next to the wall. "Nicole, did you see who got out the candy bars?"

Nickie quietly nodded her head, confirming that she knew. She didn't want Aunt Caroline to be mad at her. Nickie saw the glares from Jeremy and Zak. She decided to change her mind and shook her head "no." She paused and looked at Caroline, "You look like my daddy."

That simple statement was like a hard slap for Caroline. Here was this little girl in front of her bringing the hard sting of the death of her own brother crashing into the present. It was better to deal with the chaos than to think of the loss. "Come on, you kids. Finish up." Caroline threw a stern look at all of them. "Give me some cooperation here."

Kathy was absorbed in the television program. "Yeah, as soon as my nails are dry.

"Thanks for helping, Kathy." Caroline looked at the wrappers in the trashcan. "Okay, boys. Now you've spoiled your lunch. Sarah, let's get you cleaned up. Oh, what a day this day is turning out to be!"

Caroline shifted Sarah to her other hip and took her into the kitchen, where she turned on the faucet and wet a paper towel to wipe the chocolate-painted face.

Zak came up to Nickie nose-to-nose. "Nice going, Nickie! Just blame everything on Sarah. Mom never gets mad at her. Here, you wanna take these wrappers and throw them away?"

Nickie held out her hands and took another pile of wrappers showing the real amount of candies that had been consumed. She went over to Kathy to see if she, too, wanted to contribute to the little paper mountain. Kathy looked at Nickie and got up from the couch, stretching like a feline, and strutted out of the room mimicking the model she'd just seen on television.

Zak saw Caroline cleaning up Sarah and thought just maybe he could have some fun getting his cousin in trouble with his mom. It felt good when someone other than him was in trouble. He looked at Nickie's pile of candy wrappers. He knew his mother hadn't seen the size of the stack.

"The garbage is by the refrigerator." He pointed to the kitchen. He looked at Nickie and gave her a gentle push. "Go on and throw them away." He peered over her head to see if his mother was there to notice. He then turned to his brother. "Come on, let's play Xbox!"

"Yeah let's play *Halo*!"

Nickie looked at the heap of candy wrappers in her hands. She thought maybe Aunt Caroline was going to be mad at all the candy they'd eaten. She looked up, and then the candy made no difference. There on the wall was a picture of Daddy and Aunt Caroline. It was her daddy looking into her eyes telling her to be a good girl. Nickie ran into the kitchen.

Caroline cradled Sarah in her arms, oblivious to Nickie, and washed the little chocolate-smeared face. "Such a pretty little girl. Mommy's little girl. How can I be mad at you when you're so cute? Ooh, such a cute lidda one. Yes, you are." Caroline tickled Sarah, and they both giggled.

Nickie watched them as she stood holding all the candy wrappers. Right now she was thinking about her daddy, and she wanted to be cuddled, too.

Caroline lifted Sarah and put her on the floor. "Oh, you're getting to be such a big girl. Now run and play."

Sarah took off with the wobbly steps of a toddler who's teetering between running and falling.

Nickie tugged on Caroline's pants.

Caroline looked down to see another chocolaty face. "Oh, Nickie! What have you done now? Come here to the sink and let me wash that off." She took a washrag and ran it under the water. There were too many things to handle today of all days. It was Christmas Eve, and there was still so much to manage with Steve stuck in Chicago.

"Nickie, Auntie Caroline just can't keep cleaning up after you today, honey. You need to take better care of yourself. You're a big girl now, and you need to—"

Nickie yanked on her apron. "My daddy is your brother."

Caroline hesitated before answering. "Yes...yes...he was, Nickie...and now he's gone." At a loss for anything more to say, she decided to try to distract her little charge. "Now you need to run along and play with the boys. I've got to finish making these cookies for tomorrow."

Nickie touched the brass knob of the cabinet door under the sink and looked up at Caroline. "My daddy is coming for my birthday."

Caroline felt the impatience rising, but knew she needed to control her emotions. She put aside the cloth now smeared with chocolate and knelt down to Nickie's level. "Nickie, we'll all come for your birthday tomorrow, but your daddy can't come. He's...he's not here anymore."

"Daddy's gonna bring me a puppy for my birthday."

Caroline took Nickie's hand. "Nickie! Now listen to me. Your daddy was my brother. I loved him very much. But he died, Nickie! He's dead. And he won't come back." Caroline stifled a sob. "He can't come back, little girl...and I love him very much, too...and miss him just like you do." It was now all too real and back in the present. Caroline had carefully filed away the memory of her brother in her heart and mind so it would no longer hurt. She burst into tears and pulled Nickie into her arms.

Nickie started crying, too. "I miss my daddy. Where is he? Where is he?"

Caroline hugged her tighter and stroked her back. "Oh, Nickie. I'm sorry. I'm sorry. Listen, your daddy is happy. He's in Heaven. Do you understand? And I know he misses you, too, honey, but he can't be with us right now. He's in Heaven, okay?"

Caroline pushed her back to look into her glistening blue eyes and forced a smiled. "Nickie, your daddy wouldn't want you to be unhappy at Christmastime. I know! I have a nice book we can look at. Do you want to?"

Nickie nodded.

"All right, honey, I'll be right back." Today everything seemed to be an interruption. Just as Caroline was about to retrieve the book, the telephone rang. "Nickie, I have to get the phone. I'll be right back!"

Nickie felt all alone, and even more alone when she thought about what Aunt Caroline had said. Her eyes filled with tears, and there, through the tears, was a picture of her daddy with Aunt Caroline. She looked at the picture and touched her daddy's face. "He said he'd come to my birthday party. I know you'll come, Daddy, because you said so."

She pulled out the chair next to the table, climbed on it, and knelt in front of the nativity scene. She put the small sheep back in the manger. "You need to go back in your house now. And all you other animals, you need to stay over here in the corner of the house." She took the other sheep, cow, and camel, and put them in the right side of the manger.

Nickie took a framed picture of Zak and placed it as a divider in the manger. "'Kay. Here's your own room, and you can't come over here on this side unless you knock." She took Mary, Joseph, and the wise men, and placed them behind the makeshift partition. "'Kay, now this is your room. All the animals are sleeping, so you have to be quiet." She picked up the cradle with baby Jesus and placed it in between Mary and Joseph.

Kathy came back and sat on the couch with a soda. She started buffing her nails.

Nickie turned, holding onto the back of the chair. "You wanna play with the animals?"

Kathy raised an eyebrow. "Get real. That's not a toy."

Nickie sat on the chair and picked up the angel and looked back at her father. Suddenly, it all made sense.

Nickie slid off the chair and walked over to Zak, who was engrossed in a video game, and pulled on his sleeve. "Zak!"

He yanked his sleeve back and barked, "What?"

Nickie put her fists on her hips and glared at him. "Do you know where Heaven is?"

Zak went back to his game and pushed on the buttons of the joystick. "Is it the latest Xbox game?"

"What's an Xbox?"

"I can't believe you don't know. If you don't know, I'm not going to tell you."

Nickie frowned and went back to the nativity scene. She picked up one of the angels and set it next to the picture of her daddy.

***

Becca pulled into her parking slot, turned off the ignition, and looked in the rearview mirror. "I certainly look pale." She took a blush stick from her purse and readjusted the mirror to see better. She made two circles on each cheek and rubbed the color into her skin. She got out, pulling her purse and briefcase with her, slammed the door, and clicked the automatic door lock.

She walked with stiff legs up the icy walkway trying not to slip and muttered, "Why did I decide to wear boots with heels?" As she got to the door, it automatically opened.

"Hey, you made it."

"Thanks, Russell. No thanks to the traffic."

"Well, do you want to see a demo of MacroScope? We've got a big airline client that really wants to use it."

"For what?"

"We're going to build an automated airport."

"To do what?"

"Make it simple for the agents."

"What a concept! I swear they're typing a novel just to check in."

Russell grinned as he opened the door to her office. "Take off your coat. I've got it loaded on your computer."

She threw her coat on the couch and sat in David's wing-backed executive chair. She looked at the screen with all its icons. "So what am I looking at?"

"This is a prototype of the ticket counter. It actually works. You want to reissue a ticket?"

"I don't have a ticket."

"Let's issue one then."

"For real?"

"No, we're working off the test system."

"Well, then issue it for somewhere exotic, like the Bahamas for the holidays."

"Okay, just let me put in your name and pick a few parameters from this graphic interface and click on ISSUE."

Russell heard the ticket printer snap a coupon out of the slot. "Your ticket, ma'am."

"Wow, that's amazing! What did the software do?"

"It basically simulated the decision logic of the best airline agent. It took all the information I gave it and constructed those cryptic commands that get sent to the reservation system, which the agent has to type. Then it interpreted the response, which was equally cryptic, and figured out what it needed to send next to ultimately issue the ticket. And *voilà*, your ticket to Austria."

"Better reissue it back to Cedarwood because this is where the holidays are going to be this year." Becca stared at the airport screen. "This must have taken forever to build. I didn't even see it in the budget for marketing expenses."

"It was simple. We built it with a couple of sociology major interns in a month."

"That seems impossible."

"That's where David's idea paid off. It's simple and fast to build this with MacroScope, our new product offering."

"So what's MacroScope?"

"David wanted to surprise you, kind of like a Christmas gift. It's a language we've been working on for months. It's like programming with big LEGOs."

"So what's the significance of this language?"

"It means that the computer science know-how is in the building material. It's going to allow someone with no computer science training to write really complicated software. Think about how we're going to market this. Look at what was possible in a few weeks in creating an automated ticket counter."

Becca picked up a stack of pink phone message sheets and sighed. "I'd rather be dealing with your technology than having to return these calls, most of which relate to open issues surrounding David's business transactions. Maybe we'll sell MacroScope to widows who would rather be at home with their kids instead of dealing with office parties."

"Don't worry about the party. I've got it covered."

Becca shuffled through the messages trying to establish a sequence of priority. "Well, got to make some calls. Let me know if I'm needed."

Russell went to the door and hesitated. "By the way, say hi to Nickie for me. Maybe we can all get together after the holidays."

"Yeah, sure. Now go, so I can make these calls" She paused and set the phone messages on the desk. "I would love that."

Russell frowned. "Love what?"

"Both of us going out together with Nickie after the holidays."

"I would like that very much."

"Me, too."

Russell closed the door. "Becca, I really would do anything to make everything better for you. Since David's death I want to make sure that you're all right." He thought back to when he met Becca for the first time. It was a crisp spring day when he walked to the psychology building. All he could think about was making it through his last obligatory science credit, PSY101. Here he found himself as a senior taking a freshman level course, but a credit was a credit and all he wanted to do was graduate, get out of college, and get on with living instead of surviving.

The auditorium-style room was full as he made his way to the last row to be out of sight of the instructor. It seemed like a safe place to hide from being called on to answer questions or comment. Then his attention was drawn to the overcrowded doorway filled with students surveying the room for open seats. When they realized the class was filled beyond the room's capacity, they decided the only place to sit was on the stairs lining the room.

It was at that moment that he saw Becca as she pushed her way through the crowd with a deep blue canvas backpack slung over her shoulder. What he noticed especially was the glint of copper and gold hair that cascaded to the small of her back and caught the light when she moved. She seemed timid as she tried to find an empty seat. He moved his coat that he had flung over the seat in front of him when he entered earlier and waved at her, indicating the seat was free.

She smiled and waved back, picking her way up the stairs and around students sitting on the steps. She made her way across folded legs and backpacks to the empty seat and turned to him. "Thank you. It's my first day today, and it's all a bit intimidating."

"I've been here for four years, and these big classes are still scary."

His entire attention was on Becca's hair and the way she took endless notes on a subject that seemed unimportant at the moment. When the instructor finished, Russell pulled on his jacket and tapped Becca on the shoulder. "Hey, would you like to go the student union for a cup of coffee?"

She smiled. "I'd love to, but I think I better go get some help with my computer course. I don't think I understood anything the professor said today."

"I'll tell you what. Let's get a cup of coffee, and I'll introduce you to my friend David who knows computers from every angle."

Russell thought back to that first meeting. He hadn't really thought about getting involved, least of all with a freshman who still had four years to go. Yet Becca fell in love with David, and he went into business with David in high technology. He thought about the first encounter with Becca so long ago and how she still stopped the world for him, but the first Christmas without her husband was not the time to tell her how he felt the first day he saw her confused and stranded in a group of students.

Chapter Eleven

Reverend Woods loved music, and Christmas was a great day for magnificent songs that filled the heart with joy. It made him feel happy to hum along with the choir as he went about arranging the chairs. His Baptist church seemed somehow bigger and more alive when the voices of the choir filled the space with lively gospel songs. He liked to listen to the rehearsal for the big pageant. Even the mistakes sounded perfect to him. Here he was sixty-five years old, and yet it seemed like only yesterday when he was a little boy playing at being a minister.

Reverend Woods was a tall man with a powerful frame, but he exuded a gentleness that contradicted his stature. The rich brown planes of his face were smooth despite his age, and he always had a smile or word of encouragement for the parishioners in his care. Only the dusting of white hairs betrayed that he was older than he appeared. He was like a gentle bear.

Reverend Woods knew Christmas Eve was filled with preparations and paying attention to last minute details that got overlooked every year. He told himself this year it would be different and everything would run without flaw.

He was deep in thought when he heard the clapping from the back of the church. He looked in the direction of the noise and saw Santiago, who had entered and was moved to spontaneous clapping as the choir finished their song.

"Oh, sorry, Reverend Woods. I guess I shouldn't clap in here."

Reverend Woods and the choir burst into laughter. "Well, we can see how often you attend here, Officer. Please don't feel badly. We're happy you like our song, aren't we, choir?"

"Amen and hallelujah!" The choir clapped their hands in unison.

"And we think the Lord would have us be happy at Christmastime." Reverend Woods winked at the choir. "Praise the Lord!"

"Praise the Lord!" The choir clapped again as if finishing a song.

"So, may I help you, Officer?"

"I need to talk to you, Reverend Woods."

Reverend Woods turned to the choir with another wink. "Oh, they finally tracked me down! I'll go quietly." He turned to one of the choir members. "Aunt Pearl, will you take over, please?" He suppressed a slight smile as he motioned for Santiago to follow him to his office.

The choir resumed their rehearsal as Santiago entered the small room. Reverend Woods closed the door, shutting out the sound of the choir. Every wall was lined with shelves filled with old books that smelled musty and the occasional modern novel stuck in between.

Santiago took off his hat and pointed at the shelves. "Do you collect old books?"

"Old books, old radios, old things in general, like me." He laughed. "Take this silly old radio. It doesn't sound all that good, but it belongs to my dad." He reached over and moved the radio closer and turned it on. "But nothing sounds that bad when it's Christmas music. So, are you going to come to our little performance?"

"Well, I wish I could be here for the whole program, but, you know, latecomers and all. If you don't mind, though, the other officers and me, well, we'll just stand in the back."

"Oh, no. Perhaps we could rope off the last row on the right, and you could sit there."

"Mighty kind of you, but I think the back will be just fine, thanks. Reverend, what I came for may seem silly." Santiago pulled a piece of paper out of his heavy jacket and passed it over to the Reverend. "But I looked at your application for traffic control, and, well…it seems sorta stupid, but you didn't sign it, and Sergeant Kim is a real stickler for this kind of stuff."

"Oh, well, that's easily taken care of. Very kind of you, Officer."

"Uh...Officer Santiago Moreno, sir."

"Yes, Officer Moreno."

Reverend Woods looked at the official-looking document. "Deck the Halls" finished playing on the radio, and Roger Dodger's voice crashed into their midst. The voice caught Reverend Woods's attention, and he leaned over his desk to turn up the volume.

Roger's voice filled the room. "And we'd like to remind everyone of tonight's youth pageant at the Grace Community Baptist Church. Eight sharp. And you surely won't want to miss midnight mass tonight at the Church of the Madeleine. They work very hard to get ready for this mass, and it is certainly one of the most meaningful moments of the year."

Reverend Woods smiled listening to his own announcement being made with stifled enthusiasm. "I'm sorry for the interruption. It's a little tedious at Christmastime dealing with details." He looked up at Santiago and turned off the radio. "Silence can be a pleasure."

Reverend Woods looked over the paper for the signature line, signed it, and handed it back to Santiago.

Santiago took the paper and looked to make sure the signature was in the right place. "Not to upset your silence, Reverend, but I have a more...um...a personal question."

Reverend Woods studied Santiago's serious face, "Oh? Very well, by all means."

All of a sudden the door burst open, and there stood an elderly man frowning ominously and dressed as one of the three wise men. He was wearing a long flowing striped caftan and carrying a huge turban covered with gems and sprouting enormous feathers.

"Michael! I'm over eighty years old. This is ridiculous! Look at this hat Pearl wants me to wear. It looks absolutely ludicrous. I'm going to look like an idiot!"

"Excuse him, Officer. This is my father, Robert Woods." He pointed his finger at his father. "Dad, you wanted to be a king. Kings wear crowns, so for one hour tonight you will wear this contraption, all right? It's too late to find another crown."

Robert Woods scowled. "It's absurd!"

Reverend Woods leaned on the desk. "Wear it!"

Robert turned to leave and mumbled, "What does my son know? This stupid head thing makes me look like a loony chicken."

Reverend Woods waited until the door was closed. "I'm sorry about the interruption. You were saying, Officer?"

Santiago cleared his throat and played with the brim of his hat. "Well, do you think…do you suppose you folks will finish at the time you said? Because last year you started a half hour late and ended forty-five minutes late, and that made the traffic cops late for the traffic control at the Catholic church, and I'm the one that had to face Father McCurdy…you know…"

Reverend Woods laughed deeply imagining the sight of the irate priest.

"Well, it's not so funny, Reverend! If you had to face him, you'd understand!"

Reverend Woods laughed. "Oh, I know, I know. I don't think even the Lord would want to meet Father McCurdy when he's upset."

"He about took my head off…in not so many words."

"No, no, rest your mind, Officer Santiago Moreno. May I call you Santiago? This year we won't have a sick Christ child, and I promise that everything will be on schedule."

Santiago was relieved. He stood and put on his police hat. "I guess that'll do it, then. Good luck tonight!"

Reverend Woods extended his hand. "You're very welcome here. You're sure you don't want that row?"

"No, we need to come in late and leave early, so it's all right. Bye!" Santiago raised his hand as he departed.

Reverend Woods nodded. "Bye. See you tonight."

Santiago left the office, shutting the door behind him.

Reverend Woods sighed. There were so many details that still needed attention. He reached for the phone book and flipped through the pages. "Okay, where's the number for that radio station?"

***

Roger Dodger checked the sequence of songs that would be next in his program. "Jingle Bells" played in the background, filling the time slot.

Geronimo tried to get Roger's attention by holding a piece of paper to the glass of the broadcast booth. On it he had written REVEREND WOODS in big, bold black Magic Marker letters.

Roger nodded in acknowledgement and picked up the phone. "Hello, Reverend Woods. Did you have something to say on the air?"

Reverend Woods flustered. "Oh, no, no, no. I, uh, just wanted to be sure you have all the information on our youth pageant."

"Oh yes, Reverend, we have all the information." He picked up the list of announcements and peered through the bottom of his glasses. "That's tonight at—" He paused moving his finger down the list. "Eight o'clock sharp, yes. We've been giving out your information all day long."

Geronimo listened to the call. He made contorted faces through the window hoping to make Roger laugh at an inappropriate moment in the conversation.

Roger put his hand over his brow like a visor, but kept getting glimpses in his peripheral vision. "Yes, and there seems to be a great deal of interest in the program this year. You've got some good word-of-mouth...Yes, mine to be exact...well, thank you, Reverend, but I'm on the air tonight. That's right. Somebody has to do it. Thank you, Reverend. Good-bye."

Roger hung up the phone and snapped a pencil in half. "Man! These guys! I swear!"

Geronimo opened the door to the broadcast booth. "Look at it this way. They're tuning in."

"And turning on me! Maybe even counting the words! Who knows? Boy, I'm glad I'm just about off for a few hours. Andrews can deal with this stuff for a while. I need a little rest without Christmas carols!"

Geronimo smiled. "Dig it, dude."

Chapter Twelve

Becca ended the call, stepped outside her office, and leaned on Gloria's desk. "What's all the fuss out here? I can barely hear myself think, let alone pay attention to my calls. Don't tell me you actually need my decorating skills out here?"

David's longtime secretary peered up at Becca over the top of her red-framed glasses and slammed the phone back into the cradle. "The caterer just called and said they can't do the meatballs."

"Why not?"

"Don't know. I guess they must have run out of meat."

"Not funny, Gloria. What did David normally do in these situations?"

"Punt."

"Well, short of making them myself, see if they can do something else, like a smoked salmon." Becca walked back into the office that only six months ago had been David's. She took off her navy blue suit jacket and rolled up the sleeves of her cream silk blouse.

Gloria knocked on the door and entered. "Good news. They've got salmon." Gloria had been David's assistant since she graduated from college twenty years ago. She had grown plump over the years, but still dressed smartly in a crisp, gray A-line skirt and bright red sweater. It seemed strange not to have him walk in any moment and bark enthusiastic orders on organizing the Christmas party. Gloria remembered how much David loved for the party to transport everyone back to their childhood.

Becca sifted through the documents on her desk. "Great! At least something's going right. So now let's talk about Santa's cue."

Gloria half listened to Becca. She didn't mean to be disrespectful to her new boss, but it just felt different this year—less organized or maybe less heartfelt. She just didn't know how to get into the spirit of the moment.

Becca noticed Gloria seemed distracted. "So that'll be it, then. When Santa hears the words 'jolly old elf,' he comes through the door."

"Okay, but what if he can't hear through the door or he's hard of hearing or…you know?"

Becca sighed. "Gloria, why does this have to be so complicated? Right. Great. Okay, you stand by the door and knock three or four times so he knows it's you, okay? For Pete's sake, I can't stand much more of this. Christmas is supposed to be fun."

Gloria picked up the memos in the out basket. "Where'd you get that idea?"

"Go make sure this party will be merry. With my luck Santa will have forgotten his costume. Did you wrap the presents for everyone?"

"Yep."

"Great! David picked them out for everyone nearly a year ago. Thanks, Gloria." Becca watched as Gloria left the office. She was feeling the effects of not sleeping well the night before. She stretched and rubbed her face, hoping that stimulating the circulation would also provide the motivation to be enthusiastic about the party. She exhaled and said to no one but herself, as if expecting a response, "I'm too tired for this." She thought about the morning. Maybe she should call Caroline to check that Nickie was all right.

***

Caroline's day was unfolding into a continuous sequence of disasters. As the telephone rang, she was dealing with a spaghetti fiasco. Every time she turned her back for what seemed like only a second, Sarah would engage in new games of mischief. She picked up the phone and put her hand over the mouthpiece to talk to Sarah, who was off on another adventure, with noodles in hand and heading to the fish tank. "Please! Don't touch anything. Just stand still."

Caroline returned to the phone. "Hello? Oh, hi, Becca...fine, if you like spaghetti as a Christmas decoration."

"Mm! Sounds delicious. So when is your white knight flying home to rescue you?"

"Not today."

"What? You're kidding!"

Caroline looked at the mess in the kitchen. Out of the corner of her eye she saw Sarah dumping a handful of spaghetti into the fish tank. "Sarah, fish don't eat noodles. Come back here."

Sarah teetered back. "Feed fish, Mommy."

"I know, sweetie, but they don't like spaghetti."

She turned her attention back to Becca. "When the airline doesn't fly on Christmas Eve, you can bet it must be pretty bad. Well, I have some errands—the cleaners, the grocery store, and last-minute things to pick up at the mall. The kids aren't supposed to see them, so this is going to be pretty tricky."

"Hey, Caroline, are you still figuring on going to the pageant?"

"I don't know. I'm not much in the mood this year."

"I'm not much in the mood, either. Well, this makes everything harder on you, having Nickie and all. Thanks, Caroline. It really helps me out. How's she doing anyway?"

"Well, I'm afraid she's not very happy today." Caroline scanned the living room for Nickie and saw her kneeling on the chair by herself playing with the nativity scene. "Kind of keeping to herself, and well, you know me, Becca. I'm a worrywart."

"Well, she's not hurt or anything, is she?"

"No, no, nothing like that, but she's a little hard to... Well, Becca, frankly, she seems obsessed with her father's death. She won't eat. She's been going around the house asking everyone where Heaven is. I mean, I just think it's, you know...weird."

Becca sighed. "Just get her through the day, Caroline. I'm sorry. I'll be there to get her as soon as I can. We'll get some help to deal with this. I promise."

"I think that's smart. But don't worry about her today, Becca. Everything is completely under control."

As though to illustrate the contrary, Sarah grabbed another handful of spaghetti from her high chair and threw it at her mother with peals of laughter.

Becca heard the commotion. "Caroline? Caroline!"

Caroline glared at Sarah, silently communicating an order to behave. "Nothing, nothing. Bye."

Caroline hung up the phone and turned to Sarah. "Sarah! This is food. We don't throw it. We eat it." She took the half-empty plate and dumped it in the garbage disposal. "Sarah, I want you to come here to mommy. I'm going to put you in the tub, honey, so we can get ready to go to the mall."

Chapter Thirteen

Santiago was at his desk. The telephone never seemed to stop ringing. He picked up the phone. "Police Department, Officer Santiago Moreno. May I help you?" Santiago unbent a paper clip. "No, no. 'Scuse me, ma'am, Animal Control handles barking dogs." Santiago rolled his eyes to the ceiling. "It's 555-2700. That's 5-5-5…yes, three fives…no, not 3-5-5. It's 5-5-5…yes ma'am…yes, ma'am…"

The frustration surfaced in his voice as he repeated his message still louder. "5-5-5! I was not shouting, ma'am. That's right, ma'am…you've got it…2-7-0-0. No, ma'am, no trouble at all."

Santiago slammed down the phone. "What? Are people deaf today?" No sooner had he replaced the receiver than the phone rang again. Santiago barked into the phone, "Police Department!" He immediately recognized the voice and softened his demeanor, hiding his initial irritation behind a cough. "Oh, good afternoon, Father McCurdy. Sorry' bout that. Something caught in my throat." He coughed, again trying to make it sound sincere. "Now, what can I do for you, Father?"

***

Father McCurdy motioned from the middle of the Christmas tree lot as if he were orchestrating traffic. He felt like he had to do a lot of things at the same time just to make Christmas mass a reality. He waved at Jimmy, who owned the tree lot. "Hey, Jimmy, how's business this year?"

Jimmy emerged from a forest of neatly organized pines and shook his hand. "Got a great tree set aside for you."

"You've said that every year for as long as I can remember."

"This one is extra special given it's your last year before you retire."

"Well, I guess next year I'll be looking at a skinny little sorry one."

Jimmy laughed. He had given a tree to Father McCurdy every year since he had taken over the parish.

There were at least twenty people looking through rows of pines, each pulling one into the center of the lot to see if it was perfect.

"Father, I put yours over there so it wouldn't be sold. I think it's the most beautiful fir I've ever seen." Jimmy motioned his helper, a burly high school boy to whom he had given the job of loading trees into cars. "Hey, Eric! See that tree with the red ribbon around it?"

Eric looked at the full tree standing alone next to the trailer that was a makeshift office on the vacant lot. "Yeah."

"Well, load it into this beat-up station wagon." He turned to Father McCurdy. "At least with you I don't have to worry about scratching the paint job."

"Well, it gets me from point A to B. Thank you for setting it aside. If you'll excuse me for a moment, I need to make a call about some last-minute details."

"No problem, Father." Jimmy walked toward Eric and helped carry the huge pine to the car.

Father McCurdy pushed the buttons on his cell phone and pressed SEND. He heard the phone ring.

"Police Station, Officer Santiago."

"Hello, Officer, this is Father McCurdy."

"Hello, Father. How can I help you?"

"We're expecting quite a congregation tonight, and I'm checking on the parking situation. I remember the problems we had last year."

"Well, that wasn't really the fault of the officers, sir."

"Certainly not, certainly not."

Santiago was relieved that he wasn't to blame for last year's logistics problems.

Father McCurdy brushed the snow off his coat. "Nonetheless, in spite of the excuses, we still had parking problems down there."

Santiago clenched his teeth trying to keep from being rude. "Well, we've been assured that all will go smoothly tonight, and you shouldn't worry about it, Father."

Father McCurdy sensed the tension. "Not worried, Officer, just taking care of the details."

Santiago pulled the phone away from his ear, rolled his eyes and mouthed, "Just taking care of the details."

Hearing nothing, Father McCurdy wondered whether he had lost the cell connection. "Officer? Officer?"

"Uh, sorry, sir. Very busy here today."

"Right, right. Well, pretty busy just about everywhere today. Merry Christmas, Officer."

Father McCurdy clicked off the phone and turned to see Jimmy supervising the process of tying an enormous Christmas tree onto the roof of his station wagon.

Jimmy held on to a large sack and motioned to the teenager. "Now tie that off right there. No, right there! Right."

Father McCurdy helped arrange the flopping branches under the rope. "Hey, Jimmy, if he ties that up too tight, I won't be able to get it off." He reached for his wallet.

Jimmy shook his head. "Put that thing away, Father. Do you want to deprive me of my blessings?"

Father McCurdy closed his wallet and smiled. "I'd never want to do that, Jimmy."

"How is it you remember my name, Father? I'm not Catholic."

"Well, you could chalk it up to the fact that St. James is my patron saint or the fact that year after year I come here to get trees for needy families and you never let me pay. But you're a good man, Jimmy, and there are so precious few in this world. Those are the names I like to remember. Keeps me humble. I'm glad to call you my friend."

Feeling deeply moved, Jimmy took off his glove and extended his hand. "You likewise, Father, likewise."

Father McCurdy removed his own gloves and held Jimmy's hand. "You're a good, generous man."

"Thank you, Father McCurdy. Better get goin' while the goin's good."

"Say, how is it that you recall my name, your not being Catholic and all?"

"Well, you could chalk it up to the fact that McCurdy is my grandmother's maiden name, but it isn't. Or the fact that year after year you come here and rob me blind. But the truth is, you have a reputation for going out of your way to help people, whatever their religion." Jimmy handed him the sack he'd been holding. "Here's a couple of small strings of lights and some tinsel I couldn't figure out what to do with."

"God bless you, Jimmy."

"He does, Father. He does. Merry Christmas!"

Father McCurdy opened the door of the old station wagon and looked closely at the roof. He shouted at Jimmy, who was retreating amongst the trees. "Hey, Jimmy! There's an extra tree here!"

"I know. It's a good thing there are only a few churches in town or I'd be outta business."

Father McCurdy was touched. Truly this was what Christmas was about—selfless giving. He would have to remember this experience when he talked at midnight mass about the spirit of giving. He made a mental note—yes, this was about being bigger than your ordinary self. He got into the car, turned the ignition, and waved at Jimmy, thinking what a special person this was, and drove off the lot to attend to all the little arrangements that would make this his last and best midnight mass ever.

***

Roger Dodger's apartment was in an organized state of clutter. He liked it that way. Everything was in its place as far as he was concerned. He told himself it added to visual interest whenever he had guests, which wasn't that frequently since he'd gotten divorced. Social events were the domain of his ex-wife. His social sphere was the radio station and its callers. There you didn't have to organize the disorder, which wasn't visible, so he could play with the illusion of pristine perfection.

As he entered his apartment, he ignored the stacks of papers, magazines, books, and piles of things that were dotted around. There were his two cats, High-tech and Low-tech, to greet him with purring and meows of anticipation at being fed.

"Looks like it's going to be another solo Christmas."

The cats mewed, acknowledging the conversation.

"All right, all right. There's the three of us—the High-tech cat, the Low-tech cat, and *me*, the very cool cat." He opened a can of chili and offered a morsel to the cats. They weren't particularly interested and turned up their noses, purring and wanting something else. Roger poured the contents of the can into a bowl and put it into the microwave. It wasn't elegant, but it worked for his lifestyle. It didn't seem interesting to fix anything special for just himself. If the cats could eat food from the can, so could he.

He picked up Low-tech and felt High-tech rubbing against his leg. "What? You mean you don't like my chili? Yeah, well, I don't much either, but it's all I got time or energy for."

Roger reached into the cupboard and retrieved another can. He opened it for the cats and divided it out into their bowls. "Mm! Just smell that horse gizzard and cow belly. Mm, with that gourmet touch of tuna."

He took his bowl from the microwave and sat down in his recliner. Just then his peace was interrupted by the phone ringing.

"Hello?"

A recorded woman's voice started as if cued. "Hey, friend, need some cash for those Christmas extras? Have I got a deal for you!"

Roger took the phone away from his ear, staring at the receiver as though this message couldn't possibly be real. He hung up the telephone and looked at the little forlorn tree that stood there awkwardly, as if it didn't know how to fit into the room.

Roger gazed at the puny tree. It reminded him of the pathetic little tree in "Charlie Brown's Christmas" on TV. He looked past it and saw the paper snowflake hanging from his bookshelf, his only organized little corner where his old records were neatly filed and stacked.

Roger walked over to the shelf and carefully took off the snowflake. Attached to it was a small rolled-up piece of paper. He touched the letters on the outside that were written in a child's handwriting: "To My Daddy."

He ran his finger over each one of the words, and they flooded his heart with an ache. "To My Daddy." She had made this gift for him for a Christmas that seemed so long ago.

Roger opened the paper. Tears filled his eyes. Tears always filled his eyes whenever he picked up the snowflake and read the precious gift inside that his daughter had made just for him when she was seven years old.

Roger read the words out loud, but actually he knew them all by heart:

I caught a snowflake for you and held it tight
So I could make it out of paper for you just right
But it melted before I could draw its looks
And I don't know if you have one
in the picture books.

So I made up a snowflake by myself
And put it next to your records on the shelf.
I know my snowflake is only a little thing
But for you Daddy, next to your records,
my snowflake can sing.

Chapter Fourteen

Caroline pulled the minivan into the parking lot of the Hillside Mall. It was slow moving mayhem. Cars circled the full lot like sharks, ready to cut off anyone in order to slide into a slot that had just been vacated. Caroline thought she would be happy with even making a parking space in a snow bank that didn't already have a car plowed into its depth.

"I can't believe this. It's a zoo. Why did I wait?" Caroline looked into the rearview mirror at the kids shoving each other and fighting in the back seat. "Now look, you guys, no one can have treats if you act like that. No quiet, no treats!"

Jeremy gave a last elbow into Zak's ribs. "Well, Zak started it."

The mall was crowded. It looked like everyone in town had forgotten a last-minute item. The entire space was filled with people carrying brightly wrapped packages and the sound of music from the high school choir. The smell of pine wafted through the air from the Christmas trees that stood like twinkling sentinels throughout the mall, their smell intermingling with that of freshly baked cookies and cinnamon rolls. All the stores were bustling with activity. Children darted between legs into toyshops to see the wonders that had been put on their wish list, and lovers surreptitiously separated to find that last special gift.

Caroline dragged the bundled-up children through the mall to the front of a clothing store. She was on her own stealth mission to pick up toys that had been ordered, and she knew it wasn't going to be easy to buy them without arousing the curiosity of her brood. She maneuvered the stroller with Sarah in front of the window, negotiating through streams of shoppers coming from both directions carrying packages.

Nickie was glad to be in the mall. It felt good to be inside with all the bright lights and the singing. She unbuttoned her coat, took off mittens that hung from a string around her neck, and stuffed her hat in her pocket.

Caroline turned to her children and Nickie. "Okay, I know you guys don't want to go in the department store with me. The toy store is right over there. You can go in, but don't break anything and don't open anything. I'll be back in just a minute. Now, all of you hold hands so you can stay together."

Zak wrinkled his freckled forehead. "Ah, Mom. That's for girls."

Caroline turned to Kathy. "And Kathy, you're in charge of Nickie. Don't let her out of your sight."

Kathy rolled her eyes, took Nickie by the coat sleeve, and pulled her reluctantly along. Zak and Jeremy turned to go to the toy store, dodging the stream of shoppers that were in their way. Kathy watched her brothers dart into the crowd and then looked down at Nickie. "Like I'm stuck babysitting you. Geez!" She pulled her along. "You gotta come with me, I guess." Kathy dragged Nickie off down the mall.

Nickie saw they were going to go by Pets-R-Us. She couldn't contain her excitement as she looked through all the people and saw a whole window full of puppies. She yanked on Kathy's sleeve. "Look! Puppies!"

Kathy's attention was on a boutique displaying brightly colored cosmetics and accessories just past the pet shop that held Nickie's attention. Kathy dropped her hold on Nickie. "Listen, cousin. You stay right here and watch the puppies, okay? I'll be back in just a minute. Don't leave."

Nickie nodded enthusiastically, already entranced with the puppies. Kathy left her, going quickly toward the boutique where she became absorbed by all the glitter. She picked up a sample eyeshade and started to apply it.

Nickie went in the store to the front display pen, but a father and his little girl blocked her view.

"Is that the puppy you want, honey?"

The little girl leaned over the edge of the Plexiglas enclosure and petted the head of a little Labrador retriever puppy and nodded her head. "Yes, Daddy, this is the one I want. I'm going to call him Blackie."

"Okay, let's go buy him so you can have him for Christmas."

Nickie watched them. Her chin quivered and she was near tears. She put her hand on the window and took one last look at the puppies. "My daddy was going to buy me a puppy, too." Suddenly, she got an idea. She set her jaw in determination, turned, and ran out of the store and into the throng of shoppers.

***

Caroline went to the counter to buy Becca some perfume. She thought it might be just what she needed to lift her spirits. Unexpectedly she heard a loud crash from behind her. "Oh, no!"

She turned, fearing the worst. What had Sarah gotten in to now? She looked at Sarah, who smiled broadly.

Just then a little boy stood up from behind the stroller, awkwardly holding up his arms to a very coiffed and well-dressed woman shopper. He looked up, wrinkling his nose. "Yucky, Mama, yucky."

The woman turned to her son. "No, no, Tyler. No!"

She leaned down to smell him. "Oh, no! Now we clash!"

Caroline sighed in relief. At least it wasn't Sarah. She leaned down to kiss her and strolled over to the shop window to look across the mall and check on the children. With a quick glimpse through the crowds, she saw Zak and Jeremy looking at something that had caught their attention in front of the toy store.

Caroline walked back to the stroller only to find Sarah's hands full of miniature perfume bottles she had collected from a lower shelf. Caroline looked around to see if anyone had seen Sarah's antics and quickly replaced the bottles on the shelf.

"Well, Sarah, at least we don't clash," she muttered.

***

Nickie found herself next to the bookstore. She pressed her hands against the window and saw all the books about Christmas—her birthday. In the display there was a beautiful nativity scene surrounded by books with bright pretty pictures on the front. She stared riveted at the covers with glowing stars and angels. Then she looked at the nativity scene. Her little mind was working on the biggest question of her life, and she wanted answers.

She turned and searched the crowd and found an old gentleman resting on a bench. She thought he looked wise with his white hair and creased face. He looked like a grandpa. She made her way through the crowd and stood in front of him staring until the old man acknowledged her.

"Hello, little girl."

Nickie continued to stare into his weathered and watery eyes.

"Cat got your tongue, eh? What's your name?"

Nickie looked at him earnestly. "Where's Heaven?"

The old man was taken by surprise. "Well, now. That's a pretty deep question. You really want to know where?"

"Where is it? How do I go?"

The old man laughed and stroked his beard. "Well, I would say, uh…Heaven is many places."

Nickie was perplexed. How could Heaven be in many places? Daddy had to be in one place, not many. She looked at him puzzled and shrugged her shoulders. "Thank you, mister. I gotta go and find my daddy."

The old man leaned forward on his walking stick and pointed at the bookstore. "He's probably in there buying you something special."

Nickie's eyes followed the direction of his finger to the bookstore window. "No, he's somewhere else. Bye. I gotta find where he is." She wrinkled her forehead wondering who would know the answer while she gazed in between the people and packages that streamed around her. Maybe the black lady talking to the little boy would know. She walked over to her and tugged on her coat. "'Scuse me."

The woman bent down to talk to Nickie. "Yes, honey?"

"'Scuse me, but do you know where Heaven is?"

"Well, what about that! It's a big question for a little girl to ask. Heaven is up there." She pointed to the ceiling.

"Heaven is on the roof?"

The woman chuckled. "No, Heaven is beyond the roof."

Nickie looked puzzled. "Oh? Well, I gotta go and find it. Thank you. Bye."

Nickie smelled fresh cinnamon rolls and decided to follow her nose to the food court. She saw a man and a woman sitting at a small table with brightly wrapped packages in pretty bags scattered around them. She walked up to the table and stroked the head of a teddy bear that was peeking over the edge of one of the shopping bags.

The woman noticed Nickie and put down her coffee cup. "Hey, sweetheart, are you lost?"

"No. I need to know where Heaven is. Do you know where Heaven is?"

She patted her chest. "Sweetie, Heaven is in your heart."

"Oh." Nickie shook her head. "How could Heaven be in my heart? It's too small and Daddy is much too big to fit in there."

The man laughed. "You've got a point there."

"I gotta go and find my daddy."

The woman lifted the bear out of the sack and nuzzled it against Nickie. "I bet you anything he's over at the toy store getting you a great big fuzzy stuffed animal."

Nickie looked over her shoulder. "What I really want is a puppy and my daddy."

The woman put the bear back in the bag. "Well, maybe he's in the pet store right now picking out a special one for you."

Nickie sighed. "No, I don't think so. Thanks. I gotta go." She walked out of the food court and saw a man with a pipe. Curls of smoke twirled up over his head. He held on to a little boy in a harness. The little boy picked at the tape holding the wrapping paper taut on a big box that rested on the park bench. The man took the pipe out of his mouth and put it on the ledge next to the escalator. He tapped the little boy's hand. "Don't pull the tape off Mommy's present. You can unwrap the ones that Santa brings tonight."

Nickie approached the man. "'Scuse me, sir."

"Yes, little girl?"

"Do you know where I can find Heaven?"

The man made a big sweeping gesture across the area of the mall.

Nickie looked at all the people up and down the escalator. "Heaven is here?"

"Yes, that's one place."

"Well, if it's here, Daddy would have found me and given me a big hug."

The man nodded. "I'm sure your daddy's looking for you right now. He's probably just getting you a big surprise for Christmas."

"I've gotta find him." She waved at the man. "Bye."

Nickie saw a young mother hug her little girl. The little girl wiped her tears and threw her arms around her mother's neck. Nickie tugged at the string that her mittens dangled from and thought, "If Daddy were here I'd get a big hug, too." She heard the persistent clinking of a bell coming from outside and spotted the red suit. "Oh, boy! It must be Santa Claus. He'll know for sure."

***

Caroline thought about getting a book for all the children. As far as she was concerned, they weren't reading enough because they were spending too much time watching television and playing video games. She wheeled Sarah's stroller into the bookstore determined to find them each something interesting that would catch their imagination.

After the side trip into the bookstore, she returned to the toy store to check on the children. She jostled the sacks hanging from the back of the stroller that insisted on banging into her knees. Everything today seemed to be taking longer than she anticipated. She parked the stroller next to the gift-wrapping booth where a high school girl was laboring over presents. To Caroline it looked like not even the tape was cooperating.

Out of the corner of her eye she caught sight of Zak. "Zak! *Zachary!*" Caroline tried to get his attention by waving her arms.

Zak was oblivious. He dashed around the corner to get a better view of a new video game.

Just at that moment, a woman hurriedly shoved past Caroline to the gift-wrap booth.

"Miss? Miss? I want to return this SpeedoRacer. Is there anywhere I can take it besides the cash register? The line's a mile long."

"Uh, well, I don't really…"

Overhearing this exchange, Caroline quickly turned to the hurried lady. This predicament could really save her. "Oh! I'll take it!"

"What?"

"I said I'd take it. My kids are dying for one. How much do you want?"

The woman looked startled but grateful, "How can I thank you? I'm so—"

Caroline interrupted, pointing at the label with the price on it. "How about I give you what you paid for it?"

Chapter Fifteen

The setting sun was visible through the mall windows. It was muted in pastel tones as it hid behind a veil of lightly falling snow.

Nickie was drawn to the light and saw Santa Claus outside ringing a bell. She had an idea; maybe he would know the answer to her question. She pushed open the heavy glass door, squeezed through the crack of the opening, and went to see the Salvation Army Santa. "Santa, do you know where Heaven is?"

Santa stopped ringing the bell and knelt down to be at her level. He adjusted his white beard. "Honey, Heaven is out there." He pointed across the parking lot.

"Well, then, I'm not in the right place. I gotta go find it. Thanks, Santa." She waved good-bye and walked toward the cars.

***

Caroline was thrilled and relieved that she had found this final gift her boys wanted. She carefully arranged the bag with the SpeedoRacer in it so that it wouldn't be visible and slid the package across the counter to the gift-wrap girl. "I can't tell you how happy I am to have found this. Can you wrap it so my kids can't see it?"

"Sure thing." The girl took it to the table and pulled a long piece of red wrapping paper from the roll.

Caroline turned back to find Sarah removing the bottom corner of a display. She lunged and grabbed Sarah's hand, but it was too late. The display made a spectacular crash on the tile floor. Sarah was thrilled, laughing and clapping at the noise and confusion of scurrying assistants ready to remedy the damage.

The store came to a virtual stop as everyone in the vicinity stared at the mess on the floor. Caroline knelt down and started to pick up the broken ornaments and statues that had fallen.

A shop assistant came over with a broom and dustpan. "Excuse me, ma'am. I'll get that cleaned up."

Caroline stood up and handed him the broken glass and ceramic pieces. "I'm so sorry."

"It's okay. These things happen."

***

The sun was low in the sky. Christmas was only a heartbeat away. The cold and light snow made it seem like the world was blanketed into a serene cocoon of warmth.

As Nickie walked through the parking lot, she saw a small man struggling to put a large package into his subcompact car. She tugged at his coat as he struggled with the logistics of getting the package into the trunk. "Mister? Mister, do you know where Heaven is?"

The small man held onto the package that was precariously perching on the rim of the trunk. "Too busy, too busy, kid. Ask the cop or somebody." He continued to struggle, determined to squeeze the package into a space that looked impossibly small.

Nickie looked around trying to figure out what he meant. Then she saw the cop directing traffic. "Thank you, sir." She pointed at the intersection. "I'm going to talk to that policeman over there."

"Yeah, well, be careful crossing the road." He gave a final shove, forcing the package into the trunk.

Nickie headed off toward the policeman determined to talk to him. All of a sudden, a car backed out of a slot. She jumped back and nearly slipped on the frozen snow. The window opened automatically. "Hey, kid, are you trying to get killed? Watch out for the cars."

"I'm sorry."

"You should be more careful." He rolled up the window.

Santiago was in a foul mood. He hated directing traffic even more than he hated Christmas. He blew his whistle. Why couldn't people go the way he directed them to go, and more particularly when he directed them?

Nickie stood on the border of the sidewalk and tried to get Santiago's attention.

He saw Nickie as he shifted the direction of the traffic. He thought she needed to cross the street, so he blew his whistle to stop the traffic.

Nickie checked both directions to make sure there were no cars, as her daddy had told her to do so many times. She stepped off the curb and walked straight over to Santiago. "The man over there," she pointed at the mall, "he said you know where it is."

Santiago was surprised that her focus was on him. "Move along, little girl. They'll wait for ya...I think." He sensed the impatience of the drivers, who had all come to a complete stop. He put his hand on her shoulder giving a little push indicating it was safe to cross the street while everything was at a standstill, but she stayed rooted at his side.

Realizing she was going nowhere, he pulled on her coat and positioned her in front of him so that he could face her while still keeping an eye on the stopped traffic. "Where what is?"

"Where Heaven is."

Horns started honking. Santiago blew his whistle and waved his arm to move cars through the intersection. He yelled at an old blue Honda Civic that spun its tires on the ice. "Move along there." Cars started to inch by on the slippery surface. He watched the progress from his peripheral vision while trying to work out what Nickie had just asked. "Say what?"

Nickie put her hands on her hips. "How do I go to Heaven?"

Santiago stared at her, lifted his hat, and scratched his forehead. "Huh? What? Little girl, did you say—"

Before he could give her his full attention, the motorist directly in front of him honked his horn to show his mounting impatience at not being able to get on his way. As if by spontaneous ignition, several others joined in to a chorus of blaring horns.

Santiago twisted his head in the direction of the car emitting irritating staccato beeps. "Ah, keep your clothes on!" He knew he had to return to directing traffic. Tempers were starting to erupt, and he had to keep things moving. He raised his hand and glared at the driver in front of him, acknowledging he knew it was his turn next. He bent over to be face-to-face with Nickie and pointed across the street. "The only…look, kid, ask over at the Catholic church. They know all about that stuff."

"Huh?"

"It's right over there, a couple blocks across from the park. You can see it through the trees."

Nickie shifted her focus to where he was pointing. He was right. Just through the bare trees was a church.

Santiago was glancing over his shoulder trying to see how many cars were stacking up when he heard a horn blare. He turned and saw Nickie crossing the street heading for the church, totally oblivious to the traffic that was starting to flow on its own. Santiago was in a panic. He blew his whistle and raised his hand to stop automobiles from both sides while running to save Nickie. He swooped her up, jogged to the other side of the street, and deposited her safely on the curb. "Geez, kid! You wanna get yerself killed? 'Bout gave me a heart attack."

Santiago stepped back into the street and blew his whistle. "Hey, slow down! Come on, move it! It's your turn." He pointed at the first car and then at the street to his right. "Okay, you next. Come on, let's go!"

Car horns blasted from behind.

"Yeah, I'll get to you next. Show some patience. It's Christmas." He shouted to Nickie over the engine sounds. "Go home, little girl. You shouldn't be out here without your daddy."

Nickie pouted. "I'm looking for him."

Santiago motioned for the next car to turn. "Now, don't run off in the street. Be careful, okay?"

"'Kay. Thank you." Nickie put on her mittens.

Santiago took control of the center of the intersecting streets.

An angry motorist leaned out the window as his car rolled past Santiago. "Hey, what's the problem? I've been stuck here smelling fumes for twenty minutes."

Santiago tipped the brim of his hat. "Well, sir, sometimes we've got some traffic light malfunctions. And a merry Christmas to you."

"Sorry, Officer. Didn't mean to bark at you. You know how it is when you got to get that last-minute thing before the stores close."

"Can't say. Move it along and don't speed."

"Funny, like that's possible on this snow and ice."

Nickie stood on the curb on the far side of the street watching the traffic creep by.

Santiago saw her standing there with a forlorn expression—or was it quizzical? He couldn't decide, but something tugged at his heart. He waved at her. Suddenly, a car came to a screeching halt. Santiago glared at the driver who had mistaken his wave as a demand to come to a stop. In an instant a colony of cars screeched to a halt to avoid a collision. Santiago wondered how he was going clear the intersection from the near pileup and yelled at the driver in the lead car. *"Get that thing outta here now!"*

Nickie stood shivering in the cold air for a moment, her clear blue eyes fixed on the frantically gesticulating policeman standing amid the cluster of honking vehicles. Finally she realized she would have to find the answers on her own. She gazed past Santiago and contemplated the mall with lights twinkling on the inside. She knew her answer wasn't in there. She turned and headed for the spires of the church oblivious to the sound of ice and snow crunching under her red rubber boots. Yes, maybe she could get an answer to her question there.

***

Caroline gathered all her children. Zak, Jeremy, and Sarah looking on from her stroller surrounded her, as she frantically interviewed Kathy, who was becoming equally emotional.

"But how could you not see her?"

"Well, I just didn't. That's all!"

"After you got into the store, what happened?"

"I told you, I don't remember." It was rare for Kathy to get teary eyed. Most of the time she exuded teenage defiance.

Caroline realized she wasn't getting anywhere with this inquisition. She looked at them all. "Now, you stay right here, and—No, no, no! Everybody follow me."

Frightened and jittery, the little troop found a store clerk, who busied himself straightening ties on the counter, hoping if he ignored them they would go away.

Caroline cleared her throat. "Excuse me."

The clerk continued to line up the ties in neatly spaced lines pretending not to have noticed their presence.

"Excuse me. Have you seen a lost little girl?"

Pursing his lips in a mock grin, he looked at them and merely raised an eyebrow.

Chapter Sixteen

Mrs. Kelly was the backbone of the rectory. She couldn't even remember how long she had been with Father McCurdy. Even though she was just the housekeeper and cook, she felt a maternal calling to her station of caring for the priests she tucked under her wing. Mrs. Kelly felt the part. In her mind she never thought of herself as attractive. Instead, now in her late seventies, short and plump, she felt like a mother with all the comforts of an old bathrobe and slippers. She knew she belonged here in the old rectory with its groaning pipes. Yes, she was the mother of the house, and she took that position seriously.

Father McCurdy sat down at the table to scribble a to-do list and pulled the loose papers that contained his sermon from his pocket. "Mrs. Kelly, remind me to put this on the pulpit."

She dried her hands on her skirt. "What is it?"

"Hopefully the best sermon I ever wrote, saved for last."

"I'll put it here on the counter so you won't forget. Now here's something to eat." She shoved a plate of steaming food in front of him. "Eat, Father! You need your energy tonight. It'll be a long one, y'know. Midnight mass shouldn't be said on an empty stomach."

"Thank you for your concern, Mrs. Kelly. I'll have plenty of time to eat later. Let's see here. Cheesecake to the McDaniels, Morgans, Noltes. Do you know if Elmar and Gabriella Reiter have a tree this year?"

"They'd never admit it, but I'm sure they don't. And such sweet people. Remember when someone vandalized the nativity scene and broke off Mary's head? Elmar Reiter fixed it."

"Wouldn't let me pay him either. Fine people, Mrs. Kelly. Thanks. Just put it in the fridge. I don't know how late I'll be." Father McCurdy's mind was filled with all the things he still needed to do. As he turned to leave, he heard Mrs. Kelly mumbling under her breath.

"Santa himself couldn't turn down my turkey à la king, but this man? His knees will give way right at the pulpit. I don't want to see it. I don't want to see it!"

He stood up from the table and pushed the half-eaten plate aside. "Mrs. Kelly, I've got to go and see if everything is ready at the church. I'll eat the rest of this later."

Mrs. Kelly started to rinse the dishes in the sink and put them in the drainer on the counter. "You always say that, and then you microwave it and it explodes all over."

"Okay, I promise this time I'll put cellophane over it."

"Promises, promises."

Father McCurdy took the keys from his pocket and went out the side door. He grabbed the railing as he nearly slipped on the ice and packed snow on the steps. He opened the car door, slid onto the cold vinyl cracked bench seat, put the key in the ignition, and turned it. The engine groaned as it tried to turn over. "Come on, you can do it." He patted the dashboard. Suddenly the engine caught as a big puff of blue-gray smoke shot out the exhaust pipe.

He pulled his beat-up car alongside the church. The car seemed as old as the church and as worn out as he sometimes felt making sure everyone in his parish was okay. He looked up and saw movement next to the life-sized nativity. Maybe it was vandals again this year. He swerved toward the curb, screeched to a halt, and jumped out of the car. His adrenaline was in full swing as he ran toward the nativity. It was his to protect, and protect it he would, particularly on Christmas Eve just before mass.

"Hey! Hey, you. Hey! *Hey!*" Father McCurdy saw a shadow move behind the stable, and he raced forward to try to intercept whoever it was. He ran full out. No one was going to destroy his nativity this year. He rounded the corner of the little shed. It was slippery on the packed snow, and he lost his footing. His feet slid out from underneath his husky frame, making him fall on his back and knocking out his breath. He groaned and looked up, and there he saw the compassionate face of Nickie looking down with enormous eyes.

"Did you hurt yourself?"

He tried to get up, but couldn't get his footing and fell back gasping. "Oh, I shouldn't have tried it."

"You shouldn't run so fast."

When he looked at Nickie, even though in pain, he was struck by the humor of the situation and laughed in spite of himself. "You're certainly right there, young lady. Serves me right. I just—"

"You have a funny shirt on." Nickie looked closer, then put her hand up to her mouth and giggled. "Oh, it's a dress!"

Father McCurdy saw how ludicrous it all was and laughed even harder.

Nickie stared at him as the laughter subsided. "What are you laughing at?"

"Oh, I needed this. I needed this. I feel much better. Oh, my." He rolled over to get on his knees, got up, and dusted the snow off his cassock.

Nickie pointed at the stable. "Is this where Jesus lives? Is this Heaven?"

"This is the stable. Jesus was born in the stable, and they put him in the manger. See, over there's where little baby Jesus will be at midnight."

Nickie wrinkled her forehead with curiosity and started to walk over to the cradle.

Father McCurdy stopped her before she had a chance to reach it. "Here, here! Don't touch the crèche. It's only for looking. Don't touch anything! You might break something."

"'Kay."

He checked his watch. It was getting late, and he still had what felt like a hundred things to do. "Now, you'd better run in. Is your daddy in the church?"

"Daddy's with Jesus."

"Good, well, go back in." Father McCurdy led Nickie to the chapel door and held it open. "You really shouldn't be out here without your daddy. I've got to go now and check on some things for tonight."

Nickie looked inside at the statues and paintings of angels. She put her hand on the door underneath Father McCurdy's. "Is that where Heaven is?"

Father McCurdy looked at his watch and tried to remember the items on the to-do list he had left on the table in the rectory. "Yes, yes. Go right in. Come back and see me another time, and merry Christmas."

He opened the enormous door wider and let Nickie inside. He motioned toward the altar. "Go, go, and join your daddy." As the door closed behind her, he checked his watch again. "Yes, I've got to hurry," he thought. He quickly went back to his car, lifting the cassock so that he could see the ice and carefully make his way back.

Nickie entered the church. It was quiet, imposing, and cool. She looked all around the big main section, but couldn't find anyone that she could ask her question. She padded forward silently. It was so big and tall. Everywhere she saw paintings of angels and people in the clouds, even on the ceiling. She felt intimidated and very small. She looked around and in a quiet voice she spoke. "Daddy?"

Her voice made a slight echo that was disconcerting to Nickie. She walked toward the altar, and there she saw a vivid statue of Christ on the cross. She turned her head to the left and saw the Virgin Mary holding baby Jesus in her arms. She didn't quite know which statue to ask her question. She looked back and forth and puzzled over the decision. Finally she stood in front of the cross and looked up at it for a moment. "'Scuse me. Do you know where my daddy is?"

***

Caroline couldn't believe they had lost Nickie in the mall. Surely security could find her, wherever she was. She was weeping and flustered at not knowing how this possibly could have happened. Where could Nickie be?

She sat on a chair facing Mr. Norton, who was dressed in a purple official-looking jacket. He was finishing a crackled conversation on the walkie-talkie with someone who identified himself as Fourteen, who was somewhere in the mall.

"It's just about impossible, chief. Kids everywhere. We'll keep looking, but nothing so far."

"Right, Fourteen. Do the best y'can. Norton out." He put down the walkie-talkie and turned to talk directly to Caroline. "Well, Mrs. Astee..."

"Mrs. Hastings."

"Right, Ulsting, whatever. Heckuva night to lose a kid. All righty. I dunno. My guys have done their best."

Caroline frowned. "Could I use your phone?"

"O' course, Mrs. Osteen."

"Hastings! Mrs. Hastings."

"Sure, ma'am. You can use my phone. That's what it's here for." He pushed the phone toward her.

Caroline hurriedly dialed the number, misdialing twice before she connected the call.

***

The office party was in full swing. After several glasses of punch and general jolliness, the staff was loudly singing Christmas songs that drowned out all background noises.

Gloria heard the telephone. At first she thought she would ignore it, but something told her it was important to answer this call. She lifted the receiver and pulled the phone around the corner to better hear. She looked around to see where Becca was in the crowd and saw her talking to one of the managers. Gloria waved her arms frantically to get Becca's attention. It was too noisy to try to shout a message in Becca's direction, so as soon as she caught her eye, she simply mimed the need to come to the phone now.

Becca acknowledged her with a nod and made her way to the phone. She held one finger in her free ear trying to block out the noise. "Yes? Caroline? You'll have to speak up. There's a lot of noise. At the mall, yes..."

Caroline's voice sounded distant and echoic. "Well, I don't know how to say this..."

Becca held the phone tighter to her ear and shouted, "What? The noise, sorry."

Caroline repeated loudly, "Nickie! We've lost Nickie at the mall. I'm with security right now." She couldn't hide her emotions anymore and started to cry.

"You *lost* her! But how could you? Okay, okay, calm down. I'm sure she's somewhere. I'll be right there."

Becca was visibly frightened. What had happened to her little girl? She slammed down the phone and went into her office to grab her coat, purse, and keys. She felt like the ground was becoming quicksand. She left her office and dashed toward the front door.

Russell Ford blocked her path. "Hey, where are you going? The party only started."

"Nickie's lost. I've got to go right away."

"Oh, my God. Let me go with you."

"Russell, you'll be more helpful to me if you handle the party."

"Are you sure?"

"I'm sure." Becca pushed open the door, letting a burst of cold air into the warm lobby. "Okay, I just really have to go now."

Russell held the door so that it wouldn't spring back on Becca. He took her by the arm, steadying her to make sure she didn't slip on the fine snow covering the recently shoveled walkway. "Let me walk you to the car. Are you okay to drive?"

"Yes, I'm fine. I just have to find out where she is and what happened." She fumbled to get the key into the ignition. Finally she connected.

Chapter Seventeen

Nickie left the church. She searched all directions trying to decide where to go next and finally just wandered down the street. Everything seemed strange. Maybe it was strange because it was getting dark and unfamiliar or because it looked rough and smelled funny. Nickie heard a sound coming from behind. She turned around, and there was a scruffy mutt following her.

The dog was the color of deep gray smoke with tan markings over his amber eyes making him look quizzical as he cocked his head and raised a brow staring at Nickie. He looked like a mix between an Australian shepherd and a Border collie with a pointed nose and ears. The fur behind his ears was matted like Rastafarian braids, and his coat was dirty and tangled, badly in need of a bath and brushing to make it soft and shiny again. He wagged his long tail caked with snow.

"Hi! Hi, doggie. C'mere, boy. C'mon!"

The dog looked at Nickie, watchful and cautious. She tried to approach him, but he ran away from her just a short distance out of reach. Then he stopped, turned, and stared at her again.

"Don't you wanna be my friend? Come on. C'mon!" She put her hand in her pocket and pulled out the whistle. "Here, boy. You want a toy to play with?"

The dog looked at Nickie and ducked behind a group of garbage cans.

"What's wrong, boy? Don't you want to be with me? Come back." Nickie craned her neck in the direction of where the dog went. She walked toward the trashcans. "Here, boy. Here, boy. Where are you, doggie?" She pushed a plastic garbage can aside and looked behind one of the other cans. "Well, you must have gone home then."

She turned and saw a light coming from the alley and out of curiosity walked toward it. Sparks sputtered and spewed from a large metal barrel as cinders drifted up and mingled with big, fat flakes of falling snow. Acrid smoke swirled around the three men who were warming their hands over the blaze.

One of them extended a brown paper bag that was molded around a bottle. "Thanks for sharing your fire. Here, buddy, want a swig to warm your insides, too?" He stroked his bristled chin. "Name's Drifter Joe from Chicago." They slapped each other's palm in a high five.

The other man pulled his hand out of a torn coat pocket and took off a frayed brown glove. Then he grasped the bottle and took a gulp. "Hey, thanks, man. By the way, my name's Fred, just plain Fred from nowhere special, and this here is Pete. Pete, want a drink?"

"Nah. They don't like it at the shelter when you smell like booze."

Fred waved the bottle in front of his face and laughed. "But they don't care that you smell like a dead rat."

Pete pushed the bottle away. "When was the last time you took a bath?"

"Who needs a bath when you have the sweet aftershave smell of whiskey?"

Nickie saw the light of the blaze. "Hey, what's that over there?" She came closer, but wrinkled her nose and coughed as soon as she reached the smoke.

Pete saw a shadow of a figure against the building wall coming toward them. "Hey, better put that bottle back in your pocket. Someone's coming." He backed up and stumbled over several cartons of glass that spilled out and clanked on the pavement. The sound reverberated throughout the alley as Pete peered into the darkness.

Fred bent down and picked up two bottles and threw them back into the carton. "Can you see anything? Who is it? Is it a cop? I don't want any trouble tonight."

"Can't tell yet!" Pete got up and went closer to the light. "Well, I'll be! It's a little girl."

Nickie came closer to the motley group clustered around the makeshift fire. She walked up to Pete and looked up and down at him. "Do you know that you have holes in your shoes and clothes?"

"I guess I didn't inherit my dad's best funeral suit." They all laughed and went back to warming their hands.

She pulled on his pant leg. "You know it's almost Christmas, and Santa Claus might bring you a new suit."

They laughed, holding their sides and slapping each other's backs. Pete leaned down toward Nickie. "Yeah, I wrote him a letter, and he wrote back and said 'Ask the guy at the pearly gate.'"

"What's the pearly gate?"

"You know." He pointed at the sky. "Heaven."

Nickie scowled and stood directly in front of Fred, who was ignoring her, mesmerized by the sparks that turned to ashes and floated like suspended snowflakes going up instead of falling down.

"Do you know where Heaven is?" Nickie stomped her foot and tugged on his sleeve.

"Hey, little kiddo. Whatcha pullin' on me for?"

Nickie cocked her head and looked at him with a serious expression. "Do you know where Heaven is? I just gotta find it."

Fred leaned against Joe and stared at Nickie through blurred vision. "Oh, my. Ain't you asking a lot of questions?" He poked Joe on the collarbone and burst into huge guffaws.

"Oh, yeah! He knows where Heaven is. We all go there every day."

Nickie brightened, "You do?"

Fred bent down, picked up some empty cereal boxes, and threw them onto the fire. The flames flared. He nodded in the direction of the street and winked at Pete. "Sure. It's just about six blocks from here. They serve really great soup." He pulled a half-eaten sandwich from his pocket, took a bite, and swallowed. "I know where Heaven is."

They all looked at him as he paused and waved the bread and turkey in a dramatic, grand, heavenly sweep. "Sure! I carry it with me wherever I go!" He burped and leaned over to Nickie, talking in a confidential tone as he looked over his shoulder. "Just kidding." He burped again. "Truth is, Heaven is right over there in that box." He gestured toward a large cardboard box with a dirty quilted blanket draped over it.

Nickie looked at him with big astounded eyes. "In the box?"

Fred pulled off the corner of the stale bread crust and threw it in the fire. He bent down to Nickie's level and looked her in the eyes. "Yes, but be careful when you look."

Pete rubbed his hands. "Fred, quit teasing her."

Nickie turned her head toward the box, wrinkled her brow, and stared back at Fred. "Are you sure that's where it is? It looks kinda small."

"Heaven comes in small packages. Now run along and go home or something."

Nickie cautiously approached the box. She walked over to the opening, pulled back the blanket, and peered inside at what looked like a bag of rags. She looked back at the men, who watched her, laughing as if they'd just heard a joke.

Fred yelled out, "Just shake the box."

Nickie turned around and pushed on the corner of the box. A piercing scream erupted from the rags. A waving hand slithered from out of the piles of rags and tried to grab Nickie, who jumped back out of reach and turned to look at the vagrants who watched from the warmth of the blaze.

All of a sudden, the rags came alive, and an old woman sprang out of the box. She shook her fist at the vagrants down the alley and yelled, "When are you loons going to understand that I hate to have my box shaken?" The alley amplified her angry voice.

Nickie stood stiff with wide eyes staring at the wrinkled old woman and then screamed.

Unexpectedly, from out of the shadows, a dog bolted down the alley, growling and barking. He stayed at Nickie's side, bouncing toward the woman with his body stiff, challenging her to keep her distance as he growled and nipped at the air.

Fred made a mock bow and yelled back, "Thought you could be of assistance, Princess Liz." The men around the fire laughed even harder.

Liz raised her forearm in case the dog was going to lunge. She peeked over it and saw for the first time that there was a little girl standing in front of her frozen with fear. She lowered her arm and put her hand in front of the dog's nose. "Okay, little mutt, calm down. I'm not going to hurt anyone."

The dog sniffed her hand and turned to sit next to Nickie. He leaned against her leg with his head nuzzled against her belly as if to reassure her that he was there to protect her.

Liz relaxed once the dog was quiet. She tightened a faded green and red striped scarf that was wrapped around her head and tucked the ends into a blue winter jacket that had been patched with duct tape. She took a step toward Nickie. "'Scuse me, kid. I didn't know it was you that was coming a callin' tonight. I thought it was those jerks bothering me again. I didn't mean to scare you. What do you want, honey?"

Nickie scratched the tangled hair behind the dog's ear and stared at a smudge across Liz's forehead. "I was looking for Heaven."

Something about Nickie's earnestness touched Liz, and she smiled and pointed at the box. "Do you think I'd be here if I knew where it was?"

"I don't know."

"Well, let me tell you where it is. Go straight ahead and turn left. Go! Quick! And never look back. Go! Say, and if you find it, kid, I hope there's lots of free food. Let me know. I'm always hungry. Go on. Beat it! Go!"

Nickie tilted her head, looked back toward the street, and smiled. "Thank you, ma'am."

Liz smiled back. She felt a tinge of sadness surface from a place she thought she'd long forgotten. She turned back to Nickie. "You're welcome, angel."

The vagrants jeered in unison. "You're welcome, angel."

Liz picked up an empty can by her feet and threw it in their direction. It rattled as it rolled down toward the metal barrel. "Shut up, you idiots."

Nickie ran away from the frightening noise as fast as she could and almost slipped on a patch of ice. The dog ran protectively alongside, keeping himself between her and the men. Once she was out of the alley, she stopped running and looked behind to make sure the men were all far behind and it was safe.

The dog stopped with Nickie, pushed his head under her arm, and looked up at her.

"Hi, boy. Hey, boy, you're great. You saved me from that scary lady. Wow! You were really great." She bent down to pet her new friend.

The dog jumped back in a playful movement with his rump in the air, wagging his tail and barking. The sudden backward leap startled Nickie, who also jumped back. This motion made the dog jump forward in playful response, and she jumped forward, too.

She petted his head and started running down the street. "Come on. See if you can catch me."

The dog ran after her. She giggled with delight and shrieked with laughter, oblivious to her surroundings. She raced around as her friend bounded behind, ready to catch her until finally she slipped and fell into a snow bank.

The dog enthusiastically wagged his tail. He was panting with his tongue hanging out of his mouth. He pounced on top of Nickie lying in the snow and licked her face. Nickie felt his tongue on her cheeks, which tickled. She sat up in the pile of snow and pushed the dog back slightly so she could wipe her face.

"Okay, boy, okay." He lay down next to her with his paws resting on her lap as she stroked his neck. "Hey, doggie. I know you're not really a little puppy anymore, but you can be my puppy. I can give you a bath and make your fur all soft and shiny again. Mommy has this white stuff that smells like flowers and it's s'posed to take out tangles. And you gotta lot of tangles. I don't know 'bout these behind your ears. Mommy may have to cut them out like when she had to cut out my tangles when I got gum in my hair."

Nickie watched him cock his head with every word. When she reached over to pet him, for the first time he turned over and let her scratch his belly, which was dotted with black spots just like the puppies in *101 Dalmatians*.

"You must be a really smart dog. I mean, a *really* smart one! Do you have a home? You probably don't because you don't have a collar, and puppies with a home are s'pose to wear one. You're really skinny. Don't worry. I'll feed you."

He rolled back over, sat up, and shook off the snow.

Nickie laughed. "You look silly with those yellow eyebrows."

He moved closer and leaned against Nickie as though he wanted to be petted some more, put a paw in her lap, and woofed.

Nickie looked into his amber eyes. "I know. You must be all alone, like me. Did your daddy go away, too? I bet you don't even have a name, do you? Okay, let's see…a good name for you…my name is Nicole because St. Nicholas and I were born on Christmas, but you can just call me Nickie. I know! You can be Christmas. Yeah, Christmas." Nickie held the dog's face and brought it close to hers. "Do you like that name, Christmas?"

The dog gently licked her nose.

She giggled. "Christmas, that tickles." She got up and brushed the snow from the seat of her pants, felt the whistle in her pocket, and pulled it out. She blew it once. Christmas raced around her in a circle and barked. "You like the whistle? Come on, let's go."

Christmas grabbed her mitten and pulled on it as he loped alongside.

***

Caroline's children watched wearily as she poured coffee in a Styrofoam cup. It seemed like they'd been sitting in this office at the mall all day.

Becca paced anxiously while she talked to Norton, the head of security. Exasperated, she slammed her keys down on the desk. "But *somebody* must have seen her!"

"Now, now, Mrs. Helsbed."

Becca leaned forward and glared. "Mrs. Halstead. Please."

"Right! Mrs. Elseenstead, we're just trying to help. We're doing all we can do right now."

"Little girls don't disappear like this!"

"They do till ya find 'em, Mrs. Helvenhead."

Becca stood up and shook her head in disbelief.

"Now, Mrs. Hasselstead, we're lookin' everywhere and doin' everything we can to help ya. Just try and be patient."

Becca stopped pacing and picked up her purse from the desk. "Well, it's not good, not good staying here. I've gotta do something, go out there."

Becca turned to leave and bumped into Caroline, who was approaching her with a cup of coffee. The children laughed as they watched the coffee stain spread across Becca's blouse.

Caroline jumped back to keep the coffee from dripping on her. "Oh! Oh, I'm sorry, Becca. I was bringing you some…"

Caroline gave a quick apologetic look and scrambled to get a paper towel. Norton slid his box of tissues toward Becca. She pulled out several and wiped off her hands, then pulled the blouse away from her skin and looked at the wet patch.

"Oh, for Pete's sake! Couldn't you be more careful?" she fumed.

Caroline quickly tried to repair the damages that could be addressed immediately. "Here, just let me—"

Becca glared at Caroline as she began to wipe off the coffee mess as if she were cleaning one of her own children. "Here, give me those towels. Haven't you done enough damage for one day?"

Caroline handed her the towels. "I'm so sorry, Becca…I'm really sorry." She felt big tears starting to form and pool in her eyes. She felt frazzled and unsure what to do next. She backed away and turned to go toward her children. She lowered her head as she retraced their every step in her mind. When was the last time she saw Nickie?

Becca looked at Caroline as she retreated. She realized she had been overly harsh with Caroline, who was also obviously distraught, and she felt her temper subside. "I'm sorry, Caroline. I'm sorry. I just…"

"I know, I know."

"Caroline…" Becca put her hand on Caroline's shoulder.

Caroline felt the gentle touch and turned around to face her. "Becca, you know I'm sorry about this, really sorry, Becca. But I'm sorry about something else, too."

"I didn't mean to—"

Caroline interrupted. "Ever since the death of my brother, we haven't seen you much."

"Caroline…"

"Please let me say this. We haven't seen you much in the last six months, and I don't know. I think maybe I've just been scared. I just…I don't know. Death is so final, and so much a reminder of losing someone precious forever. That's so stupid. I just really…I miss David. I miss my brother…a lot, see, but I really miss you and Nickie, too. I think you've handled this all so well. I've been pretty critical of Nickie and I…I just wasn't thinking clearly. I don't think I've been very helpful to you, and I want to apologize. I'm sorry, Becca. When this is all over—"

There was a long silence with nobody knowing what to say. All of the sudden the quiet was broken by the pop of the radio as it crackled to life. "Nine to Chief. Nine to Chief. Do you read? Over!"

Norton pressed the button and put the radio close to his mouth. "Gotcha, Carl. Come back." He released the button to hear.

"Chief, we've got a witness to the little girl that's lost. The cop doing the traffic. He's on his way in there right now. I'm takin' over for him out here."

"Roger, Carl, we'll be here."

Becca and Caroline looked at each other, each reflecting a glimmer of hope for the first time since they discovered Nickie was missing. Becca reached out to Caroline and drew her close in a strong hug. Yes, she felt maybe it would be all right. In a low voice she whispered, "Thank you, Caroline, for opening up to me. I needed to hear this. Thank you."

Suddenly, a loud crash disrupted the optimistic atmosphere. Everyone turned and saw Sarah smile sheepishly at the sight of the chalkboard that had been pulled down and now lay on the floor. Chalk was still rolling across the linoleum floor.

Chapter Eighteen

Today was a long day at the deli. Mrs. Kirschbaum felt good about the steady stream of customers they had all day long. It was going to feel deliciously soothing to go home and have a nice cup of tea and a piece of holiday bread.

She looked around the now empty deli, checking to see that all the chairs had been put on top of the tables. She turned and leaned over the final table that still needed cleaning and started to wipe away the crumbs and coffee spills.

"Harry, that's it. I guess everybody's finished mit us. I lock up, yes?"

Harry called out from the kitchen. "Sure. Vatever. That Mrs. Klinghoffer never picked up her order."

"Ach! So, vat's new?" Mrs. Kirschbaum moved toward the door and fumbled in her apron pocket for the keys. She sifted through several until she found the one she wanted. "Put it in der 'frigerator. I'm goink to charge her anyvays this time."

Mrs. Kirschbaum stared out the window, initially focusing on the Christmas lights across the street until her attention was caught by a little girl and a stray dog. She looked at them in front of her display window that was still decorated to show off the baked delights that tempted passersby to come inside to indulge the senses. She thought the little girl looked hungry with her wide-eyed scrutiny of all the goodies lining the window. "So, Harry, ve're not close yet."

Harry still answered from the kitchen, "So, ve close, ve don't close. Vat is all dis?" Harry entered the deli from the kitchen wiping his hands on the white apron tied around his waist. "Maybe ve don't got to put in 'frigerator—" He stopped mid-sentence as he saw his wife waving at someone through the window. He watched as the little girl waved back.

Mrs. Kirschbaum mumbled, "Vat is dis girl doink out there mitout her parents?"

Harry went to the counter and poured himself a cup of coffee. "Vat, you pickink up a little stray elf from the Santa Claus?"

"Look how skinny she is! Harry, who feeds this girl? Ve lettink her in."

Harry looked at his wife as she exited the door and went outside. He watched with interest through the window as she tried to coax the little girl to come inside. The girl shook her head that she wouldn't come in. Finally, Mrs. Kirschbaum pointed at something in the window that made her nod approvingly. She turned and reentered the deli.

Harry laughed as his wife entered. He couldn't believe she hadn't been able to entice the child to come inside. "Vat's that, Esther? You losink your touch mit the little vons?"

"Vell, at least her momma teach her not speakink to strangers. She say's her name is Nickie." Mrs. Kirschbaum retrieved a muffin from the window display and showed it to Nickie, who nodded and looked down at her dog. Mrs. Kirschbaum understood the message. She took a second muffin and walked out on the sidewalk, handing one to Nickie and one to the dog.

Nickie turned around and saw a bench nearby where a young girl was sitting staring out at the traffic. She looked at the girl, who turned and smiled and patted the bench next to her. The girl was older than Nickie. She had big green eyes framed with long, Bambi-like eyelashes and soft, fine golden hair that fell to her shoulders in big curls. There was something gentle and kind about her.

Nickie sat at the end of the bench and looked at Christmas as he inhaled the muffin and then busied himself licking up the wayward crumbs. Nickie was hungry. She looked at the girl. "Do you want to share this with me?"

The girl smiled and shook her head no.

Nickie took big bites out of the muffin, periodically wiping her mouth with the back of mitten.

Mrs. Kirschbaum stood with her hand on the door of the deli ready to go in. She smiled with contentment as she watched Nickie remove her mitten and take a bite out of the last piece of muffin and give the rest to the scruffy dog.

Christmas sat next to Nickie and squirmed, ready to take the final morsel. He took it gently from her hand and inhaled it in one gulp without chewing.

Mrs. Kirschbaum peered intensely at Nickie's face. "And ver is your mama?"

"At the office."

"So vu's taking care of you today?"

"My auntie Caroline."

"Oh, and vat is she doink?"

"Shopping for everybody."

Mrs. Kirschbaum glanced at the Cedarwood bookstore next to the deli and nodded. "Vell, don't catch a cold and go inside to your aunt. It's vinter and already dark so soon."

Nickie smiled. "'Kay."

Harry saw his wife wave at a passing police car as she was ready to come inside. He turned his attention to Nickie and the dog through the window. They really seemed to have enjoyed the baked treats his wife had made that afternoon.

Nickie noticed the older girl stand and take a fuzzy scarf from around her neck and offer it to her. It was made of cream-colored fleece and had fringes edged with beads. Nickie touched the beads and smiled. The older girl wrapped it around Nickie's head and stared across the street, pointing into the dark, and whispered, "There's what you are searching for."

***

Becca looked out the window at the night and the falling snow. The lights in the parking lot illuminated the crystals as they fell silently and accumulated on the pavement. "If you just come back to me, I promise I'll get you a puppy," she said to her reflection. She heard the door open and turned to see a medium height, well-built, Hispanic police officer enter. His black hair was starting to be interlaced with white that looked like fiber-optic strands as they caught the light from the fluorescent bulbs. His hair was combed back neatly, and he had an air of confidence that gave her hope.

Santiago walked in, took off his hat, and surveyed the assembled group. He saw Becca over by the window and stepped on a wayward piece of chalk that crunched under his foot as he walked towards her.

Becca looked at him with wide-eyed anticipation. "Did you find her?"

He fumbled with the brim of his hat. "No, sorry, ma'am. I only saw her. When was the last time you saw her?"

"I didn't. I was at the office party. She was with my sister-in-law, Caroline, who was doing some last-minute shopping." She pointed at Caroline and her children, who were huddled together in the corner. Becca put her hand over her mouth to stifle a cry. She turned her back to Santiago to wipe away a tear that streamed down her face. She looked out into the dark again and put a hand on the cold window. "Where are you, my angel? Where did you go? How's mommy going to find you?"

Santiago saw Becca's reflection and the look of desperation. He walked over to Caroline. "You go home with the kids and wait. There's nothing you can do here. I'll contact you the minute we find out anything." He turned to Becca and held out her coat. "Mrs. Halstead, come with me in my cruiser. Let's see if we can't find her."

Becca put on the coat and picked up her gloves and purse. "Thank you, Officer."

Santiago held open the door. "Here, we can go the back way. My patrol car is just by the door."

Becca waited for him to open the passenger door. It was warm inside with the motor still running. The police radio crackled with dispatcher messages.

"Do you think there may have been a message that someone found Nickie?"

"Not yet or they would have contacted me on my mobile unit."

Becca fell silent, listening to the slush hitting the undercarriage as they left the parking lot. She stared out the window.

"This is the street I last saw her coming from. She may be trying to come back this way to get back to the mall." He slowed the cruiser to five miles per hour.

Becca looked furtively from sidewalk to sidewalk, searching for her precious child. At least she was doing something riding in the police cruiser with Officer Santiago searching for Nickie. She strained and thought she saw a shadow, but when they got closer it was only a heap of garbage bags.

Santiago clutched the wheel, looking left and right as well. He turned on his spotlight and searched every porch and alleyway, looking for any sign or clue of this little girl he had seen a while ago.

Finally he broke the tense silence. "Well, you can't stop 'em from worryin'. They always worry. But it was best to send your sister-in-law home. I mean, there was nothing more for her to do there, right? And them little kids, they looked hungry."

The cruiser drove by the deli. Santiago saw a van parked in front of the display window obscuring his view of the bench and all the delights that were probably still displayed. He would have to remember to call it in to have it ticketed, but he just didn't have the time right now. He saw Mrs. Kirschbaum standing by the door ready to go inside. Santiago slowed to a crawl, beeped his horn, and waved.

Mrs. Kirschbaum noticed the police car. She saw Santiago, who only this morning had had hot chocolate there by the window. She waved at him as he drove by, catching a glimpse of a passenger. "I vonder vu?" she thought absently and turned to look at Nickie still sitting on the bench letting the dog lick the last taste of muffin from her hand.

Becca stared absently at Mrs. Kirschbaum as she returned Santiago's wave. She was numb and saw the pleasant gesture without looking at anything in particular.

Mrs. Kirschbaum watched the cruiser as it continued down the street, turned right, and disappeared from view.

Becca gazed into the dark. "You're sure she went to the church, Officer Santiago?"

"No, I'm not sure, but those were the directions I gave her. I mean, who knows where she went? This is one brave little kid, if you ask my opinion, and she coulda gone anywhere after me, but that's where I thought she was goin'."

"Now, what exactly did she say again?"

"Look, I was in the middle of traffic, Mrs. Halstead."

Becca rubbed the fog off the side window, turned to Santiago, and interrupted, "Call me Becca, Officer."

"Okay, you can call me Santiago, Mrs., uh…Becca. Right? So I'm in traffic, the worst kind, and suddenly there's this little girl pulling on my leg. So I don't know exactly. Anyway, she asked me something about did I know where Heaven is. So…"

He shrugged and looked back at both sidewalks while keeping an eye on the car ahead that insisted on constantly applying the brake. "I pointed her to the Catholic church, and she took off across the street. Scared me spitless, y'know. The little girl…geez…here we are."

***

The work just never seemed to end at the rectory. Mrs. Kelly took care of all the needs of Father McCurdy and the other priests that she took into her charge. She stood over the sink shaking the water drops off the last dish she was rinsing and placed it into the drainer next to the sink. She was deep in thought as she started to wipe off the counters, absently listening to the radio playing in the background.

She was startled by a loud knock on the door. She shuffled to the door, wiping her hands on the dishtowel that was still draped over her shoulder. She looked through the peephole to see who might be calling at this hour and saw a police officer with a lady she didn't recognize. She wondered what they would want. "Oh, dear," she whispered as she reached for the lock. "What could be the problem?" She quickly unlocked and unbolted the door. "Oh, dear, Officer, is something the matter?"

Santiago tipped the bill of his hat. "Well, ma'am, we've got a missing person report here."

Becca stepped slightly forward into the light spilling out of the foyer and interrupted Santiago, "My daughter, Nicole, she's about this tall."

Santiago put his hand out to reassure her.

She shook her head. "No! I'm fine."

Mrs. Kelly looked at both of them and frowned. "Oh, no! A missing girl? The night before Christmas? How terrible for you!"

Santiago cleared his throat. "She's five years old, around three-and-a-half feet tall, blonde, blue eyes, and was last seen wearing a light red jacket and a red knit cap. Does this…"

Mrs. Kelly shook her head. "No, I've been inside most of the day. Haven't seen anybody. Did you lose her while you visited the church?"

Santiago leaned forward. "No, see, she was at the mall, and for some reason…"

"Oh, at the mall—the mall? What in the world are you looking clear over here for? Gracious sakes! It's several blocks to the mall from here. I don't think…"

"Is the Father here?"

"No, he's gone out to run some errands. He certainly would've mentioned a lost girl."

"No, he wouldn't. He doesn't know. Will you tell him?"

"Well, I was just finishing up. I could leave him a—I know! Let's call him on his portable phone." She motioned for them to enter and follow her to the next room where the phone stood on a polished, worn credenza.

Mrs. Kelly picked up the phone and turned to Santiago and Becca. "It's more than I can understand how you can have a phone like a radio without a cord, but he's got one. It's called a cellular phone. Let's see the number…It's something what they can do now, isn't it?" She turned and slowly pressed the numbers. "Not my generation…Here it is." She beamed. "It's ringing!"

***

The phone rang persistently on the seat of Father McCurdy's empty car. He opened the door of the rectory while holding on to the pine tree when he heard the faint sound of a ring and reached into his coat pocket, realizing he had left his cell phone in the car. Oh, well. It would just have to wait. He was already running late getting the Christmas tree and preparing for his last midnight mass.

***

Nighttime at the radio station was typically low-key. However, today it was more quiet than usual given that it was Christmas Eve and the majority of the staff was off doing last-minute preparations for the festivities.

Roger Dodger leaned into the microphone. "And this is the last call for the youth pageant, which starts tonight at eight o'clock. Better get there quick if you want a parking place within a country mile. And here's one more reminder of midnight mass at the Church of the Madeleine. Father McCurdy informs me that all are invited, Catholic or not, for an evening of spiritual renewal, reflection, and the celebration of the birth of Christ. That's the midnight mass, I think you know what time it starts."

Roger switched on a commercial and leaned back, satisfied with his announcement. He held up a piece of paper for Geronimo, who was peering at him through the window. Roger mouthed what he had written in order to emphasize the message, "Fifty words each! Now let 'em call!"

As if on cue, the phone bank lit up obligingly.

Roger frantically waved to get Geronimo's attention. He shook his head and mouthed insistently, "Oh, no! I didn't mean it. Didn't mean it!"

Geronimo ran his fingers through his hair as he looked down at the illuminated switchboard. He waited for a few seconds and punched a button as he braced the receiver against his shoulder. He quickly scribbled something on a piece of paper and held it up to the window for Roger to read.

Roger squinted to decipher the message. MRS. KELLY ABOUT MISSING CHILD. Roger slowly made out the words and then immediately picked up the phone. "Hello?"

Chapter Nineteen

Nickie wasn't sure where to go next to fulfill her quest. She reached down and scratched behind Christmas's ears, and then she knelt down and held his head. "It's cold! Brrr! That girl on the bench was so nice to give me her scarf."

She looked down the block through the mist escaping through her breath. In the distance there was a steady flow of cars and lights that streamed out of the buildings. "Wonder what that is over there, Christmas. Let's go see." She stood up and beckoned for him to follow as she marched toward the glowing lights that cast sparkles in the snow. As she got closer, her attention focused on a young black boy who was playing on the snowy steps of what looked like a church.

Seth looked up from the snowman he was starting to shape and saw Nickie and the dog walking down the sidewalk. He hadn't ever seen her before, not even in kindergarten where just about all the kids his age in town went. He was about to reach for some more snow to pack for the snowman's head, when he saw Christmas bounding toward him to investigate. His heart started to race. He was afraid of dogs and remembered his grandmother's warning to him. "Don't touch those mangy critters or they'll likely bite your head off." The words rang in his head, and here was this dog coming straight at him. He looked around, panicked, and started to run away, shouting at the dog, "No, no! Get away, get away!"

Christmas thought this must be a game, and he wanted to play. He leaped through the snow toward Seth and bounced after him.

Seth was terrified. He fled toward Nickie and grabbed her shoulders as he spun around and hid behind her. "Ow! Ow! Help me! Help!"

"No, no! No, no, Christmas. No! Now stay, *stay*!"

Nickie jumped forward toward Christmas to rescue Seth. She caught Christmas by the neck, as he wiggled with delight. He panted and licked Nickie's hand and gave her a woof. Nickie held him with both hands. "Settle down, boy."

He nudged her legs with his nose and sat next to her, starting to pant again.

"Don't worry. He's a good dog. He won't hurt you."

Seth tried to act cool and relaxed. "I knew that." His stare never wavered from Christmas just in case it looked like he would come after him again.

Nickie backed up and turned toward Seth just as Christmas yawned and lay down in the snow. "You know, he can talk. Watch." She pulled the whistle out of her pocket and blew on it.

Christmas raised his head and barked.

"That's cool. Can I try?" With new confidence he stood next to Nickie, who handed him the whistle.

"I bet he'll talk for you, too."

Seth blew the whistle and Christmas perked his floppy ears.

"Woof!"

"Hey, he did talked for me."

Nickie felt she needed to say something to Seth, who stayed close to her, still wary. "He's a nice dog, you know. He helped me escape from a scary, screaming woman."

"He did?"

Nickie nodded.

"Did she look like a witch?"

"Yeah, and she was made out of rags that became her body, and she came right out of a big box."

"She did?"

"Yeah! She yelled and almost grabbed my arm, and Christmas…"

At the sound of his name and the tone of Nickie's voice, Christmas raised his head and growled.

"Christmas tried to bite her hand off."

"Is Christmas his name?"

"Yes, because tomorrow is Christmas, see?"

"I know it is. That's why we gonna have the pageant tonight."

"What's a p-p-pagnant?"

"No, pageant! It's where we sing and do a play for Jesus."

"You sing for Jesus?"

"Yeah."

"Does he comes down from Heaven for you to sing to him?"

"Yeah!"

"Wow!"

Seth straightened and looked around to see who else might be listening. He felt a newfound confidence given that he had a captive audience, and Christmas didn't seem to be a threat anymore. He puffed out his chest and found his bragging tone. "Yup! He gets wrapped up in sweating cloths and limes in a manger."

Nickie looked at Seth quizzically and totally lost. She wrinkled her forehead, trying to understand. Even though she was confused, she was fascinated by Seth's knowledge.

"You wanna see?"

"Yeah."

Seth shifted his stance to get ready to go to the church.

Christmas saw him move. He jumped up and came toward him.

As Seth watched the dog advancing, new terror erupted within him. "Hey, he's after me again! Let's run!" He ran toward the steps of the side door with Nickie in close pursuit.

"Hey, slow down!"

Both stopped at the door panting.

"I don't want him to tear off my hand."

"He won't. He only tears off hands of bad people, like scary people."

Nickie turned to address the dog, which also panted. "Now stay! Stay, Christmas, stay right here." She turned back to her new friend, "What's your name?"

"Seth Daniel Woods. My grandpa is the minister."

"Oh, I'm looking for Jesus."

"What kind?"

Nickie looked at him, flabbergasted. "What do you mean?"

Seth tried to look taller and puffed out his chest again. "We've got two kinds of Jesus here. One baby Jesus for Santa Claus at Christmastime, and a big Jesus with a beard, who's in big trouble when the Easter bunny comes." Seth looked at Nickie and proudly resumed. "Which one?"

Nickie was puzzled. "I don't know."

Seth opened the side door. "Let's go ask my grandpa; he knows everything." He pulled Nickie by the sleeve of her coat inside the church and quickly closed the door, looking out the window to make sure Christmas remained outside.

Christmas looked up with an expectant expression on his face, but sat down on the stoop panting and staring at the window.

Nickie walked with Seth down a long corridor. In the distance she heard the beautiful sounds of a choir. It was far away at first, but as they came closer to stairs that led backstage, it was loud and awe inspiring. Seth pushed Nickie forward as they climbed the steps, and soon they found themselves behind the curtains. Nickie stumbled as one of the actresses accidentally bumped into her. Everywhere she looked there was a quick, unorganized bustle of actors, children, helpers, and parents.

"Seth, who's singing behind the curtains?"

"Oh, that's on the stage. It's the angels. They're rehearsing."

Nickie opened her eyes wide. "You have angels?"

"You can't have Christmas without angels, y'know?"

Nickie nodded knowingly. "Oh, yeah. Can I see 'em?"

"Sure."

They both moved to the edge of the curtains.

Seth whispered, "Just a peek! They aren't s'posed to see us."

Nickie nodded in silent agreement, as Seth pushed back the curtain just enough for both of them to look out at the choir dressed in their white robes.

"Wow! You've got black angels!"

Seth stepped back from the curtain. "We've got all kinds a angels here—black ones, white ones, yellow ones, brown ones, all colors."

Suddenly, they were both startled by the deep voice of Reverend Woods, who stood behind them. "Hey, kids, you wouldn't want to spoil the show, would you?"

Seth turned and smiled. "Grandpa!"

Reverend Woods picked up Seth and shut the curtain.

Seth looked down at Nickie. "This is my grandpa!"

Reverend Woods looked down and saw Nickie. "And who's your new friend?"

Seth beamed and said, "Christmas."

Nickie frowned. "No, I'm Nickie. Christmas is my dog. Am I going to see Jesus in the pagert?"

Seth giggled. "Pageant!"

Reverend Woods put Seth back down on the floor. "Well, we're all hoping we can see him someday." He gazed up toward the ceiling. "When he gets here."

Nickie thought for a moment and then yanked Reverend Woods's hand with excitement. "You mean Jesus is really coming here?"

The reverend stared at the entrance of the backstage. "We'll have a baby Jesus, yes, if his parents can be on time for once." He saw two statuesque black women with long, curly salt-and-pepper colored hair in choir robes coming toward him from the entrance. "Good evening, Sister Fort, Sister Harley. Have you seen the Millers?"

Sister Fort shook her head and waved over her shoulder as both women continued toward the exit on the left side of the backstage area. "No, Reverend Woods. Sorry."

Reverend Woods frowned and looked at his watch. He tapped his foot and glanced at the entrance. He mumbled under his breath, "Why can't people be on time, especially the star of the show?" He rubbed his forehead. "My, this pageant gives me a production headache every year!" He patted Seth and Nickie on the head. "Can't have a pageant without the baby Jesus!"

Seth squeezed his grandfather around the leg to emphasize his important point. "Nickie wants to talk to Jesus."

Reverend Woods grinned. "Really? And what do we want to disturb the Lord for?"

Nickie put her hands on her hips and stared up at the face of the tall, black man with the big smile. "My daddy is with him and he needs to be back with me for Christmas because it's my birthday and I miss him a lot and I would like to—"

"Whoa, whoa, whoa! Hold your horses, little girl." Reverend Woods scratched his head and chuckled, but when he saw Nickie's determined look, he bent down. "Time out! Let's talk."

Nickie beamed. "He's coming from Heaven."

Reverend Woods saw a big man dressed as a shepherd coming toward him. "Excuse me, Nickie." He straightened upright and cleared his throat. "Brother Joseph, have you seen the Millers?"

Brother Joseph hustled by toward the split in the curtain, mumbling his lines. "Just arrived, Reverend. Downstairs."

Reverend Woods let out a long, audible breath as he felt huge relief passing through him. Finally, one of his many problems was solved. He said more to the air than to Brother Joseph, who was about to disappear offstage, "Wonderful, wonderful!"

Reverend Woods caught movement in his peripheral vision and looked in the direction of the yellow-robed man approaching him. He thought, "Well, it must be my father, the wise man." He saw the deep furrows of a disapproving frown etched on his father's face as he pointed at an elaborate headdress that he carried under his yellow flowing sleeved gown.

"Michael…"

Reverend Woods was exasperated by all the little details needing attention and threatening the smooth performance of the pageant. He looked to the ceiling, rolling his eyes, and said silently, "Dear God, give me patience and a little assistance here, please."

"Michael, I've got a big problem with this head contraption."

"Wear it!"

Robert Woods scoffed at his son. He audibly huffed, turned, and, with his chin up in indignation, left the backstage area.

Nickie was not to be deterred. She pushed on Reverend Woods's leg to make him notice her, but he seemed to be lost in his own thoughts. She insisted on getting his attention and pulled on his pant leg. "I gotta find Heaven, but I don't know where it is."

A glimmer of understanding of what Nickie sought filled him. He bent down on one knee to be at her eye level and stroked her cheek. "We're all looking to find Heaven, sweetheart."

Nickie's eyes widened in anticipation. "I gotta get there."

"Well, let's hope you aren't going there for a long while."

"I want to go there now! It's important!"

"You want to go there *now*? What's the hurry, really?"

"My daddy is there! He needs me."

"What about your mommy? Don't you think she needs you, also?"

"Yes, but my daddy misses me."

"Well, the quickest way to reach someone in Heaven that I know about is prayer, Nickie. Would you like me to say a prayer with you to Jesus for your daddy?"

Nickie nodded. "Yes, please. I've gotta find my daddy."

Seth watched the exchange between Nickie and his grandpa with great intensity. He leaned over and whispered to Nickie in a proud voice, "My grandpa says the bestest prayers."

Reverend Woods reached out and gathered the two children closer toward him and placed a hand on each of their heads.

Seth came closer to Nickie and whispered, "You gotta close your eyes. You don't want to see the Holy Host."

"Who's the Holy Host?"

"He's going around invisible."

"Oh, I see."

"No! You can't see."

"Quiet, children." The Reverend looked up to Heaven and started the prayer. "Let us pray. O, great heavenly Lord, our Master, help us in our time of need that we may seek you in our hearts and in our minds and in our closed places. Help these two young children to grow strong and good. And help young Nickie here, that she may have her heart's desire, for she is harrowed in her heart."

Puzzled, Nickie stared at Reverend Woods, trying to interpret what he had said.

Reverend Woods saw her apparent confusion. "It means you're doing right, Nickie, to look for Heaven in your trouble and your time of need."

He paused, organizing his thoughts. "O, that this child, in her time, Lord, may find you, like the prophets of old, in the desert place and on the high mountain."

Nickie stared at Reverend Woods's face deep in thought. She had a flicker of a new insight, and an idea started to form in her mind.

Reverend Woods raised his eyes to the heavens and then closed them in reverence. "Yes, and found you, Lord, in the high places. Bless this child with your spirit, this Christmastime. In the holy name of Jesus, amen. Hallelujah!" He opened his eyes and looked down.

Nickie stared at him with a new understanding and in an enthusiastic voice said, "I didn't know Jesus was on the mountain."

Reverend Woods muttered, "Okay now back to…I still have to check on the refreshments, see if all the choir members are ready, make sure the mike works, get dressed, make sure they plowed the parking lot…" He looked at his watch. "The parishioners are going to start coming in less than an hour." He shooed the two children along in order to get ready. "Now go on and have yourselves a good time tonight and enjoy the pageant."

Seth hugged his leg. "Okay, Grandpa."

Reverend Woods bent down to Nickie's level and took her hand in his. "Nice to have met you, Nickie. Are you here with your mommy?"

Just as Nickie was about to answer, a man approached the reverend, breathless. "Pardon, Reverend. Everybody's looking for you. Aunt Pearl can't find the recorders. Herbert says you told him to start on time, but—"

Reverend Woods stopped him with a gesture of his hand. He squeezed Nickie's little hand. "I'll talk to you about Heaven again sometime, Nickie. Now you go find the folks you came with, and Seth, you go find your mama. I'll see you two later."

Nickie and Seth watched as Reverend Woods rushed off in the direction of the man who had just left. They looked at each other.

Nickie heard the commotion of the pageant's last-minute preparations being addressed with barked commands.

"Will someone check the lighting? Are the shepherds here? Where are Mary and Joseph? Angels, I need you in your places to check the sound."

"You wanna watch the pageant?" Seth asked.

"I gotta go check on Christmas. How do I get back outside?"

"Down that way. I'll walk you back to the back door." They walked together down the corridor. As they reached the exit, Seth put his hand in his pocket. "Hey, wait! I still have your whistle."

"You can keep it. I don't need it. I'm getting my daddy for Christmas."

"Hey, thanks. Wow, cool!"

She turned and waved at Seth. "Bye."

"Bye." He put the whistle in his mouth and blew, and heard Christmas answer with a bark from outside. "Hey, this really works! He *can* talk!"

***

Becca fidgeted, tapping her finger on the handle of the door as Santiago inched the cruiser through the Christmas traffic. It appeared everyone at once was crawling toward their ultimate destination in anticipation of arriving at parties, buying last-minute presents, and being on time for other festivities.

To Becca it seemed like a nightmare with no certain outcome. Where could Nickie possibly be? She had to be somewhere. Becca didn't allow herself to think of all the terrible things the news reported could happen to missing children.

Santiago clutched the wheel in frustration and craned his neck to see if he could spot what was slowing traffic to this unbelievably slow pace. He adjusted the volume on the police radio, which was the only sound breaking the silence, along with an occasional honking horn. He glanced over at Becca and then back at the traffic. "Every year it's like this. Lucky they let me off to help you."

Becca stared out the window at the brake light of the car obstructing their progress. "I've been thinking, Officer."

"Please, just call me Santiago. Everybody does."

"The reason she went to church was to find Heaven. Now, I don't know, but I'm just thinking, how many life-sized manger scenes are there in town?"

"Geez, who knows? Half dozen, maybe. Let's see, there's one at..." Santiago studied the traffic situation ahead and the slow progress of the oncoming traffic, where headlights inched by like a line of slow tin soldiers. "Aw, we'll never get to the church at this rate." He reached over and flipped a switch. Instantly, lights started to twirl, flooding the street with oscillating red and blue beacons. Immediately, the traffic started to part slowly, looking much like the biblical Red Sea as cars pulled to the side. The cruiser moved ahead in the cleared path. "That's more like it. You were saying?"

"We really don't have any way of knowing."

At this moment another police car approached from the opposite direction. Both cars stopped.

Santiago waved his hand and rolled down his window. "Hey, Pacino!"

"Hey, give me a break tonight. I was raised in Brooklyn. My name is Cliff. Actually for you, Moreno, it's Officer Palmore. Show a little respect in front of the lady here."

"Okay, Officer Pacino Palmore. We're out looking for a little lost girl about three foot five."

"Yeah, I picked it up from the dispatcher."

"Have you seen anything?"

"Not a trace of her, but I came from the opposite direction from where she was spotted. I'll keep my eyes open and check some of the side streets."

"Appreciate it. Say merry Christmas to all the relatives, like Pavarotti, Sophia Loren, and the Godfather."

"*Feliz Navidad* to you, too. Say hi to Gloria Estefan and Andy Garcia."

"Wrong, man, Estefan and Garcia are *cubanos*. I'm *mexicano* and proud of it!" He rolled up the window and turned back to Becca. "Sorry. You was sayin'?"

"Maybe she's gone around to all the manger scenes." Becca clenched her fist and hit the door panel. "Why would she do that?"

Santiago slowly turned the corner toward the Baptist church at the end of the block with a quick glance at Becca. "I think it's probably because you told her that her father was in Heaven."

"Look, Officer Santiago, I'm sorry if I seem to be overanxious, but this is my daughter that's lost!"

Santiago saw the Baptist church ahead. Already all the parking in front was taken. He pulled alongside a station wagon and double-parked the cruiser. He shut the engine off, but left on the police lights.

One of the older parishioners held onto the arm of her husband and leaned close to his ear. "Look, Cyrus, something important must be goin' on. That cop just arrived with a lady."

"Are you sure, Jean-Ann?"

"Uh-huh."

Becca opened the door, climbed out of the cruiser, and raced toward the church. Santiago followed her cue and got out as well. He trotted up to the church steps, trying to catch up with Becca. He was slightly out of breath and looked embarrassed.

"I'm sorry, Mrs. Halstead. Becca? Please…"

Chapter Twenty

Nickie opened the door and there was Christmas. As soon as he saw her, he jumped up, rested his front paws on her chest, and licked her face, wagging his tail like a fast tempo metronome. She gave Christmas a big hug, pushed him down, and stepped off the stoop. "Christmas, I know zactly where we need to go. Come on."

She noticed all the people arriving for the pageant as they streamed up the stairs and into the church. She knew at the moment she didn't have time to see the pageant because her goal was now within reach and there was no time to waste. With one last look over her shoulder, she noticed the police car with its whirling lights. She stroked the top of Christmas's head between his ears. "Somebody must be in trouble. Sure glad it's not me."

Nickie's focus shifted to the silhouette of a majestic snow-covered hill that glistened in the distance over the rooftops of the houses that stood in the way. It looked imposing and yet it attracted her with an inviting allure. She was transfixed by the sight. "There it is, boy. We finally found where Heaven is. I know my daddy is there." With one last look, she turned her back to the church.

Across the street, she noticed the girl she'd met while eating her muffin and thought, "She must be going to the pageant, too."

Nickie waved, feeling special that she had made friends on her journey toward finding her father. Even if the girl had only said a few words to her, she was somehow a comforting presence. After all, she had given her a soft off-white fleece scarf and pointed the way. She saw a smile cross the young girl's face as she waved back, acknowledging they had met earlier.

The young girl pointed up at something beyond the houses.

Nickie looked where she was gesturing. She put her hand over her brow like a visor to see past the falling snow and again saw the huge snow-blanketed hill. "See, boy, she knows that's where we gotta go...the 'high mountain.'"

Christmas barked and ran ahead.

The snow squeaked under her boots as she ran after him down the street toward the big hill. "Wait for me, boy!"

***

Geronimo enjoyed the opportunity to be with Roger in the broadcast booth. Music played quietly in the background, filling the dimly lit space. He felt relaxed with Roger and confident enough in their relationship to put his feet up on the board. He read the childlike printing on the paper he picked up from Roger. So Alexis had written this poem. He turned to Roger. "Cute. That's real nice. You gonna read it on the air?"

"Heck, no!"

"Well, what'd ya bring it down for, then?"

Suddenly the telephone rang. Geronimo popped his feet off the board and laid the poem back down in front of Roger. "I got it." He sprinted back around to his side of the glass partition and reached for the receiver.

Roger looked down at the poem. "Yeah, why did I bring it here?"

Geronimo answered the call. "Hello? Oh yeah, the lost little girl. Right." He cringed when he heard the identity of the caller. "O-Officer. So give me the specifics...I mean, if we can help...yeah, yeah...lemme get this down."

Roger Dodger thoughtfully eyed his daughter's poem for a moment. He picked it up and looked up at Geronimo, who was still on the call. He made his decision on impulse. He quickly went down his list of carts, picked one out, and loaded it into the sound equipment just as Geronimo entered with the information he'd received.

"Hey, you know, like the lady wasn't off her rocker after all. P-p-police called. There *is* a lost kid." He handed Roger his scribbled note. "Imagine losin' yer kid the night before Christmas!"

Roger took the note. "Great! Great! That's a great lead-in!"

"What do you mean, lead-in?" At that moment the music ended. Roger leaned into the microphone. "You're tuned to WPRA, the 'Pleasures of Christmas.' Hope you're having a great Christmas Eve. Unfortunately, one of your neighbors is not. We've got a WPRA exclusive on a very sad story developing out there tonight. Apparently a little girl named Nicole Halstead wandered away from the mall tonight, and police are looking for anyone who's seen her and might know her whereabouts."

***

Mrs. Kelly was busying herself in the rectory kitchen wiping all the counters and the stove until they gleamed. There were always last-minute things to do to get Father McCurdy ready for midnight mass, and it seemed important to fuss over tonight's preparations. She listened to the radio every night. It was like having a trusted companion, and the disk jockey's voice had grown to be a familiar one over the years. She heard Roger's voice.

"Nicole, AKA Nickie, will be five years old tomorrow. That's right, a Christmas girl."

Mrs. Kelly dried her hands on her apron, came closer to the radio, and turned up the volume. She wrung her hands. "Oh, my goodness!"

"Nickie is three feet six inches tall, with blonde hair and blue eyes."

Across town in her kitchen, Caroline cradled Sarah in her arms as she rocked back and forth. The constant motion had put Sarah into a deep sleep, contentedly snoring little baby snores. Caroline took a sip of lukewarm tea and placed the cup on the kitchen table.

The radio filled the silence as she twirled a lock of her baby's hair around her finger. She felt anxious as she listened to the announcement.

Roger's presence cascaded into the kitchen. "She was last seen leaving the east side of Hillside Mall wearing red boots, jeans, a red coat, and a red knit hat."

She rocked harder, clutching Sarah. "Oh, little Nickie, where are you?"

Zak came into the room. "Mom, I heard on the radio that they're still looking for Nickie. Are they going to find her? They have to find Nickie, right, Mom?

Kathy stood next to him. "Mom, I didn't mean to lose her. You think they'll really find her?"

"Yes, they're going to find her. This is all my fault. I have to go and help." Caroline picked up the phone and dialed the number of her neighbor. "Patty, something awful has happened to my little niece."

"That's not the little girl they've been talking about on the radio?"

"Yes, it is."

"Look, send your kids over here and I'll take care of them."

"Are you sure that's okay?"

"Absolutely."

***

Marie turned up the volume on her old radio on the kitchen counter just as the kettle started to whistle.

"...We have a lost little girl in Cedarwood...anyone who wants to help come down to WPRA..."

"Oh, *madre de Dios*. I have to go see if there's something I can do."

Chapter Twenty-One

The night was muted, and the looming trees were encased in muffled silence as sounds receded into oblivion and the snow started to fall harder, accentuating a hushed tranquility.

Nickie's feet sank through the layers of snow while Christmas darted back and forth, crisscrossing their footprints in the newly fallen virgin blanket. He played excitedly, snapping at the falling snowflakes and burying his nose in the snow with his rump and wagging tail in the air.

Nickie stopped as her gaze went upward in the distance. She pointed. "Look, Christmas. That's gotta be where Heaven is. I know I'll find Daddy there."

Christmas lifted his head, which was buried in snow, trotted to her side, and nuzzled his nose under her hand.

The lights of the city faded as she started up the mountain, yet the snow made everything glow with a soft, gentle luminescence. The only sounds that penetrated the quietude were her breathing, Christmas's panting, and the sound of the crunching snow as she followed the path through the trees.

***

The pizza parlor was filled with teenagers hanging around with their friends celebrating their own holidays. The radio in the background added to the noise.

Roger's voice intermingled with the dozens of simultaneous conversations. "So if anybody may have seen little Nickie this Christmas Eve, please let us know. Call WPRA. Tell us where you saw her, the place and the time. Let's get Nickie home for Christmas. I can't think of a better Christmas present."

No one paid much attention to the message. Alexis vaguely heard her father's voice over the din.

Jerry leaned toward her. "Hey, that's your ol' man on the radio."

She looked over at the speaker. "So what?" She turned back to preside over a captive audience of punk friends.

Jerry visually scoured his pizza slice options and grabbed the piece that was disproportionately laden with sausage and pepperoni.

Alexis picked off the black olives from her slice and put them on Jerry's. "I hate these. You can have them." She turned to the punk next to her. "So you said your name was what?"

"Spike."

"Like your parents actually named you Spike?"

"No, like, I mean…like, I named myself Spike."

"I think your hair is kinda rad."

"Thanks…like, I bleach it myself…you know…with something that smells like Clorox."

"Well, you better put that head in a bucket of it again, because you've got at least an inch of brown roots."

"That's really funny, Lexi. Wow, like I might give it a try…could be a radioactive kind of trip. So what d'ya think of the spikes?" He brushed his hand over a stiff rooster comb.

"How much gel did it take?"

"Like, a whole tube."

Bored, Alexis put her arms across the back of the booth and surveyed the other tables. Jerry picked up another slice of pizza, leaned back against the booth, and talked to Spike. She ignored what he was saying, choosing instead to watch a TV mounted to the wall that was broadcasting a surfing contest on mute.

The punk swallowed a piece of pizza and leaned closer to Jerry. "So he goes, 'Wow!' And I go, 'Nuclear *wow!*'"

Everyone laughed, with the exception of Alexis, who turned her attention to picking the onions off her slice.

Spike picked up two pieces of pizza that were stuck together. "And this guy starts to laugh so hard, he's flippin' out, y'know, like this." As he waved his hands in the air to illustrate the point, the top of the pizza slid off and landed on Alexis's shirt.

She pulled the cheese and pepperoni off her shirt and threw the pieces on the table as she glared at him.

"Look what you did, you idiot!"

"Geez, sorry, Lex. Hey, kinda matches your shirt."

She threw a piece of pepperoni at him. "Which kind of matches your zits, barfhead."

Spike rolled his eyes and feigned mock fear. He stood up, putting his knuckles on the table. "Ooh, tough talk! Well, you've got a whopper on your forehead. Check it out."

"Oh, yeah! What?" She squinted her eyes and glared. "You moron!"

He picked up another slice of pizza. "Wanna slam into this piece, too?"

Alexis continued to stare at him and replied through clenched teeth, "Excuse me while I wash your face off my shirt." She got up to go to the restroom.

The punk placed his hands on his hips and assumed an air of mock terror. "Ooh!"

Alexis turned to see his antics, to the amusement of the others at the table, and glowered. "Slimeballs!" She stormed into the bathroom, went straight to the sink, and stared at her shirt in the mirror. "Oh, man!"

Alexis furiously yanked several paper towels from the dispenser. She turned on the hot water, soaked the towel, and started wiping the pizza remnants and stains off. She heard her dad's voice coming from the speaker mounted in the corner.

"And now something in honor of little lost Nickie. I'd like to read something my daughter wrote years ago. This is for you, Nickie, and for Alexis, wherever you are tonight."

Alexis rolled her eyes and addressed the speaker. "Oh, please!" She listened incredulously.

"It's called 'For My Christmas Daddy.' '*I caught a snow flake for you and held it tight…So I could make it out of paper for you just right…But it melted before I could draw its looks…And I don't know if you have one in the picture books.*'"

Alexis stood mortified by what she was hearing. How could he embarrass her that way? She looked at the speaker for the volume knob, but found it had been broken off. She cringed in horror as the simple little poem continued to flow over the airways. She stomped back to the table where Jerry was engrossed in a story from another one of their punk gang.

The punk with the pink streaked hair leaned toward Jerry as if to convey a deep secret. "So I says, 'Well, that's okay, 'cuz, like, I got my rights and you got yours and…'"

Alexis charged up to the table with hot tears stinging down her face, leaving a stream of mascara. With her hand planted firmly on the table, she confronted Jerry through clenched teeth. "I gotta have your keys."

Jerry looked at her puzzled and shrugged. "Huh? What for?"

"None of your stinking business! Now, *give me those keys!*"

The restaurant became quiet as everyone looked at Alexis, waiting for the imminent explosion.

A couple of punk teenagers in the corner booth looked up and gave an exaggerated grin toward Alexis. "Ooh!"

Alexis shot them a venomous glare. "What's your problem?"

"Nothin'!"

They sat back down. "What's with her?"

Jerry raised an eyebrow. "Okay, I see you're pissed at something. I'll give you the keys, but no speeding!" He dug out the keys from the deep pockets of his oversized pants, put them on the table, and pushed them toward her. "Right? Here."

Alexis snatched the keys. "I've got someplace to go, all right? I'll give them back to you when I'm done." She stormed to the door.

Jerry picked up one of Alexis's olives and looked toward the door. "Man, that's as mad as I've ever seen her."

Spike looked in the same direction. "I wouldn't want to cross her right now and I barely know her."

Chapter Twenty-Two

Nickie stood at the base of the mountain. She turned around and saw a faint glow of city lights through the curtain of snowflakes. Christmas went ahead, leaving leaping tracks. He barked at her to come. She slapped her thighs. "Come here, Christmas."

He stopped. "Woof!" He stuck his nose in the snow, lifted his head, threw a clump in the air, and snapped at it as it came down. "Woof!"

"Come here, boy."

He put his front paws down with his hindquarters in the air and wagged his tail.

"'Kay, you want me to come to you?"

"Woof!"

Nickie looked back at the lights and then to the top of the hill, which was obscured by low clouds that dropped snowflakes like angels shaking a pillow filled with feathers. She reached Christmas, who waited for her, and hugged him around the neck, feeling the cold of the snow that had caked onto his fur. "Christmas, that's a really big mountain. Will you come with me?"

He barked, pulled away, and trotted up the slope. He stopped after several yards, turned toward Nickie, and sat, panting.

"'Kay, boy, I'm coming." She trudged through virgin snow until she reached him. "I'm not scared. Are you scared?"

Christmas put his head under her arm.

***

Becca walked around the ornate manger in the center of the lawn of the Lutheran church. Her breath condensed in the cold night air. "Come on, Nickie. Please…where are you?" She walked around it one more time. "Come on, Nickie. Please be here." She turned around in a full circle and whispered, "All these churches are starting to look alike. I can't remember where I've already been or whether I should look there again just in case." Exhausted, she slid back onto the seat of the police cruiser.

Santiago kept his hands on the steering wheel as he watched Becca return. He looked forward at the street ahead and waited for Becca to break the awkward silence.

Becca also stared out the windshield at the dark. "Nothing. Where's the next one?"

"Look, Mrs. Halstead, we're both pretty beat. A lot of stress and strain. This is the last one in an area that could barely have been close enough for her to come to."

"So, what are you saying?"

"I'm saying…I'm saying we need a little break. Look, all of our available officers are on this. Why don't we stop by Kirschbaums' Deli for some coffee?"

"I can't give up."

"We're not giving up, just getting a quick cup of coffee, okay?" Becca opened her wallet to Nickie's picture and stared out the frosted side window. "All right."

Santiago slapped the steering wheel. "That's more like it. We could use something positive." He sharply turned the wheel, making a U-turn, and proceeded down the street. He reached to touch her arm, but then decided not to. "Mrs. Halstead…"

Becca saw him put his hand back on the steering wheel. "Becca, Officer Santiago Moreno."

Santiago cleared his throat. "Okay, Mrs. Halstead... Mrs. Becca...I gotta say somethin'. Look, a cop's job is not too glamorous. You know what I mean? I mean, criminals, victims, hurt people, drunk people, unhappy people...it can get pretty ugly."

Just as he was finishing the sentence a VW van raced by from the opposite direction.

"Man, that guy is speeding! I ought to turn around and pull him over."

Becca looked at him.

"But I won't. We've got to find your daughter. That guy should consider himself lucky tonight." He followed the car in his side mirror. "Geez! Slow it down! See what I mean? And, well, anyway, what you said back there at the church..."

Becca rubbed her eyes and stared in between the snowflakes that hit the windshield, hoping her daughter would materialize from the dark. "Oh, please, I'm just very tired."

Santiago remembered how his mother reacted when he ran away from home for a day. "No, no. You're right. You're right. My head wasn't in it. Or rather, my heart wasn't in it. I mean, she is your kid. A cute little girl, too, by the way." He pointed to the photograph.

Becca stared at the picture of Nickie in the wallet on her lap. "Thank you."

Santiago turned the wheel and listened to the slow beat of the wipers as they pushed the heavy snow to the side. "And having lost her dad and with her birthday tomorrow and all, well, the poor little kid, who knows what she's thinkin'."

"Officer, you don't have to..."

Santiago glanced at the picture and then out the windshield, staring into the snow falling in mesmerizing patterns in front of the headlights. "Santiago. Everybody calls me Santiago...please. What I'm sayin' is that I've been thinkin' about what you said. And you're right. I'm out here actin' like a jerk!"

Becca started to interrupt, but Santiago stopped her with a halting gesture. He found he was angry with himself. He stared into the night and turned up the speed of the wipers. "What I'm sayin' is, if I hadn't of been so lamebrained, this never would have happened. I mean, she pulled on my pant leg for help. The night before Christmas, and she pulls on *my* pant leg. I reached down and touched her. I got her across the street, and, hell, I even lectured her on crosswalk safety."

Becca saw that Santiago was getting emotional. She was touched by the genuineness of his concern, and it made her soften toward him. "Hey, it's not your fault."

Santiago swallowed hard and gripped the steering wheel. "So, I'm sayin' I'm into this thing now, Mrs. Becca. I mean it. I'm here to help, one hundred percent for sure."

Becca managed a faint smile as tears threatened to spill down her face. She wiped her eyes with her index finger. "Okay, I know you're doing everything you can and…"

Santiago reached in his pant pocket, extracted a white handkerchief, and gave it to her. "Here, this may help."

"Thank you. I'll wash it and give it back to you."

"Go ahead and keep it. My mother gave it to me. I want you to hang on to it. She always told me that when your tears spill into it, everything would be all right." He looked at Becca and then at the falling snow hitting the windshield. He turned up the heat and the speed of the defroster fan. "I'm in it big time. She's just a little kid, y'know."

Becca extended her hand, and he took it. She whispered to him through choked tears, "Thank you, Santiago."

He squeezed her hand. "Have faith, Becca. We're going to find her." Santiago saw the deli sign and pulled in front of the shop. He frowned when he saw that only the kitchen shone with what looked like the small illumination from a nightlight. He leaned forward with his arms resting against the top of the steering wheel and peered at the shop's front window. "Oh, no! You gotta be kiddin'. It looks like they're closed."

Becca rubbed the frost from her window with the sleeve of her coat and looked at the dark deli. "It *is* late, you know."

"Yah, well, let's see if there's still somebody inside."

Santiago stopped the police car against the curb in front of the delicatessen and got out. "The Kirschbaums might still be there cleaning up. Stay here and let me see."

He knocked insistently on the glass of the door until finally he saw movement from within the kitchen. The swing door opened slightly, and he could see Mrs. Kirschbaum's frame. The door opened a bit wider with warm light from the kitchen outlining her silhouette. Then he saw a shotgun in her hand pointed at the front door. He stepped aside. "Geez, Mrs. K. Put that thing away before you hurt someone." He waved his hand. "It's me, Santiago."

Mrs. Kirschbaum raised her hand and put up one finger. "Give me a minute. I gettink the keys." She let the door swing shut and propped the gun in the broom closet next to the sink. "Harry, ver are your keys? Ver? It's Santiago."

Steam escaped from his mouth as he said to himself, "What's a sweet little old lady doing with a gun?" He shook his head in disbelief. He turned and waved to Becca to come join him.

***

"That's right, folks. We've got a little missing girl, Nicole. If anyone has any information, call WPRA at..." Roger looked up at the control booth where all the phone lights lit up almost simultaneously.

Geronimo punched the first blinking button. "WPRA, please hold." He punched the next button. "WPRA, please hold." He looked at Roger and shrugged his shoulders, overwhelmed.

Since Roger's announcement of the missing girl on the radio, Geronimo was inundated with a flood of incoming calls he couldn't answer by himself. Roger saw the banks light up, demanding immediate attention. He lifted the receiver of his own handset and motioned to Geronimo that he would also start picking up the calls. "Winter Wonderland" faded in the background as they turned their focus on each call.

Geronimo, preoccupied, acknowledged an "affirmative" to Roger and returned to his caller. "That's all right, but the mall was the last place she was seen, so thank you for callin'. Bye." He hung up the phone in time to hear Roger finishing his own telephone conversation.

"You have a nice time yourself, and merry Christmas." Roger put the phone back in the cradle. "Whew!"

Geronimo got up and poked his head around the corner of the broadcast booth. "Man! That's twelve calls in twenty minutes, man, and look at the phone lines! Looks like a Christmas tree, man!"

Roger saw the CALL button light up. "Beats boredom! And remember, you dared me to." He punched the blinking button. "WPRA. Can I help you?"

Geronimo went back to his producer's desk. He rubbed his bloodshot eyes and picked up the phone. "WPRA, a station for the nation. What's yer pleasure? Yeah…yeah…"

Suddenly, an insistent ringing of the station's side doorbell interrupted Geronimo's concentration. He looked through the glass and noticed that Roger hadn't even heard it. He came back to his caller. "Hey, can I, like, put you on hold?"

Without waiting for a response he punched the HOLD button and put the phone down on the desk as he headed for the door. He walked through the lobby and saw the blinking handset on the reception desk. He talked to the blinking phone. "Can I put you on hold?" He laughed. "Now I know how secretaries feel."

Geronimo yanked open the self-closing steel door, stepped into a small foyer, and heard the door snap shut behind him. He was amazed to find Alexis at the door.

Alexis saw him through the window and pounded on the door. "Come on! Will you open this blasted door?"

He opened the door with trepidation, trying to sound upbeat. "Lex! Hey, sorry, babe. I can't get off right now."

Alexis brushed by him and turned with her hands on her hips. "Where's my old man?"

Geronimo hesitated. "Oh, hey, you caught us at, like, this very crucial time." He stepped past her and forced open the door going to the secretary's desk. He picked up the phone, punched one of the lit buttons, and watched the door close with Alexis standing rigid and immobile in the foyer glaring at him.

She pushed open the door and stomped to the desk. "Hey, I asked you a question. Where's my old man?"

He put his hand over the mouthpiece. "I'm on the phone, babe. Hang on. We got a lost little girl tonight."

"Where is he?"

"Just chill." He removed his hand and talked to the caller. "Right, so I'm back. So did you see this little girl? She's five years old with a red coat on. Yep, got lost at the mall, and then took off....That's what we're trying to figure out."

The telephones kept ringing, demanding immediate attention. Geronimo motioned to Alexis and pointed to the phone in the office across from the secretary's station.

Alexis shook her head. "I'm not a secretary. I didn't come to answer stupid phone calls."

Geronimo put his hand over the mouthpiece and whispered to Alexis, "Could really use some backup, babe. Plenty o' calls, plenty o' calls. Savin' a little kid…"

"So what? It's your job, not mine, and I don't want to do it." She crossed her arms.

"Babe, I got to deal with this call. The guy is a real talker." He spoke into the phone again. "Mm-hm, mm-hm." Geronimo pushed the MUTE button and kept listening to the caller. "Here's the situation. It's her birthday tomorrow, and there's, like, a heavy freeze and snow forecast tonight. Do ya get it?" He took the call off mute. "Mm-hm, …That's right, last seen at the mall."

Chapter Twenty-Three

Mrs. Kirschbaum flicked on the light switch of the deli, letting warm, comforting yellow light flood the room. She looked at the radio on the counter that emanated the gentle notes of "Do You Hear What I Hear?" and went to unlock the door. "Come, come, sit, sit." She ushered Santiago and Becca to a booth by the window. "I brink you some nice hot coffee." She went to the counter and grabbed two white mugs by their handles and the pot of coffee and brought them to the table.

"You vant that *mit milch* or *kreme*?"

Becca took off her gloves and put her hands around the steaming cup. "I'll take it with milk, please."

"Harry, ver's the *milch*?"

Harry popped open the kitchen door and pointed to the refrigerator. "*Im Kuehlschrank beim Kaese* right by the cheddar."

"*Ach so*! Yah, yah, now I rememba." She set the pot on the table and walked to the refrigerator, pulled out a carton, and poured the contents into a little silver pitcher, which she brought back and set next to Becca. "Here is the *milch*. And Santiago de Chile?"

"I'll drink it just black tonight."

"Ve already tryink to close vunce. Is all right, is all right, and nobody drinks from the Styrofoam and the plastic in this deli. You von't stay. You drink from vatever. You people looking like you need a rest. Sit! Rest! Vat is so important you out on Christmas Eve mitout coffee?"

Santiago replied, "Well, we're looking for a little girl that got lost today."

"Is awful, no? Yah, ve been tryink to call the radio for Nickie."

Becca put down her cup. "What? You know her name?"

Mrs. Kirschbaum shrugged her shoulders. "Sure, she told me. Ve tryink to call up the radio station."

Becca put her arm across the back of the booth and turned to the source of the Christmas music. "The radio?"

Santiago followed her gaze. "Now, how in the heck?"

"Listen to vat I'm talkink!" Mrs. Kirschbaum poked Becca's arm "Vat's your name?"

"Rebecca. Everyone calls me Becca."

"Becca, listen to vat I'm sayink to you. Yes, they askink for help on the radio. Ve know little Nickie. She vas here tonight."

Becca wrinkled her forehead. "What?"

Mrs. Kirschbaum picked up the pot and filled Becca's cup. "Yah, a cute girl."

Becca put her hand onto Mrs. Kirschbaum's wrist. "Please, I'm her mother."

Mrs. Kirschbaum put the back of her hand against her forehead. "*Oy ve! Mein Gott! Ach du lieber!* You are dee mutter." She raised her eyes upward. She set down the pot and took Becca's hands into both of her own and held them tight. "No! Can't be! Harry!" she yelled in the direction of the kitchen as she stroked Becca's hand. "Der coffee for free!"

Harry came out of the kitchen holding a bowl with a wooden spoon in his hand and continued to mix cream cheese with bits of lox he had just cut. "Vat is it?"

Mrs. Kirschbaum looked at her husband. "Harry, *das ist* Mrs. Becca...Haleved, right? Is Nickie's mama."

Harry nodded at Becca. "Oy! Ve vere ready to close, and the girl, nice girl, looks in vindow. Ve thinkink 'she looks so good girl, but hungry.' So ve decide to give her muffin to eat. Ve invite her in. She small girl, nice girl. She von't come in because—"

Mrs. Kirschbaum flicked a napkin in his direction. "Harry, shut up for vunce. He's talkink more than for tventy years! You been drinkink from the Maneshevitz, already! I vas mit the girl outside, not you! Please, I tellink story. Yes, ve give vun muffin for her, unt vun for the dog."

Becca exclaimed unnoticed, "Dog?"

Santiago lifted his empty cup. "You said the radio station is gathering information?"

Mrs. Kirschbaum poured him another cup and nodded toward the set. "Is busy. Radio alvays busy." She patted Becca's shoulder. "Yes, so Nickie vas here mit the dog, Hanukkah. No, vat vas? Harry! Vat's the name I told you the dog vas?"

Harry stopped stirring. "Uh...Christmas!"

Mrs. Kirschbaum beamed. "Christmas! Christmas, Hanukkah, so vat?"

Becca looked puzzled. "But she doesn't have a dog!"

Mrs. Kirschbaum leaned forward. "Vell, she got vun now!"

Becca stiffened and looked out the window thinking, "Oh, Nickie, I'm sorry I didn't pay more attention to you this morning. You can have a dog. Just let us find you. Please let us find you."

Mrs. Kirschbaum felt Becca's rigidity and saw her sad reflection in the window. "In fact, she vas sittink on dat bench." She pointed outside and poked Santiago. "Ven you vave at me, rememba?"

Becca turned to Santiago. "I remember you waving at Mrs. Kirschbaum."

"Yeah, me, too. I was going to call in the van that parked in front of the deli."

Becca shook her head and stared at the bench. "She was sitting on that bench?"

Mrs. Kirschbaum nodded. "Yah! Eating the muffin ve give her. Vun for her and vun for the dog. She vasn't actink like she vas lost. Actink like hungry. Oy! If I only know."

"That's okay, Mrs. Kirschbaum. You didn't know. This is the best news we've had so far. Well, where did she, I mean, which way did she go?"

Mrs. Kirschbaum put the palm of her hand against her forehead and looked out the window. "Oy, should I only know! I come back in to talk to Harry." She laid the hand against her cheek and shook her head. "She is gone!"

Santiago slid his cup to the side. "How long ago was this?"

"Vell, you know yourself. Ven you vave at me. Two, three hour? I don't know."

"You mean to tell me that when I waved at you she was sitting on the bench behind the van?"

"Vell, yes. I didn't know she vas lost."

"I know you didn't. May I use your phone?"

Mrs. Kirschbaum pointed toward the phone on the wall, "Use. Use. Go."

Santiago went to the phone, lifted the receiver, and proceeded to dial. He looked over at Becca and Mrs. Kirschbaum. "I've got to find out if there's any more information. He turned back and stared at the touch pad of the phone. "Come on, connect!"

Mrs. Kirschbaum stroked Becca's hand and talked to her in a soothing and reassuring voice. "And vat a goot mommy. You know, she vouldn't comink in the deli because ve vas stranger. You teach vell. Goot mom."

Becca frowned and sighed. "Not so good mom. We can't find her."

Mrs. Kirschbaum patted Becca's hand, "Oh, you find, you find!"

Santiago replaced the receiver and came back to the table. "She's right. The radio station's busy. I suggest we go over there. They might have some information we don't." He offered his hand to Becca, who was sliding out of the booth. "Thanks, Mrs. Kirschbaum."

Mrs. Kirschbaum put her hand up. "Vate. I give you sumsink to go for das cold wetter out there." She went to the counter, took the glass coffee pot from the burner, and poured the hot liquid into two Styrofoam cups. She retrieved two plastic lids from the basket beneath the counter and scrunched them on the top of the cups. She came back carrying the cups and handed one each to Becca and Santiago. "Here. You takink coffee mit you. Ve gotta know vat happen. Tell you vat. All you people lookink, you need coffee. You come here. Ve stayink open. Harry?"

Harry put the bowl on the counter and looked over the rim of his glasses. "For the little child?"

Mrs. Kirschbaum scowled. "Yes, the little girl."

"Vel then, ve stay open."

She raised her eyes to the heavens and continued, "Oy! Please. You needink coffee? Sanviches? You come back! Ve gonna stay open, right, Harry?"

"Of course! Ve stay open all night if necessary. Ve vill do vatever it takes to brink das little girl back to her mama. I go and start makink some more sanviches."

Becca was ready to open the door, but turned. "You're a sweet lady. Thank you very much."

Mrs. Kirschbaum waved as they both left to get into the cruiser. "Go! You find!"

Santiago called over his shoulder as he opened the door for Becca, "Thank you, Mrs. Kirschbaum."

Mrs. Kirschbaum yelled at him with a shooing motion. "Find, Santiago de Chile! Find!"

Chapter Twenty-Four

Reverend Woods surveyed the mess of papers and tracked-in footprints on the floor. He unbuttoned his cuffs and rolled his sleeves up above his elbows, and then he reached for the broom leaning against the chair in the aisle and started to sweep along with several of the elders. "What's so funny over there?"

"Nothin', brother. Just talking about tonight's pageant and its little screw ups." Reverend Woods picked up a glove, put it on the chair, and continued sweeping the paper into the center of the aisle while half listening to one of the elders.

"And then when the angel of God was supposed to announce the birth, she says, 'I don't want to, I don't want to,' and everybody heard it. I thought we'd lost it all then. I mean, when the angels ain't interested, who is?"

Everyone laughed.

"And then did you see when baby Jesus grabbed the ear of the lamb? I thought he was goin' to pull that little kid's costume right off his head."

One of the elders stopped sweeping and leaned on his broom. "Well, what about when the kid carrying the star on stage for the wise men to follow looked at the audience, got scared, threw the star at the front row, and walked back off stage crying?"

Out of the corner of his eye, Reverend Woods saw a big, imposing black woman coming toward him with a stack of papers in her hand.

"Reverend Woods."

He stopped sweeping and straightened. "What is it, Aunt Pearl?"

She put one hand on her hip and stood in the path of his sweeping. "Reverend, I'm all done. Everything's all accounted for, and I'm happy to say we done even better this year than last. But we gonna have to get a whole new church house just for the pageant next year. I mean, there wasn't enough room for a mouse, much less me." She took the pages and fanned her face. "And it was hot!"

Reverend Woods unbuttoned his collar. "Yes, it was, Aunt Pearl."

She continued to fan herself with a brisk staccato motion. "Why they don't make a fan big enough to cool me off when I'm hot? If hell is half that hot, I don't wanna go."

Reverend Woods looked to the heavens. "Amen, sister."

"And I do believe the only air conditioner in that great beyond is with Jesus, Reverend."

"I believe that's a good way to look at it, Aunt Pearl. And thank you for all your good work tonight."

Reverend Woods paused, temporarily distracted by his father's sweeping two rows away. "And, by the way, Dad, you looked terrific tonight."

Robert Woods smiled and touched his elaborate headdress. "Thanks, son. And I'm keeping the hat."

Everyone started to laugh. One elder stopped. "Brother Robert, that was one stupendous outfit."

He bowed slightly to the group. "It was indeed, brothers and sisters." He started sweeping again.

Aunt Pearl tapped her foot. "Reverend, there's something important I've got to tell you."

"What is it?"

"Oh, Reverend, anybody tell you the police came by just as we was about to start?"

Reverend Woods leaned his broom against a chair and turned to Aunt Pearl, "No. About what?"

"Told us to keep an eye out for a lost little girl named Nickie."

Reverend Woods gasped. "Nickie?"

"Yes, a little white girl, about five years old."

He frowned and held his chin in a cupped hand. "Oh, Lord have mercy!"

Aunt Pearl looked alarmed and held his elbow. "Whooee! What's a matter, Reverend?"

"Aunt Pearl, she was here!"

"Who? The little girl?"

"Yes! Right before the pageant started. I was so...she was with Seth! I better call the police. Any of you men want to form a search party?"

The elders all stopped sweeping and picking up papers and replied like a chorus, "Yes! Sure! You bet! I'll go."

Aunt Pearl put her hands on her hips and glowered. "I don't talk like a man, I don't walk like a man, and I certainly don't look like a man, but I can search just as good as any man born!"

Reverend Woods shook his head and smiled. "Fine, Pearl, fine. Women, too. And think of anybody we might call. I'll see if she's still lost."

He started to walk toward his office. "I knew I should have attended to that little girl. Forgive me, Lord."

Seth came running to him. "Grandpa! Grandpa!" He stopped in front of him panting, out of breath. "They said on the radio that Nickie's lost."

"I know, Seth. We're going to find her."

"Grandpa, do you think she opened her eyes and saw the Holy Host and that's why she's lost?"

Reverend Woods laughed. "No, she just must have wandered off."

"Grandpa, you got to find her. She's my friend. Look, she even gave me her whistle that makes Christmas talk."

"That's a mighty nice gift she gave you."

"Grandpa, here take it. When you find her, you gotta tell her that she has to come back so we can play and make Christmas talk."

He rubbed the top of Seth's head. "Okay, son. I'll make sure she comes back to play." He slipped the whistle into his pocket.

Chapter Twenty-Five

Alexis paced. She stopped and put both hands on the desk and glared. "Come on, Geronimo, answer me."

He turned his back to her. "Thank you, ma'am, we're, like, doin' what we can, okay?…Right. Good-bye." He put down the phone and crossed his arms on the desk. "So, I don't get it. Like, what did you even come over here for?"

Alexis took a rigid, stern stance and crossed her arms. "Didn't you hear that stupid thing he read over the radio?"

Geronimo chuckled. "Yeah, yeah, but it wasn't stupid. He wasn't going to, but I dared him to read it."

Alexis looked at him, stunned. "You did what?"

"Yeah, Alexis, I did. I liked it. Pretty awesome stuff for a little kid. I thought people would like it. They do like it, see?" Geronimo swept his hand over the phone bank, which had every button blinking with callers on hold. "A lot of them called in after your dad read your poem. And you wanna know what? I like your dad, too."

"Yeah, well, he shouldn't have done it without asking; and anyway, he didn't leave you."

"He didn't leave you, either. He only, like, divorced your mom, and he's really cool when you get to know him."

Alexis clenched her fists and stuffed them in her pocket. "Oh! Not this again."

Geronimo stood up. "Yeah, this again. I don't get it. Why are you so pissed off?"

"Okay, well, you don't have to live with him."

"Right, right. And you don't either, babe, or haven't you noticed lately? Haven't for some time, right? Look, I know you don't think much of your old man, okay? Me, I'm workin' fer money. I need it, right? But he's workin' extra shifts tonight. Christmas Eve, babe, so like, everybody else can have the night off with their families, because, like, as he sees it, y'know, he doesn't have one. Get it?"

Geronimo dragged Alexis over to the self-closing door, forcing her to look through the window to see her father talking animatedly into the microphone.   He said in a proud voice, "Look at him in there. He didn't have to do this, any of it. He's workin' hard to find this little kid that's lost, and all you wanna do is dump on him? Wake up, babe. You got a cool old man, and you're the only one who doesn't know it!"

Geronimo turned and saw the phone lines blinking. "I got to answer these, babe. Think about what I said." He picked up the handset and pushed one of the buttons. "WPRA. Can I help you? Yes, we're checkin' out the search for the lost girl."

Alexis chewed her fingernails. She looked at Geronimo, who stared back, pointing to a phone on an adjacent desk while he listened to the caller. She turned back and contemplated her father. She put her hand on the window. "I don't know what to think anymore." She pulled at a hangnail and then with uncertainty walked over to a desk opposite Geronimo. She watched Geronimo and with a little apprehension picked up the phone and pushed a button to answer the next call. "WPRA. How can I help you?"

Alexis and Geronimo were both preoccupied with the endless calls needing to be answered from their accidentally acquired makeshift command post in the lobby of the radio station. They were both intensely involved in conversation with their respective callers, scribbling snippets of notes on legal pads. Suddenly the doorbell rang, and they both jumped at the unanticipated sound.

Alexis heard the persistent *brrring, brrring, brrring* of the doorbell. She looked at Geronimo, who was busy writing notes and wanted to temporarily ignore the interruption. He wedged the receiver tighter between his ear and shoulder to hear better, and without looking up from his paper he waved toward Alexis, motioning her to get the door.

Alexis hurried along her caller. "Okay, okay, gotta go. Bye." She quickly hung up the telephone. She chewed her gum, making a bubble and sucking it back in her mouth to pop. She looked over at Geronimo, who was engrossed in a new call. She stood up and passed his desk. "What do you think I am, your slave or something?"

He put his hand over the mouthpiece. "Will you please just get it?"

She stepped into the foyer and yanked open the outside door without looking through the window. She stretched the gum over her tongue and blew another bubble. When the door opened, she saw Santiago in uniform. She recoiled at the sight of a cop. She popped the bubble, took the gum out of her mouth, and put it in the ashtray by the door. Immediately her feeling changed to guilt and nervousness. She consciously made a mental inventory of her appearance and scrutinized from memory the contents of all her pockets. It was safe.

She opened the door further to reveal that Santiago was not alone. Next to him was a woman. Both of them wore a surprised expression. Alexis thought they must be taken aback by her appearance. She looked at her black fingernails and conjured a mental image of what they must be seeing. Alexis dismissed their shock. After all, the gothic look was seriously cool.

Alexis straightened and with authority turned to Santiago. "What?"

"We're here about a lost little girl."

"Yeah."

"We'd like to talk to everyone involved."

"Yeah."

Annoyed, Santiago took Becca by the arm and stepped toward Alexis into the foyer. "This is the girl's mother, miss."

Alexis looked at Becca and then back to Santiago.

Santiago took off his hat and tucked it under his arm. "Look, miss, this is a serious situation. We need to know if you have any information or clues on this little girl's whereabouts."

"Oh, right!" Alexis opened the door to the lobby. "Come on in. I'll take you to the broadcast booth and you can talk to my da-...uh...the DJ."

Geronimo saw the door open as Alexis held it back. His eyes widened when he saw the uniform. He rolled back his chair and busied himself shuffling pink message slips and thought, "Geez, what're the police doing here?" He raked his fingers through his hair.

Alexis leaned on the desk. "Hey, Geronimo, they're here to talk to my…I mean they're here to talk to Roger. This is the little girl's mom."

Geronimo rolled his chair back to face Becca and Santiago. "Hey, I'm really sorry. We've been getting tons of calls after we aired the story. See? Look at this board. It's been lit like a Christmas tree all night."

Santiago ran his fingers across the buttons and looked around the station. "You got anything, kid?"

"Nothin' much so far, but Roger's been taking calls, too. You may wanna talk to him."

"Sure do. Come on, Becca, let's see what the DJ knows." He walked toward the broadcast booth door.

Alexis looked at Geronimo, who pointed to the door. "Hey, Lex, show some station hospitality and lead the way."

She hurried around Becca and Santiago, reaching the door before them, and opened it. "Well, come in. He's in here."

Geronimo saw them entering the booth and sighed with relief. "Man, I thought they were after me; about gave me a heart attack."

Roger hung up the phone as he flipped through the ad cards in his hand. He was startled and surprised to see Alexis opening the booth door. "Alexis! What a surprise! " For the first time he saw the policeman behind his daughter. His heart sank. Once again he thought she was definitely in trouble. "Alexis, what are you doing here?"

He mumbled to himself, "Oh, no! Not again. Alexis, what kind of trouble did you get yourself into now? I don't need this aggravation today."

Roger stood up and glared at Alexis, but turned to smile at Santiago. "What can I do for you, Officer?"

Santiago put out his hand to shake Roger's. "You're Roger Dodger, eh?"

Roger took his hand and shook it. "Yep! That's me."

Santiago picked up a CD from Roger's desk. "Santana! I love this album."

"It's a throwback to great memories, isn't it?" Roger handed him another CD. "How about this one? *Bare Trees*."

Santiago took the CD and turned it over. "Fleetwood Mac. I listen to you all the time in my cruiser. I'm a big fan."

Roger looked surreptitiously at Alexis, who was annoyed and avoided making any eye contact with him. He thought, "I wonder what she's done?"

Santiago gave him back the two CDs. "Look, you've been broadcasting about a lost little girl, Nickie Halstead?"

"That's right. I've been getting a lot of phone calls in response."

Santiago took Becca's arm and drew her closer. "Here's her mother, Becca." He looked into her eyes. "Becca, this is Roger Dodger."

Roger launched out of his chair to greet Becca and extended his hand. She took it as he put his other hand over it. "Mrs. Halstead. Boy, am I ever sorry for what happened. Come on in here. We're doin' everything we can to help. Have a chair. Here, I'd like to put you on the air. Can we do that? Are you up to it?"

Becca turned to Santiago. "What do you think? Should I do it?"

Santiago gave her a nod. "Well, sure, if it'll help—and I think it will help. The more people understand the situation, the better."

She approached Roger. "Then I'll do it. Tell me what I need to do."

Alexis felt she was not privileged to hear the conversation that was occurring. She quietly left the room, watching the interaction between her father and Becca behind the glass that separated the sound booth from the rest of the office. She looked at him, pensive. "Daddy, you've just got to help them," she whispered.

Roger motioned to Becca. "Sit here and as close as you can to the microphone."

Becca moved the chair and put her elbows on his desk.

He moved the boom closer to where she was sitting. "Good. All right. Here, sit right there...and we'll pull this right up here. See if you can come just a little bit closer."

Roger arranged the mike once more for Becca. "Just stay right where you are while I adjust the feed." He turned his concentration on adjusting the myriad dials on the sound table.

"Okay, Mrs. Halstead."

"Becca, please."

"Okay, Becca, this song is almost over. Are you ready?"

"I think so."

He leaned toward the mike in front of Becca. "Hey, you're listening to the sounds of Christmas on WPRA. Now for an update on the continuing story of little Nickie Halstead, who's been lost." He looked at Becca and gave her a thumbs-up. "We'd like to thank all of our concerned listeners who called in. We're now happy to have with us in the studio little Nickie's mother, Rebecca Halstead."

***

Father McCurdy drove back to the rectory, half listening to the radio in the background while staring at the flakes slamming into his windshield and accumulating on the sides. He turned up the speed of the windshield wipers and the defroster fan just as the announcement aired.

"Oh, Jesus, Mary, and Joseph! What was that?" He reached over to turn down the fan speed to better hear.

Roger's voice boomed out of the speakers. "Welcome, Mrs. Halstead."

Father McCurdy listened to the anxious female voice. "You can call me Becca."

He listened to Roger respond. "Well, happy to have you with us, Becca."

An uncomfortable female voice responded. "Thank you."

Father McCurdy sensed Roger was trying to make his guest feel at ease. "Now we know little Nickie, a blonde five year old, whose birthday is tomorrow, incidentally, was last seen wearing jeans, red boots, and a red coat, right?"

Father McCurdy reached over and turned up the volume. He put his hand over his mouth. "Oh, my! I think I've seen that little girl. Now when was it?"

Becca's voice came through the radio and broke his thoughts. "And a red knit hat, yes."

Roger picked up the conversation on the air. "Yeah. Sadly, she got lost at the mall today. And after that? Bring us up to date, please."

Becca paused. "Well, uh, the best we can figure, she started off toward the Catholic church. Whether she made it or not…"

Father McCurdy talked to himself in despair. "Oh, Lord, give me the strength! What did I do?"

He pulled over to the curb and retrieved his cell phone from inside his coat pocket. He fumbled in his other pocket and pulled out a little address book. He quickly paged through the entries until settling on the number he needed. He looked at the touch pad, quickly dialed the number, and pressed SEND.

An insistent busy signal broadcast through the earpiece. Father McCurdy pondered this obstacle for a moment. He checked his watch, looked in the side mirror for traffic, quickly made a U-turn, and headed toward the radio station.

***

Mrs. Kirschbaum was nervously busying herself in the deli while listening to the radio interview. "Harry, do you believe ve saw das little child?"

Harry stopped wiping the counter. "I know, and now she's lost somever."

"Harry, be kviet. I'm trying to hear vat they sayink." She moved the radio closer. She looked at Harry as they both nodded their heads in silent acknowledgement of the gravity of the situation. They listened solemnly to the unfolding story in which they had had an involvement.

Becca's voice resonated through the speakers and reverberated in the now empty deli. "We don't know, but somehow around that time she got to the Kirschbaums' Deli downtown, where the owner, Mrs. Kirschbaum, was kind enough to give her a muffin, and uh, one to her dog."

Roger paused. "Dog? She has a dog?"

Mrs. Kirschbaum nodded an emphatic "yes" at the voice coming from the radio.

A perplexed Becca filled the silence. "I guess she does now. A kind of a scruffy-looking, smoky gray dog she calls, according to Mrs. Kirschbaum, 'Christmas.'"

Mrs. Kirschbaum quietly confirmed the dog's name in conjunction with Roger. "Christmas, okay."

She became quiet and listened intently to Becca's statement. "Unfortunately, after she left the deli...well, after that, it's a total mystery."

Mrs. Kirschbaum became pensive. "Harry, do you know ver she go from here? I don't rememba."

"I only saw her on the bench feeding the dog."

"Harry, did you see her go? Did she cross the street?"

He shrugged his shoulders. "I don't know."

"Harry, ven vill you pay attention?" She went closer to the radio. "Kviet, Harry. I vant to hear vat he is sayink."

Roger's voice sounded concerned. "The deli downtown? A rough neighborhood or two around there, isn't there?"

Mrs. Kirschbaum threw her hands in the air in mock horror and replied to the speaker, "Vat rough neighborhood, my deli? He is talkink stupid this...this Roger, mm...Hammerstein!

She half heard Becca's anxious response. "Yes, a little spooky."

Mrs. Kirschbaum stared at the speaker. "Vat, spooky? I give her a muffin. Vat is this spooky nonsense? This is a friendly place. Harry did you hear these spooky things? Vat spooky? It's not spooky. Vat kind of vord is spooky?"

"Relax. Vat do they know?" He started to sweep behind the counter.

Roger's voice continued to fill the empty space. "So, listeners, those of you who saw little Nickie at the mall or headed toward the Catholic church, we already have that information. You don't need to call, all right? And this news about the dog we'll explore in a moment."

Harry watched his wife pace in front of the radio, lamenting in Yiddish. He put down the broom and put his arm around her. "It vill be all right. They vill find her."

"Vat if they don't? Then it vill be all my fault. I saw her."

"But you didn't know that the child vas lost."

"I should have known."

"How?"

"*Ich bin eine Mutter.* I should have known. She sat on that bench right there, and I should have asked, 'Ver your mama und papa?'"

Chapter Twenty-Five

He squeezed her shoulder. "You didn't know. She didn't vant to come inside."

"I should have taken her by the hand and made her come." She watched the snow falling outside the window. "Harry, it was only hours ago. I vorry about her…in the dark and mit der *snow*."

"They vill find her, and ve vill do our part to help now. Come, ve have vork to do."

Chapter Twenty-Six

Santiago and Alexis looked through the window and watched Roger busily shuffling his cards to cue what to play next. Santiago turned to Alexis. "So, have any of the callers said more than that, miss?"

"Not to me." She continued staring at her father.

Santiago nodded. "Right."

Geronimo entered the control room and stood next to Becca. "Hey, Mrs. Halstead, sure is a bummer, ma'am. I gotta say this is deep stuff. Sorry, ma'am."

Becca stopped stirring the coffee with the powdered cream that floated random flakes on top of the cup. "Thank you. I really appreciate your concern."

Becca looked over at Santiago, who stood awkwardly nearby. Her eyes met his. He immediately looked down and then over at the window separating the control booth from the broadcast space.

Geronimo picked up a school photo of Nickie that Becca had brought to the radio station and looked at the impish, smiling face. "I mean, looks like she just sorta disappeared...unless, of course, somebody picked her up."

This statement was the one unspoken fear that everyone had suppressed. The mention of it made everybody tense. Geronimo was anxious that he had spoken without thinking. A long silence permeated the room.

Alexis whispered to Geronimo through clenched teeth, "That was way uncool, Geronimo."

Roger looked through the glass of his booth and called to Becca, "I'm ready for you, Mrs. Halstead…uh…Becca."

Becca took a last fearful look at Santiago.

"You're doing fine, Mrs…Becca. Go in there and tell your story. We'll do the rest."

"Thank you, Offi…uh…Santiago. I'm just a little nervous."

"Don't be. You sound like a pro."

"Are we going to find my little Nickie?"

"Yes, we are, one way or another. Now go in there and give us some help."

"Thank you. I'll do my best." She went back into the broadcast booth and sat next to Roger.

Santiago turned to Alexis. "So, you guys just gonna sit around, or we gonna answer some phones?"

Alexis and Geronimo looked at each other and shrugged. They both picked up the closest telephone. Alexis found herself on the producer's handset. From her vantage point she watched her father through the glass.

All of a sudden Santiago's walkie-talkie crackled, and the voice of the dispatcher flooded the room.

"One-Charlie Extra, One-Charlie Extra."

Santiago pushed the button to speak. "One-Charlie Extra, too much static. Lemme get outside. Over." He stepped out the back door in order to minimize the distraction.

The dispatcher paused and picked up a picture of his wife and five-year-old daughter. "Be advised another witness has had contact with the missing juvenile, Nickie Halstead. Subject appeared at the Grace Community Baptist Church and spoke with the pastor, Reverend Michael Woods."

Santiago exhaled and watched his breath condense in the cold. He looked up as snowflakes hit his face and said to himself, "She's really makin' the rounds. Where could she be now?"

The dispatcher was oblivious to Santiago's preoccupation. "Subject reportedly left the property approximately 7 P.M. Destination unknown.

Subject reportedly still accompanied by gray and tan dog of unknown breed."

Santiago spoke into the enveloping night, "The mutt. At least she's not alone."

The dispatcher's voice continued to crash through the silence with an occasional crackle from the speaker. "Witness, the Reverend Woods, is gathering a search party of volunteers. Be advised that the watch commander has approved the volunteer search party. Appoints you to coordinate efforts."

"Okay."

The dispatcher put down the picture. "Where would you like the search party to gather?"

Santiago saw an old station wagon pull alongside his cruiser and park. He watched Father McCurdy get out of the car and walk toward him. He pressed the button to speak to the dispatcher. "Tell 'em to meet me down at the…no, no wait. Tell 'em to come on up to WPRA, the radio station, right away. We'll fan out from here. One-Charlie Extra, clear." He walked toward the priest. "Father McCurdy! What can I do for you?"

"I need to talk to the girl's mother—right away!"

"She's inside the building. The door's propped open. She's either in the control booth or with the DJ." Santiago scrutinized Father McCurdy as he pointed to the building.

"Thank you, Officer. I really need to speak to her."

"Here, Father, I'm sorry for being so curt. It's just a tense situation. I'll take you to her. Come this way."

Santiago and Father McCurdy made their way through the lobby and control room. Santiago opened the door of the broadcast booth just as Roger finished loading a music CD. He observed Roger punching a button and turning down the knob that adjusted the volume.

Father McCurdy fidgeted and with a beseeching look turned and saw Geronimo, Alexis, and Becca in the broadcast booth. He leaned toward Santiago, "I need to talk to the mother."

Santiago pointed at Becca and mouthed, "He wants to talk to you."

Becca nodded and put her cup of coffee on the desk next to the control panel. "I've got to go. He may have news of Nickie." She went around the corner of the control booth. "Father, do you have any information on my little girl?"

"I saw your little girl…a cute little girl. You see, I had prepared my sermon for the midnight mass, and a couple of things were bothering me about it, so I had a quick dinner served by Mrs. Kelly. She's been my helper for twenty-three years. And I decided to quickly deliver a few Christmas trees for the poor of our parish, and you know that trees are much cheaper the day before Christmas. Anyway, I was on my way out, and I saw someone next to the nativity scene. Now last year someone broke a camel and the Virgin Mary, and they even stole one of the sheep, so I'm very nervous about anyone hanging around the nativity scene, especially at night. So I ran over there and slipped on the ice. I almost broke my back, and there she was, laughing at me because she thought my cassock was a dress. Well, actually, we both laughed. You wouldn't believe what she asked me!"

Becca and Roger answered in unison. "What?"

"She asked me if my church was Heaven, if Jesus lived there in the manger scene. I was in a hurry and I misunderstood."

Becca glared at him. "You didn't ask her what she was doing there alone?"

Father McCurdy rubbed his hands and stared at the floor. "Well, I assumed her parents were in the church."

Becca clenched her fists. "Parents don't let their five-year-old children wander outside in freezing weather!"

Father McCurdy stammered. "I'm sorry. I really am. I know how you must feel."

Becca slammed her fist on Roger's desk. "I beg your pardon! How can you say that when you don't have children of your own? How can you say that? How do you know how a mother feels inside? How?"

Roger stole a glance at Alexis, who stood with her mouth open absorbing the drama she was witnessing.

Becca straightened. "Are you saying to me that after a good laugh, you sent this five-year-old child back into the church without checking on her?"

Father McCurdy rubbed the top of his leg. "But there was no way for me to know that…"

Chapter Twenty-Six

Becca came closer. "That what? That she was alone? What about asking her?"

Father McCurdy stepped back. "Well, yes, I could have, but I was so busy."

Becca stepped toward him again as he retreated. "Yes, I know, so busy delivering Christmas trees to your poor and feeling high and mighty about it that you didn't have the time to pay attention to what was happening right under your nose!"

Father McCurdy took out a handkerchief from his pocket and wiped his forehead. "Well, at the time I—"

Becca grabbed the picture of Nickie from Roger's desk and thrust it toward Father McCurdy. "I know, I know. You were busy! My daughter is lost! My only daughter! And my husband left me six months ago! A terrible car accident—gone! To Heaven, right? Nickie is lost and I may never see her again."

Father McCurdy touched the picture. "But she didn't look lost."

Becca yanked the picture back and put it on the table. "You had her right there in your hands, and you sent her away!" Becca started to sob. "It's my little angel. How could you not know that she wasn't with her parents?"

"Mrs. Halstead, I've been praying since the time I found out. I've been praying that God keep her safe and that we find her."

"You've been praying, and then what? You shouldn't have let her go in the first place. She may die out there all alone. In case you didn't notice, it's cold, dark, and snowing out there."

Alexis watched what was transpiring. She slid a can of Coke toward Geronimo. "Hey, have a sip."

Becca paced in front of Roger's desk. "I don't get it! I just don't get it! The day before Christmas, and a little girl, by herself for most of the time, can wander around a mall and the busy streets of a city in America, and no one—not the policemen, not the priests, not the shopkeepers—no one asks her where her mommy is? No one asks her what her phone number is or if she's lost or where her dad is? No one thinks to ask what she's doing all by herself. 'Oh, she was a nice little girl. What a cute little girl.' And can you imagine not a soul is asking what a cute little girl is doing out there in the street all by herself in the freezing cold asking where Heaven is?"

Santiago pushed a tissue box from Roger's desk closer. "Here, Becca."

Hot, angry tears streamed down Becca's cheeks. She took the tissue and wiped her face. "I can't stay here and do nothing." She bolted out of the self-closing doors.

Santiago put on his hat and started to follow Becca. "I've got to help her find her daughter."

Roger stood up and put his glasses on the desk. "Yeah, sure. I'll be here and call you with anything we find out from this end."

"Thanks, I appreciate it." Santiago waved at Roger and sprinted after Becca. "Hey, wait up! Don't go. Let's figure out where we need to look."

"I need to go out and walk a little bit."

"Okay, I'll go with you, and then let's come back here and organize the search."

"Okay. I need the company."

Alexis stood next to Geronimo and watched them leave. "Did you see that mom? She's really scared. And you know what? I'm scared, too. I wouldn't want to be lost in the dark with all that snow, not knowing where to go."

Geronimo placed his hand on the window to the broadcast booth. "You know what?"

"What?"

"Your old man is going to help find her."

"Do you think so?"

Geronimo nodded his head. "I know so. How can you be mad at your dad? Look at him."

Roger came around the desk and handed Father McCurdy a glass of water. "Listen, Father. Thank you for all your help."

Father McCurdy mumbled in a daze, "I was just trying to shed a little more light..." He set the glass down on the desk. "If there's anything I can do, you will call me, won't you?"

Roger Dodger moved closer and said in a soft voice, "Of course, Father. I'm sure she's going to be found...soon!"

Alexis watched her father in silence. She put her hands on the glass of the booth and thought, "Daddy, I know you can help find her."

Roger took the glass from the priest's shaking hands, set it on the table, and escorted him to the door. "She's upset, Father. It's been a tough day for her, y'know?"

Father McCurdy put his hand on the door handle, looking at the floor and then at Roger. "Yes. Well, I had better get back, I…I, uh…I have a mass tonight."

Roger held the door open. "Sure, Father. Let me see you to the door."

Roger motioned to Geronimo to take care of the broadcast booth as he escorted Father McCurdy to the exit. He cracked open the door as blowing snow swirled in. "Thanks again for coming. Every little bit of information makes the trail a little more clear."

Geronimo and Alexis watched through the small window. Alexis saw Father McCurdy look to the heavens holding his hands together and saying what appeared to be a silent prayer. "Do you think everything will be okay?" she asked.

"I hope so. We need to answer these calls. Look at that lit-up board."

"What if it doesn't matter?"

"It matters, Lex. Go over and pick up the phone."

"Are you sure?"

"I'm sure."

Alexis went back to the producer's desk and punched a blinking button. "WPRA, can I help you?"

***

Father McCurdy put on his vestments slowly as he listened to the choir singing from the other side of the door. He smoothed the front of the garment and muttered, "How could I have let that precious child go? I should have checked to see if her parents were in the church."

One of the altar boys adjusted the collar around his neck. "Excuse me, Father. Are you talking to me?"

"No, just to myself, Marc." He smoothed the front of the gold embroidered vestment. "Let's start mass. Come on, Veronique. Go out and light the candles on the altar."

"Okay, Father." She lit the end of the wick on the long lighter and went to the altar, where she stood on tiptoe trying to reach the wicks.

"Marc, go out and see if you can help; you're taller." He looked at his watch. "We need to start mass. We're already ten minutes late."

"Okay, Father."

"How could I have been so careless?"

He looked out from the side of the altar and saw the church was full, with people standing in the aisles and the narthex. "This is my last mass, and all I can think about is the safety of that girl."

He handed a cross on a long pole to another altar boy. "Here, Christopher. It's time to start the procession. Go to the back of the church. I'll be right there."

"Okay, I'll get Michael, too."

"Hurry along. It's time to start." He took the Bible and gave it to Veronique. "Here! It's time to start."

He went to Father Clancy. "Leonard, let's get mass underway. I'm worried about something I've done."

"What have you done?"

"I don't want to talk about it right now. Go and get the altar kids ready for the procession."

"Okay. Just let me know if I can do anything to help."

"You're going to say mass tonight. Now let's get ready."

They walked through the basement to the back of the church. The choir started "Joy to the World." Father McCurdy tapped Marc to start down the aisle with the cross, followed by the other altar boys and girls, along with Father Clancy, who sang in a tenor voice.

Deep in thought, Father McCurdy walked down the aisle behind the procession. He reached the altar and waited for Father Clancy to take his place at the foot of the pulpit stairs. Father McCurdy climbed the circular stairs with the Bible in his hands as if carrying a heavy burden. He opened the big leather-bound Bible on the lectern and stared at the page. He looked down at the crowd and closed the book.

"My friends, my parishioners, brothers and sisters, dear visitors. I had prepared a sermon for you tonight—refined it, rehearsed it. I was hoping it would be stimulating, that it would have made you feel good about yourselves as Christians, good about Christmas, good about making a commitment to Christ, Jesus."

The congregation watched him and listened in silence. The only sound was a baby crying in the back of the church.

"But I am not going to give that speech to you tonight. No, I will not. The truth is I haven't the heart to give it to you."

Father McCurdy looked down, gripped the podium, and paused for several seconds. "And the reason I'm not going to give you this wonderful sermon is because I am not feeling good about myself."

He looked up at the ornately painted ceiling of the church and back down to his parishioners. "You see, tonight I feel like the innkeepers who told Joseph and Mary, who was with child, that there was no room in their inn...because perhaps they looked too poor and humble. I always wondered during my many years as a priest how they must have felt when they realized they'd closed their door in the face of the earthly parents of Christ. Well, tonight I know how they felt."

He folded the pages of his sermon and put them under the Bible. "I don't know how many of you have heard about it, but a five-year-old little girl is lost in the streets of our city tonight. Her name is Nickie Halstead. No one knows where she is, if she's warm or fed, or, most importantly, if she's safe."

Father McCurdy stopped as a murmur emanated from the congregation. "I'm the one who had a chance to see her, talk with her this evening...just a few hours ago. Here! Right out here in front of our church. I spoke to her and then let her go on her way. Of course, I didn't know she was lost. She was just a cute little girl who asked me an innocent question: 'Is this were Jesus lives? Is this Heaven?' She meant our nativity scene, and I gave her the easy answer: 'Yes, Jesus was born in the manger.' And when she, in her innocence, wanted to go there, to Heaven, to the manger...to touch Joseph and Mary and the animals, to look at the manger where baby Jesus was to be lying in the next few hours, I forbade her to touch it. I did! And I sent her away."

Father McCurdy swallowed. "I...I am...a very busy priest, you understand—much to do, many good works to perform for my last Christmas as a priest, since I'm retiring next February, lots to do, my friends, especially on the day before Christmas. And I was too busy being a good Christian and congratulating myself for it to take the time to hear the wishes of a little girl who was searching for Heaven; a little girl who lost her father in a car accident some six months ago and was told her father was not coming back because he was in Heaven with Jesus; a little girl not afraid of the dark or the cold, simply trying to find out where Jesus lived and to ask him to give her back her daddy; a five-year-old little girl who, bravely, on Christmas Eve, was out looking for what she had lost—and I sent her away."

Several women put their hands over their mouths and gasped.

"She is lost. How many of us are lost? Bearing terrible burdens, burdens too heavy to share? How many of you have come to the house of God, as did little Nickie, looking for what you had lost, looking, as was Nickie, for Heaven? You were looking for a word of comfort, a shoulder to lean on, for a message of hope. And when you came here, how many of you heard the wrong message? Yes, yes, Heaven is here. Jesus is here. But don't touch the manger! It's just to look at."

He sighed. "Yes, my dear friends, Jesus is here in our sacraments, in our worship, in our hearts. And the scene outside our church that so attracted little Nickie tells a true story. The story of a humble birth, of a king born in a stable and laid in a manger, because those who were too busy turned weary travelers away from there."

He wiped the tears from his eyes. "You do not need me here tonight, my friends. I'm called to be a shepherd, and tonight I must go seek the one who is lost, the one I turned away."

Father McCurdy turned to go down the steps, paused, and returned to the microphone on the altar. "I have asked Father Clancy to celebrate mass this evening. Afterward, for those who wish to remain and pray, the doors of the church will be open for a vigil. For those who wish to be involved in the search for little Nickie, go to the WPRA radio station. I ask that you all please remember little Nickie Halstead in your prayers tonight. I wish you a merry Christmas, and may God bless you all. Amen."

The congregation replied in unison, "Amen."

He quickly descended from the pulpit. On cue, the organ started and joyous notes spilled from the choir loft. He noticed that many from the congregation were whispering among themselves. Several men quietly stood up and followed Father McCurdy to the sacristy.

Father Clancy watched Father McCurdy leave. With a disquieted uncertainty, he straightened his collar, moved to the center of the altar, and addressed the parishioners. "The Lord be with you."

The congregation replied together, "And also with you."

Father Clancy continued with his arms outstretched. "Brothers and sisters, let us prepare ourselves for these sacred mysteries by bringing before us the spirit of Christmas. Peace in our hearts..." He paused for a moment and resumed. "Lord, have mercy."

The congregation answered, "Lord, have mercy."

Chapter Twenty-Seven

The snow came down in big flakes and settled on Nickie's coat and hat. It was a muffled quiet that surrounded Nickie as she made her way through the woods with the fervor of knowing that soon she would find what she was looking for.

She pointed up the hill. "Look, boy, that's gotta be where Heaven is."

Everything looked like clouds from above had nestled down and enveloped her, yet it was cold and it made her shiver. The snow swirled around her and obscured the trees behind a gauze-like falling veil.

"Come here, Christmas. Stay close."

Christmas played in the snow, burying his nose as he looked for an imaginary rodent that may have hidden under the white blanket. He sensed Nickie wanted him and stopped frolicking. He ran up to her and bumped her leg with his nose.

"Woof!"

She knelt down in the snow and hugged him around the neck. "Christmas, I've gotta rest. Let's just sit for a while. I'm tired."

Christmas sat next to her. He looked into her eyes and then up the hill. "Woof!" He put his paw on her leg. "Woof!"

"What is it, boy? Do you want to keep going?"

"Woof!" He got up wagging his tail and extended his paw to her.

She took his paw. "'Kay, Christmas, let's go."

"Woof!"

Nickie stood up slowly and looked around. "Christmas, everything looks the same. Where do we go, boy?"

The only sign of her progress was when she turned around and saw her footprints and Christmas's tracks crisscrossing her own determined steps. She bent down and took Christmas in her arms. The dog was caked with snowflakes, and while he was cold and wet, he felt reassuring in her arms.

"Well, boy, I guess we can't go that way because that's where we came from."

Christmas wiggled loose from her hug and bounded up the hill. He stopped and turned toward her with his front paws down and his rump in the air. "Woof! Woof!"

Nickie trudged through the snow up to where Christmas waited. She stopped and again sank to her knees. She shivered. "I'm cold, Christmas, and I'm really tired. I hope Heaven is close. We've been walking for an awful long time."

Christmas licked her face, lay down, and put his head in her lap. He nuzzled his nose under her hand.

She patted his head and stood up. She hugged herself and shivered with her teeth chattering. "We gotta go up higher and find my daddy."

Nickie turned around in a circle, looking at the clearing that was surrounded by tall trees. They creaked and murmured with the wind. What were they trying to say?

Nickie slapped her thighs to have Christmas come closer. She stared into the snow that blew all around and stung her eyes. "I'm cold. Daddy...please...I want my daddy."

***

Normally the radio station was dimly lit, but today it was ablaze with lights, broadcasting that something important was unfolding. Cars streamed into the typically vacant parking lot. It appeared the entire town had heard about the little girl and wanted to assist in the search.

Inside, the lights illuminated the perplexing problem of where Becca's daughter might be. Everything seemed to unfold in a hazy slow motion as Becca leaned over the map of the city with magic-marker numbers drawn all over the surface. She only half listened to Santiago, Caroline, and Reverend Woods. She watched Roger talking to all the listeners, coaxing any information about Nickie. She surveyed the scene through the window of the door to the lobby and saw Aunt Pearl, who appeared to be snoozing in a large chair. She felt tired, like Aunt Pearl. It seemed like everyone was tired and trying to draw on an inner energy to figure out where Nickie was.

"White Christmas" played from Roger's selection and served as a solemn backdrop for the quietly constrained conversations occurring in the lobby.

Santiago ran his finger across the map, passing over the mall and the churches in the vicinity. "Well, we have almost every place covered now, unless she just went off in some crazy direction."

Becca looked at the various sites, picturing where they'd already searched and what streets were missed. "I'd like to go back out and search for her. I feel helpless just sitting here."

Caroline overheard the exchange and came toward Becca. "I can take you."

Reverend Woods cleared his throat. "Well, with all due respect, Caroline, Becca needs to be somewhere we can get hold of her quickly."

"You can call me on my cell phone." Becca pulled the black miniature phone from her purse. Just then it rang, and she fumbled to answer it. "Hi, this is Becca."

"Becca, this is Russell. Where are you? And what's happening? Have you found Nickie?"

"No, not yet."

"I know you're going to find her."

"How do you know? It's snowing and dark…"

"I just know she's okay."

"How do you know that?"

"She's your daughter, and she has your tenacity."

"Russell, I don't think that's enough."

"I'm at the office cleaning up from the party. Why don't you let me come and be with you?"

"I'm fine. You need to be at the office in case someone calls. The radio station is giving out the office number, and I want you there to answer it in case they find Nickie."

"Becca, I'll be here and I will call you with any news, but I really think I should be with you and looking for Nickie."

"I know, and I appreciate the gesture, but I'm worried that someone who might have spotted her will call the office."

"Okay, I'll be here, but call me with any news you have."

"I will, and thank you, Russell." Becca snapped the mouthpiece of the cell phone closed.

Santiago extended his hand toward the door. "Right! You wanna go, I'll take ya. We've given everyone the station numbers and the precinct numbers. They've got their areas. That leaves the Reverend, here, without a car, but he can stay and keep an eye on things."

Caroline turned to Becca. "And I can stay, too." She handed Becca her thick ski gloves. "Here, you may need these."

Becca took the gloves, not wanting to be reminded how cold the night was. "Thank you...Caroline, you don't have to..."

Santiago held open the door. "See? Plenty of backup."

Aunt Pearl opened an eye and yawned. "Ain't nobody got to stay when Aunt Pearl is here!"

Reverend Woods smiled at her exuberance. "Amen, sister. As long as you're keeping a watchful eye, everything will turn out all right."

"Darn straight, Reverend. I'm having a little word with the Lord as we speak."

Alexis noticed the tension and anxiety in the radio station. She absently reached for one of the donuts on a tray behind her desk, picked off individual brightly colored sprinkles, and popped them into her mouth. She turned to Geronimo. "Do you think maybe someone's got her?"

"Dunno, babe."

"I mean, she's been out there a long time. Do you think we'll find her?"

Geronimo gave her a broad smile.

Alexis glared. "What are you smiling at?"

"I thought you didn't give a damn about anything. Now you look and act like you're interested."

Alexis threw several candy sprinkles at him. "Look at Mr. Sarcasm here."

"Hey, hey, hey, Lexis, babe. I'm just sayin', y'know, hey! I never thought…I never saw this side of you before, I guess, y'know? And I like it, babe."

Alexis turned her back, blushed, and smiled to herself. "Well, maybe I been keeping it away from target practice, y'know. It kinda feels…oh, I better get outta here! I got Jerry's van, and…" She laughed. "I left him at the Pizza Palace."

Geronimo arched his eyebrows. "Does he know where you are?"

"No, I just took off. He had to pay for the pizza, too."

The shared thought made them both giggle as if punch drunk. Suddenly, the doorbell rang. Alexis gave Geronimo a tired look and rolled her eyes. "Can't we unlock this stupid door?"

"Sure." Geronimo got up and searched for the keys in his pocket. He moved toward the door hesitantly as he saw Roger. "Maybe I should ask your old man."

"Come on, that bell's giving me a headache. I mean, nobody's gonna try and rip off this radio station tonight."

She snatched the keys from his hand, unlocked the door, and yanked it open to find herself face-to-face with the Kirschbaums.

The Kirschbaums were laden with packages that appeared impossible to balance. They both frowned and shook their head in disapproval at the sight of Alexis and Geronimo.

Mrs. Kirschbaum handed several bags to Alexis. "Here, take these and put them on a plate." She brushed her aside and marched into the studio.

Alexis backed against the door to let her pass. "I'm not sure we have any plates."

Mrs. Kirschbaum came back to Alexis and poked one of the bags. "Vell, I vas afraid of that. There's some in here."

Alexis looked at Geronimo and started laughing hysterically, holding her sides.

"Vat is so funny?"

Alexis stifled the laugh. "I don't know. It's just funny. I guess it's because it's so serious in there with this major snowstorm and the lost little girl. I just pictured a table setting for twenty in this brown paper bag."

"Vell, there's enough for tventy in there."

"Oh!" Alexis ducked past Mrs. Kirschbaum and put the bags on the reception desk.

Mrs. Kirschbaum approached Geronimo. "You are Roger the Dodger?"

"Um, no, actually…"

"Goot! You don't lookink like your voice is soundink. You and you…" Mrs. Kirschbaum gestured to Geronimo and then to Alexis, who was staring at her. "Go helpink Harry, my husband. Ve got more out in der car!"

Geronimo was taken aback by the order. "Hey, uh, just a second…"

At that moment Santiago, Becca, Reverend Woods, and Caroline came through the self-closing doors of the broadcast booth.

Mrs. Kirschbaum put both hands on her cheek. "Oy! Becca! Have you any news?"

Becca shook her head. "No, not yet."

"*Ach du meine Liebe!*" She bit her lower lip. "Ve brinkink some food. You must be hungry mit all the vorrying. Ve vait here mit everyvun else until she is found."

She put her hand on Santiago's arm. "Hello, Santiago de Chile. You go and find her. It's dark and mit der snow…"

"Hi, Mrs. K. We're going to go out and keep looking."

"Ve don't closink down mitout ve know about Nickie und the dog. Have you found anysink?"

Santiago frowned. "No, but we have a lot of people out looking."

"Find! Please find das girl!"

Mrs. Kirschbaum took Becca's hand and affectionately kissed it. "But not on empty stomach! Look vat ve brink." She opened the bags and started to pull out wrapped sandwiches and place them on the desk. She wagged her finger at Alexis and Geronimo. "Vat? You still here? Please, DJ's helper, Harry is old, can't brink in the coffee by himself. Go help him."

Geronimo looked at Alexis and shrugged his shoulders. "Coffee?"

"That's right, Roger helper, fresh in the brewer."

Geronimo's eyes lit up. "I'm out of here." He motioned for Alexis to follow him to the parking lot to give assistance.

Mrs. Kirschbaum was full of nervous worry. She unwrapped all the different packages on the table in the lobby. "Look vat ve brinkink—ten pastrami on rye mit cheese, half mit mustard. Ve got lox and bagel, ve got the gefilte fish, ve got knockvurst, livervurst...Here! Macaroni salad, potato salad, strudel und the best cheesecake. Oy! Ve needink a bigger table."

***

Father McCurdy sped back to WPRA in a daze. He still couldn't believe he let Nickie go. The thought preoccupied him from the time he left the church until he pulled up to the station. He plowed his beat-up station wagon into a makeshift space in a snowdrift that surrounded the entrance. As he put the car into park, he saw Becca, Reverend Woods, and Santiago come out from the building. He turned off the ignition.

Santiago was drawn to the lights of Father McCurdy's car. "Hey, somebody else to look. Now we can split up and cover more territory. Reverend Woods, you could go with them and take that one last sector of Gracie Avenue. Oh! Look at that! It's Father McCurdy!"

Santiago looked at Becca. She stared at her feet and then into the dark at the mist coming from her breathing.

"Santiago, I was really mean to him earlier. I was just so angry over his negligence."

Santiago held out his arm. "I'm sure he's forgiven you. Hold on to me so you don't slip. Let's see what he wants."

Reverend Woods watched Father McCurdy get out of the car. He talked to himself, "Well, this ought to be interesting. A white try-to-be-hip Catholic priest with a black get-it-down Baptist minister. Who would have thought we'd end up together on this blessed night?"

Father McCurdy stammered, "I-I would like to help."

Santiago walked Becca to the car and opened the door. "Right, Father. We just about got everything covered. You don't have to—"

Father McCurdy put his hand on the door. "I want to! I want to...."
Father McCurdy turned to Becca. "Mrs. Halstead, I...I don't know that I have words."

Becca put her hand on top of his. "You don't have to apologize, Father. I was upset. I..."

Father McCurdy lowered his eyes. "I know you were upset, but what you said had truth in it. Now I'm here to help."

"I'm sorry, Father. I didn't mean to be hurtful before."

"I know." He took Becca's hands and held them tight. "Mrs. Halstead, I'm praying every minute that we find Nickie."

She squeezed his hands. "I know you are and...it's now in God's hands and whatever we can do. I'm grateful for your help...really." Becca wiped her eyes on the back of the gloves.

Father McCurdy for the first time felt he could make a difference, and he whispered to Becca, "Thank you. Thank you for letting me help. If you want, you can ride with me, and we'll go through all the streets."

Santiago put a protective arm around Becca over the back of the seat. "I think, if you don't mind, I'll keep Mrs. Halstead with me, radio and all." He yanked out a packet from his belt and handed it to Father McCurdy. "Here's my walkie-talkie."

Father McCurdy looked puzzled at the device. "Oh, I have my mobile phone!"

Santiago took it back. "Right! Okay, call the station if you find out anything, and they'll dispatch it to us. So we best get on the road. Come on, Becca." He leaned across her and closed the door.

Becca turned to see Father McCurdy and Reverend Woods look at each other like strangers on a blind date. She rolled down the window. "Good-bye, and thank you both."

Father McCurdy slapped the roof of the cruiser as it passed by them. "Good luck, Becca."

Santiago leaned out the window as they drove by and yelled, "Father McCurdy, take the Reverend with you and call the station on your cell phone if you find anything."

Reverend Woods addressed the priest. "Well, this is going to be an interesting night. You and me, imagine that!"

***

Father McCurdy watched the police car leave along with six other cars that joined the search. For the first time he became fully aware of Reverend Woods. He had always viewed the reverend and his church as competition, a spiritual rival.

They grinned at each other uncomfortably for a moment.

Father McCurdy broke the awkward silence. "Well, we had better get going, eh?" He proceeded to walk to the car and open the door. He turned and saw that Reverend Woods was still rooted to the same place he was before everyone left. He went around to the passenger side door and opened it. "It's pretty ugly, but it runs...and it has a heater...and I've got a phone...and it's better than walking."

Father McCurdy climbed into the driver's side and turned the ignition several times until finally the car sputtered to a start with blue-gray smoke spewing out of the tailpipe.

Reverend Woods flailed at the smoke, trying to clear it away. He walked slowly to the dilapidated car and hesitated. "Is this contraption safe?"

"Of course, it's safe. Now get in if you want to come along." He leaned over to the passenger side. "What's the matter? Got cold feet? Get in, Reverend."

Reverend Woods walked around the car and chuckled. "Man, you actually make forward motion in this rust bucket?"

Father McCurdy glared over the rim of his glasses. "What's bothering you? The color of my face or the fact that I have a dress on?"

Reverend Woods laughed, draped his arm over the passenger side door, and took in the inside of the old car. "I wonder what the good Lord must be thinking at this moment—a white Catholic priest driving in the night with a black Baptist minister at his side. Who's kidnapping whom? Who's converting whom?"

Father McCurdy waved Reverend Woods to get in the car. "Reverend, every minute is precious. Now, are you coming?"

Reverend Woods got in and slammed the door. "Okay, I'm in. Can we get going now?"

Father McCurdy took the back of his glove and wiped off the frost from the inside of the window. "Look, Reverend, if you see anyone from my congregation, can you duck please?"

Reverend Woods slapped the dashboard, laughing. "Likewise, Father, likewise."

The station wagon pulled out of the parking lot with the sound of crunching ice and snow. Father McCurdy turned up the windshield wipers and continued to scrape at the frost. "Man, it's cold out there."

"You know it." Reverend Woods scraped his side of the window. "We've just got to find that little girl. That snow is coming down pretty hard. I can barely see twenty feet in front of the car with the wind and the flakes swirling around."

Father McCurdy inched along, turning off the bright headlights. "I don't know what's better, the low beams or the high beams."

"Turn the low beams back on. At least that way maybe we can see something."

Chapter Twenty-Eight

Nickie partially closed her eyes against the wind as it whipped up ice crystals, stinging her face. She felt the snow fall heavily and blow in spirals, like a freezing whirlwind, slowing her progress. It was a hard struggle to make headway through the deep blanket, where every step seemed to take her last possible ounce of energy.

Nothing had ever felt so cold, and the wind twirled around snowflakes, making everything look unfamiliar. Tears ran down her face as she wiped her nose with the back of her mitten. It was hard to repel the bitter chill. Her teeth chattered, and she forced labored breaths through her lungs. She started to feel sleepy and numb to the cold for the first time.

Christmas was getting tired, too. He pushed his chest through the increasingly deep snow. At his side Nickie stumbled and fell to her knees. She started to cry. Christmas cuddled next to her and gave her his paw. She took it in her hand and looked in his eyes. He whimpered.

Nickie embraced him. "I don't think there's anybody here, Christmas. I'm scared." She started to sob as the dog nudged closer, licking the tears that rolled down her cheeks. He tucked his head under her arm.

Nickie took Christmas by the head, looked into his eyes, and with a tone of resignation said, "I don't think anybody knows where Heaven is."

Christmas snuggled closer and licked the snow off her mittens. He stopped and looked into her eyes.

She again burst into tears. "I'm cold. I want to see my daddy! Christmas, help me find my daddy."

The dog looked toward the top of the hill. "Woof!"

Nickie held Christmas close and rubbed her hands together to try to generate heat. It seemed like the snow blowing around them contained light in each flake.

"Look, Christmas. There's light in the snow."

Christmas cocked his ears and whimpered. He squirmed away from Nickie's grasp and circled her. He looked at the illuminated flakes and tried to catch them in midair.

Nickie shifted her attention in the direction of Christmas's focus. "Do you see it, too?"

There she saw the bright white light. The snow no longer blew around her. Instead it fell softly, accentuating the illumination that grew even more brilliant around them.

"Come here, boy." She held the dog close to her chest, both mesmerized by the intensity. She no longer felt the cold. It was all like a magical dream. She just concentrated on the amazing star-like radiance emanating from between the snowflakes.

Christmas snuggled closer, tucked his head against her neck, and stared into the intensifying glow that filled the night. He licked her ear and whimpered again. Nickie smiled and hugged Christmas's neck. The light grew stronger and enveloped her. Its radiance was warm and inviting, full of love, making everything feel like this was home, where Daddy was. She was drawn into the bright swirling, comforting, star-quality brilliance.

Suddenly, her attention was pulled to the center, which blinded her. She blinked, trying to focus on a silhouette that came toward her. She closed her eyes for just a second, feeling it must be a dream and that it was time to go to sleep. She opened her eyes and smiled. "Do you know where my daddy is?"

***

It felt like the minutes elongated into timeless eras as everyone tried to find Nickie. Patrol cars inched along streets, pointing their search beams down alleys and toward every possible crevice.

No one experienced the passage of anxious slow time more than Roger. "The Little Drummer Boy" played in the background. He wearily pulled some more CDs to queue up. From some remote intuition he was aware of someone standing behind him. He turned to see it was Alexis. He didn't know quite what to say. They hadn't really talked in a while. Roger heard the end of the carol and quickly punched the button to start another song before putting the CD of carols back into the jewel case. "We almost lost Christmas for a minute there."

"I came here to rip into you...for reading that stupid thing I wrote when I was a kid."

Roger opened another jewel case, extracted the CD, and put it into its slot. "First, you're still a kid. Second, it is not stupid. It's a very smart and touching poem for a seven year old with an attitude. Third, it was addressed to me, right? So it's mine, and I'll read it aloud or to myself when and where I want. What else do you have to say?"

Alexis picked up the CD and turned it over to read the song titles. "This is the first Christmas we've been together in a long time."

"Yeah, I guess so."

"Well, I just want you to know that what you're doing here tonight is really great."

Roger reached over and squeezed her arm. "And you're a big help. That's great, too. Are we a team again?"

Alexis blushed. "Uh...I guess. Well, we gotta find that little girl."

Roger leaned back in his chair and stared into the distance, remembering the times they'd shared when she was growing up. He picked up the picture of Nickie that Becca had left behind and touched her face. "Yeah, we do." He got up and put his arm around Alexis. "I want to tell you I'm really proud of you tonight, but don't come in here again with a cop without some forewarning."

"Hey, I didn't do anything."

"Thank God. You about gave me a heart attack."

Alexis looked at the floor and then into his eyes. "Well, I guess I just wanted to say...um... merry Christmas."

Roger felt his eyes water. He took her in his arms and whispered. "Merry Christmas to you, too, honey."

Alexis pulled away and smiled at him. "Well, I guess I got to go back to work answering the phones."

"Alexis, before you go…" He paused and picked up the picture of his daughter and the photograph of Nickie. "You know, by sheer coincidence, I just happen to have two frozen turkey dinners at home. How about eating them together Christmas Day?"

Alexis put her hand on the door handle. "Frozen turkey dinner? I'm…I…I'll think about it."

Roger watched her walk out the door of the broadcast booth. He put down the photos. "Well, Alexis, it might not be a big homemade turkey, but I'm happy we might be together for Christmas."

Alexis walked back into the lobby and began nibbling at the feast Mrs. Kirschbaum had spread on two long folding tables butted together like a banquet display. She picked up half of a Reuben sandwich. "Hey, Geronimo, want a bite?"

"Later, babe. I'm on this call. Can you answer the other line?"

"Yeah, I'll get it, but who can hear with Mr. K. snoring like that?"

"He kinda took over the couch and crashed."

Alexis took a bite, picked up the phone, and plugged her free ear. "WPRA."

Aunt Pearl and Mrs. Kirschbaum sat in office swivel chairs, bouncing them like rocking chairs. Mrs. Kirschbaum couldn't contain her nervous energy and knit furiously in time with the syncopation of her rocking.

Aunt Pearl stopped rocking. "What Nickie needs is her mama!"

"Oy! Vat they all need is a mama! Look at Harry. From the time I marry this man, I am his mama."

"Honey, do you love that man?"

"Vat you mean, love? I take care of him."

Aunt Pearl laughed and pulled her chair closer. "No, no, no. I mean, do you love your man, girl?"

Mrs. Kirschbaum looked at Harry asleep on the couch and felt a tenderness toward him. "I vork every day mit him. I fight mit him. I dress him, or he vears the wrong socks. Look at him there, sleepink like a baby, keepink the neighborhood avake mit his snorink. And you know vat? Ven he is not snorink beside me, I'm not sleepink!"

Aunt Pearl leaned toward Mrs. Kirschbaum and patted her hand. "Now, that is love, honey. That's *real* love!"

Chapter Twenty-Nine

The neighborhoods were like an endless maze. Father McCurdy drove slowly. Suddenly, the light turned red, and he stepped full force on the brake pedal as a white elderly couple entered the crosswalk. The couple recognized Father McCurdy and waved. He smiled at the two.

"Hurry! Duck! These are my parishioners." He pulled on Reverend Woods's coat. "Get down and out of sight before they see you."

Reverend Woods chuckled. "Why?"

"Because. Just do it now!"

Without thinking, Reverend Woods slid down in the seat to make himself invisible to the outside. "This is crazy."

"Oh, no! The Johnsons!" Father McCurdy opened the window and waved. "Merry Christmas. God bless you."

At that moment the light turned green and Father McCurdy floored the accelerator of the station wagon. "We got to get out of here. You can sit up now." At that instant he swerved to miss a passing dog.

Reverend Woods laughed hysterically. "Slow down, Father. You're gonna get us seein' the Maker before our time."

Father McCurdy reclaimed his composure. "What's so funny?"

Reverend Woods put his hands on the dashboard and continued to laugh. "I don't know who's more in need of a blessing—us, that elderly couple, or the dog crossing the street. You almost killed that animal! Come on. Oh! Watch out! I can see some of my brothers and sisters crossing at this intersection."

As Father McCurdy recovered and hurled down the street, he saw an elderly black couple step off the pavement and instantly step back to give passage to the car. Reverend Woods waved at them. He put his hand on Father McCurdy's head and pushed it down. "Scoot lower. I don't want them to see you."

"Hey, what are you doing?" Father McCurdy turned the wheel, hit the curb, and nearly smashed into a tree. He lay with his head on the old padding of the car, facing the ancient floorboards, and laughed uncontrollably.

Reverend Woods looked at him incredulously. "What's so funny?"

"This is so ridiculous! Can you imagine the traffic in Heaven if we were both in the same car?"

"You're the one driving! I'm only a passenger. You'd get the ticket."

They both chuckled and drove on in silence watching the snow fall in the headlights. Father McCurdy slowed to fifteen miles per hour so they could see anything in the doorways and alleys. He wiped the fog from the window with his coat sleeve and turned up the defroster fan. "You know, Reverend, I've been making an idiot of myself since around five last evening."

"And why is that?"

"Since it's almost two o'clock in the morning, I'm going to regain my sanity and apologize to you."

Reverend Woods leaned against the passenger door and crossed his arms. "For what, may I inquire?"

"For being an idiot and an old bigot."

"You are not an idiot—but you are old."

Father McCurdy stared out at the falling snow. "What about the bigot?"

"What about it? Are we so perfect? Aren't we all children of God with all our imperfections? Don't beat on yourself, Father McCurdy. I'm far from being a saint myself."

Father McCurdy gripped the steering wheel and wiped the side window. "George."

"What?"

"Call me George. Let's drop this Father-Reverend baloney."

Reverend Woods put his hand up in the air. "Michael. My name is Michael. Gimme five, George!"

They slapped their hands together over their heads.

***

The cruiser worked its way down the silent suburban street. Some houses still had on their Christmas lights, even though it was well past midnight. It added a glow and yet reminded them of the absence of Nickie. Santiago and Becca searched their respective sides of the street, hoping for any small sign.

Becca took off her gloves and put them on the dashboard. She stared at the police radio, willing some news of her little girl. "Santiago, you've been around long enough to know. How does this look?"

Santiago turned left and focused his search light at a door front. "Look."

Becca looked in the direction of the light. "What are my chances, really?"

"Boy, that's a tough one, Becca. There are so many possibilities. I've seen a lot worse."

"But you've seen better?"

"Okay, you wanna know. I say she'll be fine if she made it indoors. Chances are somebody's found her. Somebody who doesn't know—"

Suddenly, the cell phone rang. Becca rummaged through her purse, pulled it out, and punched the green button. "This is Becca."

"Hi, this is Russell. Have you got any news on Nickie?"

She stared out the window. "No, nothing yet."

"Is there anything I can do? Let me come help."

"I wouldn't know where to tell you to go. We just don't know anything yet. Russell, I'm so worried. It's so cold and dark out there."

"I know, Becca. I'll stay at the office in case anybody calls with any information. They've been giving this number on the radio and we've gotten a couple of calls, but nothing of substance."

"Thanks, Russell, but it's Christmas and it's late. You should go home."

"Remember, I'm single. There's nothing urgent waiting for me at home."

"Then maybe we need to do something about being home alone on Christmas once we find her. Say a prayer that Nickie is all right."

"Consider it done. I'll stay here, though, just in case we get a call about her. You know I love her."

"I know. We all do." She hung up the phone.

***

Father McCurdy and Reverend Woods rode slowly through the street, scouring the blocks on both sides. There was a tense seriousness between them. Father McCurdy cracked the window open to help get rid of the fog on the windshield. "I know what you're thinking about, Michael."

Reverend Woods nodded in agreement. "We both know the danger of a little girl alone in the street, but this isn't New York City."

"I know. Nevertheless, there are so many sick people, so many perverts. I couldn't bring that up in front of the mother. I'm really worried. When I think I had her with me alive and well…"

"Don't blame yourself. I gave her and my grandson a blessing."

"You have a grandson?"

"Yep! And a smart, cute one." Suddenly, Reverend Woods's face lit up. He turned to Father McCurdy. "What are you doing on Christmas Day, George?"

"I rest. I'm exhausted from the preparations and all the tasks."

"I mean socially. Do you go anywhere? Does anybody invite you for a well-deserved Christmas dinner or anything?"

"Everybody in my parish has always thought I was invited by somebody, somewhere. In all truth, I've never been invited anywhere on Christmas Day."

"Incredible! Well, George, would you like to taste a turkey with my family on Christmas Day, surrounded by grandchildren and flying peas and carrots? Would you also give me the immense pleasure of blessing the food, because if my spies are right, you Catholics also bless the food before eating it, right?"

Father McCurdy smiled and nodded. He put his hand on the seat next to Reverend Woods who saw the gesture and put his own hand over Father McCurdy's. They both smiled at each other as Father McCurdy drove slowly down the street. "I'm grateful for your generous invitation. I accept. Thanks, Michael." Father McCurdy grinned. "Will I be the only white around the table?"

"Yes! You and the turkey."

They both laughed just as they passed a patrol car. The officer waved at them to stop. Father McCurdy braked and saw that the police car was backing up to be even with him. The policeman rolled down his window as Father McCurdy opened his own.

"Seen anything, Father?"

"Nope, Officer. Nothing."

"Hope she's safe and sound."

Father McCurdy touched the rosary in his pocket. "Hope so, too."

Father McCurdy closed the window and took the car out of park and shifted back into drive. His hands trembled as he thought, "Dear God, where is Nickie? Don't let any harm come to her." He muttered, "And Jesus said, 'See that you do not despise these little ones, for I tell you that in Heaven their angels always behold the face of my Father, who is in Heaven.'"

Reverend Woods stared out the window into the night. "It is not the will of my Father who is in Heaven that one of these little ones should perish...Matthew 18:10."

"Thank you, Michael. I feel much better."

All of a sudden, Reverend Woods jumped up in his seat and shouted, "The mountain! When I gave her a blessing, I told her about the mountain. The girl was looking for Heaven. Thank you, Lord!" He turned to Father McCurdy. "Gimme your phone!"

***

Santiago and Becca rode in silence, each deep in thought and neither wanting to articulate the worst—Nickie might not be alive. They both were startled when the police radio crackled to life.

The dispatcher's voice filled the space. "One-Charlie Extra, One-Charlie Extra. Come in, please."

Santiago grabbed the microphone and dropped it out of excitement. He fumbled around Becca's feet trying to recover it. "One-Charlie Extra." Santiago released the button to hear the dispatcher.

"Be advised witness Reverend Woods remembers telling the search subject that, quote, 'God is on the mountain.'"

Becca and Santiago exchanged glances.

Becca grabbed the sleeve of Santiago's coat. "Oh, God! She's been outdoors all this time!"

The radio crackled again. "Reverend Woods asks you to meet him on Winslow Drive immediately. That's all."

"Got it. We're on the way." Santiago made a U-turn and headed toward the hill. He reached over and flipped on his lights.

The dispatcher picked up the picture of his daughter from his desk. "And good luck, you guys…from all of us here….Dispatch clear!"

Santiago saw Father McCurdy's car in the distance, parked just beyond the last house on the block. He pulled in behind it, put the car in park, and turned off the engine.

The station wagon lights were on bright. Santiago walked around the car and saw Father McCurdy and Reverend Woods crouched in the snow, as they studied the ground in the beam of the headlights, looking at footprints.

Becca leaped out of the police car and ran toward them. She looked at the marks and then at them. "Did you find her?"

Father McCurdy looked at her and pointed at the snow. "Not yet, but look at these tracks."

Reverend Woods stood up. "A child and a dog. And look at that!" He pointed down the slight incline and down the street at the footprints that led straight to his church two blocks away.

Becca was scared and shouted at the men. "The Church! Oh, no! She's been out here since the pageant! Nickie! *Nickie!* You've got to be kidding. She'll freeze out here." Panic-stricken, Becca ran off toward the mountain, following the footprints. Santiago, Father McCurdy, and Reverend Woods quickly joined in, trying to keep pace with her in the deep snow.

Santiago heard two more cars pull up behind him. He turned and saw four more men jump out to assist. He waved at them to follow. "Come on! Just follow the kid's footprints and the dog's."

Adrenalin pushed Becca forward at a fast pace. The tears and snow blinded her. She yelled, cupping her hands around her mouth. *"Nickie! Nickie!"* She slipped several times in the heavy snow on the steep incline.

Santiago, Father McCurdy, Reverend Woods, and the other searchers tried to keep up, but soon found themselves falling behind.

Father McCurdy stopped, exhausted. He bent over to support himself with his hands on his knees to catch his breath.

Reverend Woods stopped with Father McCurdy and put his arm around him. "Hey, let's rest a little. I'm getting tired, too, and I'm not going to leave you here."

"Okay, but we can only stop for a minute. We've got to help find her."

Chapter Thirty

Becca sank almost to her knees as she plowed through the deep snow, her attention focused on the footprints. "I have to find my Nickie," she said to the trees. "Come on tell me, where is she?" She turned around three hundred and sixty degrees, wondering where to go next.

Reverend Woods looked up the hill and traced Becca's path. "We better keep going, George."

Father McCurdy stood up, brushed the snow off his legs, and touched the outline of a paw print. "Okay, let's go. I'm ready."

Reverend Woods took off his glove and reached in his pocket for a tissue. He felt the whistle and pulled it out. "Hey, my grandson said this whistle makes Christmas talk. I'm going to give it a try. It can't hurt." He put the whistle to his lips and blew three times. From up the hill he heard a dog bark.

Becca heard the whistle and a sudden rustling noise from within the bushes.

"Woof!"

She called out in the direction of the bark. "Nickie! Nickie?"

"Woof! Woof!"

From behind Becca and below where she stood, she heard the others call out, "Nickie! Nickie!"

Becca pointed her flashlight at the bushes, searching where the sound had come from. She then spotted something that was pale gray and almost blended with the trees. It was a dog. She approached him, slightly wary. "Are you Nickie's friend?"

The dog cocked his head, sat, and simply stared at Becca.

"Are you…Christmas? Are you?"

At the sound of his name the dog whimpered and wagged his tail.

Becca knelt down to his level and took his head in her hands. "Where's Nickie, Christmas? Where's Nickie?"

Christmas whined and ran away from the trail of tracks. Becca looked at the dog and down at the footprints trying to decide which way to go. Christmas ran back to her, barked sharply, and once again turned and loped off in the same direction.

"What are you trying tell me, boy? Do you want me to go with you?"

He bounded back, nudged her leg with his nose, and ran up the hill. "Woof!"

"Okay, Christmas, I'm coming. Show me where Nickie is. Show me!"

Father McCurdy, Reverend Woods, and the others caught up with Santiago, who looked puzzled over the divided tracks in the snow.

Santiago shouted. "Rebecca! Where are you?"

Reverend Woods added his voice. "Mrs. Halstead!"

Becca heard them in the distance and yelled back. "I'm with the dog!"

Santiago cupped his hands to amplify his voice. "You found the dog? Great! We're close. We're real close."

Santiago pulled a flashlight from his pocket and handed it to Father McCurdy and Reverend Woods. "We'll follow the mother's tracks and the dog's." He motioned to the other group. "The rest of you fan out that way. Look for double tracks."

Everyone moved quickly on their appointed routes.

When Becca topped the ridge, she found Christmas lying next to Nickie's resting place with his paw on her chest. He looked at Becca and licked Nickie's face. Nickie was covered in snow, and looked like a little mound with only her feet and her face sticking out of the white. Becca saw that part of her body was still visible where the dog had lain up against her.

She screamed at the snowy bundle. "*Nickie*! Oh, Nickie!"

Becca ran toward Nickie, tearing off her coat as she rushed toward her. She knelt down and brushed the snow off Nickie's body and wrapped her in the coat. She shook the limp little body. "Wake up! Wake up, Nickie! It's mommy. Wake up!" She pulled her body close and screamed. "Wake up! Oh, no! Oh, no! *Oh! No*! Angel, wake up. It's mommy." She put her cheek next to Nickie's mouth to see if she was breathing. She started to cry. "Nickie, don't leave me. Come on! Breathe for mommy. Breathe!"

She wrapped the coat around Nickie tighter and held her closer. She cried out into the night, rocking Nickie in her arms. *"No!"*

Everyone stopped as they heard Becca's cry reverberate over the hill and echo in the valley.

Father McCurdy fell to his knees in the snow and made the sign of the cross. "Please, Father, spare this little innocent girl...I made a grave mistake."

Reverend Woods bowed his head and put his hands together in prayer on his lap. "We both made a mistake."

Santiago took off his hat and covered his eyes with his hand, trying to stop the tears that were threatening to spill out.

The other searchers were still and stood quietly in the distance. They looked at each other with sadness and resignation, lowering their heads as one of the searchers said in a low voice to the one standing next to him, "Man, we're too late...I can't believe it...we're too late."

Becca held Nickie close and rocked her like when she was a baby. Suddenly, she felt a little hand touching the tears that rolled down her cheek in a stream.

Nickie looked up into Becca's eyes. "Mommy, why are you crying? I was only sleeping."

Becca was in shock. She held Nickie tightly against her. "Oh, God! Nickie, oh, Nickie!" Becca couldn't stop the new flood of tears. She looked up at the heavens and gathered Nickie in her arms to carry her down the mountain. She shouted as loud as she could, "She's alive! Thank God, she's alive!"

The message echoed through the hills, reaching Father McCurdy, Reverend Woods, and Santiago. They looked at each other in disbelief.

Reverend Woods put his arms around Father McCurdy and Santiago. "She's alive, George. She's alive."

Father McCurdy folded his hands in prayer. "Thanks to the Lord!"

Reverend Woods stretched out his arms to the heavens. "Hallelujah! It's a miracle!"

Through teary eyes, Santiago nodded and watched up the hill for Becca. "*Gracias, madre de Dios!*"

Chapter Thirty-One

Roger sat quietly in the booth with his shoulders stooped. He was feeling tired, but it was an unsettled, anxious weariness. He looked up and saw a bleary-eyed Geronimo sitting next to Alexis in the control room, each propped up against the other. Both were quiet. Caroline had fallen asleep on the floor next to them. Everything was tensely subdued with the exception of "Hark! The Herald Angels Sing" playing in the background. All of a sudden, the phone rang.

Alexis was the closest and jumped to answer it. She listened intently and pulled on Geronimo's shirt, excited. "They got her! They got her!"

She turned her attention back to the receiver and listened intently while everyone held their breath. "Yes, I understand, and thank you." Alexis put the phone back in the cradle and flung herself at Geronimo. "She's alive! She made it!"

Geronimo couldn't contain the feeling of relief and happiness. He began leaping up and down in celebration.

Caroline woke up. "What! What's happening?"

Alexis held out her hands and pulled her up. "She's okay. She's alive."

Caroline looked over at Geronimo and then back at Alexis and said through tears, "They…she…she…I can't believe it!"

"I gotta go tell my dad." Alexis ran toward the booth. Roger put another Christmas CD in the slot.

"Dad, it's amazing!"

He looked over the rims of his glasses. "What is, honey?"

She ran to him and threw her arms around his neck. "Oh, Daddy. Oh, Daddy, they found her alive!"

Roger hugged her tight for a moment. A few tears escaped and he muttered, "I'm so glad. I found you again, too." He lingered for a few seconds as the phone started to ring. He held his daughter and answered the telephone. "WPRA."

***

Aunt Pearl and Mrs. Kirschbaum were asleep in two office swivel chairs while Harry snored on the sofa. Several people who had heard the announcement of a missing child and volunteered to help were asleep on the floor, while others sat against the wall too tired and anxious to sleep.

Geronimo rushed into the lobby. He shook the ladies and announced, "It's all over. They found her! She's *alive*! Man! I mean it! *Alive!*"

Caroline pushed through the door. "Wake up, everybody! We've got some celebrating to do. Nickie has been found and is okay."

Mrs. Kirschbaum rubbed her eyes. "Vell, vat goot news! They found *das* child. Harry, vake up! They found the little girl." She went over and shook him. "Harry, vake up! They found the girl. Vat goot luck , Harry. Little Nickie is alive."

Harry sat up and put on his glasses. "Vat are you sayink? I go back to sleep."

"Harry, they found her and she's all right."

Harry Kirschbaum woke up slowly. He sat up on the edge of the couch and saw everyone dancing about. He wasn't sure why everyone was singing. He took a chance at joining in the fun. "*L'chaim! Mazel tov!*"

Aunt Pearl raised her arms to the heavens. "Praise the Lord, sweet Jesus!" She began singing "Hallelujah" as the sleepy members of the choir joined in.

Caught up in the spirit of relief and happiness, Mrs. Kirschbaum clapped in time with the music and laughed at Geronimo, who was rocking with the beat. She wagged her finger at him. "That vas a goot job you did tonight. That girl was found because you helped."

"Thanks, I appreciate it, but we all helped. Can I have another one of your bagels with lox?"

"Go have some more. You too skinny. Go!" Mrs. Kirschbaum felt the draft as the entrance door opened. A shabby-looking bag lady walked in. Mrs. Kirschbaum scrutinized her. "And vu are you?"

"Elizabeth! Queen of England!" shouted the bag lady over the singing and strutted into the room. She looked around the lobby. "I was listening to the radio in my box...heard about the lost little girl."

Mrs. Kirschbaum took her aside. "You friend of Becca?"

"Oh, don't know Becca, but I told Nickie where Heaven was. Whoa! I smell food here!" She pulled back from Mrs. Kirschbaum, sniffing toward the buffet tables.

The bag lady stared at Mrs. Kirschbaum, mimicking her. "And vu are you?"

"I am the delicatessen on South Street; and you, friend of Nickie?"

"I am."

"You a friend of Nickie then you schtop in my deli, I give you free coffee...anytime!"

"Thanks. That's nice. You're kinda neat!"

"No, I am Jewish."

Mrs. Kirschbaum turned and resumed clapping her hands out of sync with the music.

Mrs. Kirschbaum and Aunt Pearl looked at each other, and then Mrs. Kirschbaum turned to laugh at Harry. "Harry, you ver dreamink. Vake up! Vee have a great zink to celebrate."

"That's right. They found the little girl. I heard that ven I vas sleepink."

Roger heard the sound of celebration in the lobby, which now filtered in as background to his broadcast.

He turned to the microphone. "For those of you still awake on this Christmas morning, we have some celebrating to do. This has been quite a day, uh, night, I guess...not the kind of thing you wish for the night before Christmas."

Chapter Thirty-Two

Roger's voice resounded through the car radio as Becca opened the door. She turned back for Nickie while a doctor and two nurses pushed her wheelchair to the car. "Thank you so much, doctor."

"You're welcome, Mrs. Halstead. That's one brave little girl. I still don't understand why she doesn't have any frostbite. Her pulse is regular. She has no sign of congestion. No hypothermia. Bring her back in a couple of days for a final checkup."

Nickie stood up to get in the car as the two nurses hugged her tight. "Bye, Nickie."

Becca stroked Nickie's head. "Doctor, I know she's brave. Are you sure there's no frostbite?"

The doctor moved toward the door and took Nickie's hand. "I'm sure there's absolutely no sign of it. Now you need to go home, put her to bed, and let her sleep as long as she needs to. She's had a long, traumatic night."

Christmas jumped in the back seat and cuddled next to Nickie, putting his head on her lap.

Becca put out her hand. "Thank you, Doctor!"

"She's fine, Mrs. Halstead. You can relax."

Becca buckled Nickie's seatbelt and got in the driver's seat. She adjusted the rearview mirror to see Nickie. "Hey, my little angel, are you tired?"

Nickie scratched behind Christmas's ears. "A little bit, Mommy."

"Well, we'll be home soon."

"'Kay."

Becca was startled by the knock on the window.

Russell brushed the snow off the front of the windshield. "It's me. Is Nickie all right?"

Becca rolled down the window.

"Russell, what are you doing here? How did you know I was here?" Becca opened the door and stepped out toward Russell.

"I've been trying to figure out where to find you. I heard on the radio that Nickie was found, and when I couldn't reach you, I could only think that you might be here at the hospital. Is she okay?"

"She's fine. No frostbite."

"Where was she?"

"We found her on top of the hill past the Baptist church."

Russell pulled Becca into his arms. "Thank goodness she's alright. Are you okay?"

"Thank you. I'm fine now. Russell, I want you to come for Christmas dinner and her birthday."

"I'd love to. By the way, I have a present for Nickie." Russell walked over to his Jeep, which was parked behind Becca's car, and picked up a shaggy sheepdog made from strips of torn material. He pulled it out for Becca to see. "What do you think? Will Nickie like it?"

Becca smiled. "I don't know. Why don't you come to the house at, say, four and give her your present? Then we can go from there to my sister-in-law's. It looks like Nickie's getting puppies this year."

"What do you mean?"

Becca winked and hugged Russell. "Tell you later."

"Okay, I look forward to it. Safe home."

"Okay, until tomorrow—or actually it's today."

Becca got back in the car and waved at Russell. She reached over and turned up the volume of the radio as Roger's voice filled the car: "But it's a Christmas a good many people in this town will never forget. A day…for a miracle."

Becca wiped a tear with the back of gloves. "Yes, a day for a miracle."

***

Steve Hastings couldn't believe it when they had been cleared for departure and his crew was finally able to leave Chicago. The time had seemed to drag as one creeping delay after another grounded him, thwarting his attempts to get back home and surprise Caroline. He switched on the lights as he walked into the house and deposited a large package on the stool by the counter.

"Hey, Caroline, I made it in time." He sprinted upstairs and into the bedroom but the bed was still made. "Caroline?" He checked the children's rooms, but they were equally empty. "What the…? Where is everybody?"

He went outside to check the cars as the neighbor, Patty Martin, intercepted him in her pajamas. She took him by the arm and escorted him back in the house. "They're not home. Your kids are sound asleep at my house."

"Where's Caroline?"

"Oh, at the radio station with all the people who volunteered to find the little girl."

"What girl?"

"Your niece."

"Nickie?"

"Yeah, that was her name. But they found her just a little while ago. It was on the radio."

Steve deposited the package under the tree and grabbed his car keys. "Patty, thanks for everything." He waved over his shoulder. "Got to go and see if Caroline's okay. We'll get the kids as soon as we get back. Just close the front door."

She waved back at him. "I'll wait up for you."

***

Father McCurdy, Reverend Woods, and Santiago pushed open the door to the lobby of the radio station. They were tired but wanted to make sure for themselves that everyone heard the news.

Santiago took off his hat and put it on the reception desk. "I can see you heard the news."

Mrs. Kirschbaum came forward and took his hands. "Ve heard. Vonderful news! You found our little Nickie."

"We did, Mrs. K."

"Is she all right?"

"She's fine and with her mother."

Geronimo, Mrs. Kirschbaum, Harry, Aunt Pearl, and Caroline encircled each other in a big hug.

Caroline stepped back from the group. "Thank God she's okay."

Mrs. Kirschbaum put her arm through Caroline's. "Ve are very lucky she is safe."

Father McCurdy took out his cell phone, punched the keys, and almost misdialed the number.

Mrs. Kelly answered on the first ring. "Hello?"

Father McCurdy pressed the phone closer to his ear to drown out the celebration noise. "Did you hear? We found her and...she's alive."

"Did I hear?" Mrs. Kelly wiped her eyes on her sleeve. "Oh, my heavens, been doin' a jig in me bathrobe in front of the radio since I heard the news."

"I'll be here at the radio station for a bit longer. Go get some well-deserved sleep and don't bother with an early breakfast. There's a feast here from Kirschbaum's Deli. I'm going to need to fast for a month after this. I'll say goodnight...or actually, good morning."

Mrs. Kelly yawned. "Good night or mornin' to you, too, Father. I can sleep now knowing you found the child. I've been sittin' here in the kitchen frettin' over the wee lass all night."

"Well, go to bed. Everything is fine." Father McCurdy placed the telephone back in the cradle. He looked through the people who milled around talking excitedly. At the other end of the room he saw Reverend Woods and waved at him before making his way through the crowd. They shook hands like two best friends.

Reverend Woods slapped him on the back. "After tonight and with what my family cooks up for Christmas, you are going to be one stuffed Catholic puppy."

"I know. I already told Mrs. Kelly that I was going to be fasting for at least a month."

Mrs. Kirschbaum noticed Santiago. She thought, "Oy! Vat a goot man. Vat is he doink standink by the door?" She reached for a Danish pastry and approached him. "Here, Santiago de Chile, eat a pastry!"

Santiago took the sweets, eyeing the other delicacies on the table. "I want chile con carne."

Mrs. Kirschbaum put her arm through his and laughed. "Ah! Ah! Santiago de Chile...chile con carne! Ah! Ah! Very funny!"

He walked with her to the side of the table, took a bite of the pastry, and with his mouth full bent closer to her ear. "Mrs. Kirschbaum, do you think Maria has plans for Christmas?"

"Vell, go and askink her. I know she's crazy for you. You blind or something? She's near Roger the Dodger!"

Santiago realized Maria was in the room and lowered his eyes. "I didn't know she was here. Why didn't you tell me?"

"Vat, and spoil the zaprize?" Mrs. Kirschbaum crossed the room and twisted her mouth as she passed near Maria. "Go over there and make conversation mit de Chile. He's ready."

Maria turned around and saw Santiago. She prowled toward him like a lioness toward her prey and caught a reflection of herself with shoulder length wavy hair and chiseled features.

Santiago saw her approaching and froze. He slowly chewed the last bite of pastry and swallowed.

Maria reached him. Without a word, she put her arms around his neck and gave him a long kiss on the lips.

Santiago stood there without resisting.

Maria moved back slowly and in a husky voice said, "*Feliz Navidad, mi* Santiago!"

Mrs. Kirschbaum saw Steve Hastings, still in his pilot uniform, enter the lobby. He looked like he was searching for someone.

Mrs. Kirschbaum moved toward him and took him by the arm. "Hello, Mr. Handsome. Vat you looking for?"

Steve answered still searching through the crowd. "I'm looking for Caroline, my wife."

Mrs. Kirschbaum took him by the arm, admiring his pilot's uniform. "Is you vife a friend of Becca's?"

Steve looked for the first time at Mrs. Kirschbaum. "And who are you?"

Mrs. Kirschbaum touched the gold braid on his sleeve. "I'm Mrs. Kirschbaum, the pushy deli owner and maker of the best cheesecake in town; and I vish I vas younger after I see you, Mr. Handsome!"

"I'm Steve Hastings and related to Rebecca. I married her sister-in-law."

Mrs. Kirschbaum took him by the arm and pulled him into the room. "Vell, Mr. Handsome, after you kiss your vife, come to me. I give you the best lox and bagel. You vish you had on your airplane. Oy! Is he gorgeous!"

Caroline saw Steve being propelled by Mrs. Kirschbaum. She just wanted to be in his arms and forget the tense nightmare of the last hours that seemed more like years. She thought how much they had to be grateful for, and how precious and fragile life was.

They ran into each other's arms and held a long embrace while Caroline sobbed quietly into his chest. "Steve…I'm so glad you're home. It's been awful."

"I heard. But she's found, home, and okay."

"But it was all my fault."

"Sh, sh, honey, she's okay. It all turned out all right."

***

Alexis walked slowly behind her father, who was still on the microphone. She put her arms around his shoulders and gave him a long tender hug.

As he prepared to speak the last lines of his broadcast, Roger grabbed her hand and squeezed it tightly. He turned to the microphone. "Little Nickie Halstead, who also has her birthday on Christmas, is five years old today. Nickie, who spent all night at the top of the hill at the edge of the north end of town has been found alive and—miraculously—well, though no one can say just why (I have my own theory on this one) with no frostbite or injury of any kind. For those of you who've followed this story, her dog was found in good shape, too. Well, well, a remarkable night last night and a remarkable early morning. Truly remarkable! I'm going to retire also as the 5:00 A.M. bell is going to ring. I'm going to go home and enjoy my family...."

He paused and pressed Alexis's hand. "What a night! This is Roger Dodger signing off for WPRA and wishing you a merry, merry Christmas."

Roger stared at Geronimo through the window and gave him the peace sign. He pushed the OFF AIR button. "Peace on Earth, dude."

Chapter Thirty-Three

Becca pulled back the blanket and sheet for Nickie, while Christmas dragged a stuffed bear from Nickie's toy box and placed it on the bed.

"Thank you, Christmas. We can share my toys." He pushed the bear closer and wagged his tail.

"You can have another animal."

"Woof!" He went to the box and picked up a stuffed kitten.

Becca tucked the comforter around her daughter's body. "Try to get some sleep, Nickie. And let's put the scarf that the girl gave you on the chair."

Nickie pushed back the covers. "No, Mommy. I want to sleep with the scarf. The nice girl gave it to me, and it kept me warm."

"Okay, but you need to sleep, angel. Santa Claus can't come unless you're asleep."

Nickie gave Becca a faint tired smile. "It's all right if Santa doesn't come, Mommy. I already had my Christmas. I don't need any presents."

Becca kissed her forehead. "What do you mean you don't need any presents?"

Nickie took her arms out from under the blanket and crossed them on top of the scarf. "I don't need any presents."

Becca readjusted the down comforter. "But...it's Christmas...and..."

Nickie patted the mattress. Christmas came closer and put his head on the bed.

"Come here, boy."

He lifted his head when he heard his name, listening attentively. Nickie sat up and braced herself on her elbows and looked at Christmas.

"I already had my Christmas. You let me keep the puppy."

Becca looked at the dog panting next to the bed. She thought he'd look much better after she could give him a bath in the morning. She pushed back Nickie's hair with her fingers and looked at Christmas. "I guess you do have your puppy!"

"And…" Nickie lay back down.

"And what?"

Nickie yawned and closed her eyes, drifting off to sleep. "Something happened when I went to sleep on the mountain."

Becca touched her cheek. "What happened on the mountain?"

Nickie yawned and closed her eyes. "It's a secret."

"I'm your mommy, angel. I won't tell."

Nickie opened her eyes. "I can't. It's personal."

Becca stroked her hair and looked at Christmas, who was rooting through the toy box. "Oh, I see."

Nickie started to sink into a deep sleep. "Only Christmas saw it," she murmured. "Only Christmas can tell."

Becca tucked the covers around Nickie again. "Tell what, angel? Please…"

Becca saw that Nickie was already asleep with a smile on her face. She looked like a little cherub. She thought she hadn't looked so peaceful since before David's death. She touched Nickie's cheeks and looked down at the dog. Christmas stared back at her, panting lightly.

Becca turned to the dog and asked, "What happened up there, boy? Can you talk? Come on!"

"Woof." He wagged his tail.

Becca paused and patted his head. "Nope, I didn't think so. Guess you'll never tell, either."

Deep in thought, Becca approached the bedroom door. She turned back to look at her daughter just in time to see Christmas hop on the bed and settle himself, curled up next to Nickie. She whispered, "Goodnight, Nickie."

She looked toward the ceiling, "Thank you, guardian angel." And then she spoke to Christmas, who looked at her from the corner of his eye. "Goodnight, Christmas, and thanks to you, too."

Becca smiled at the sight of both of them nestled peacefully together. She tiptoed out of the room and quietly closed the door.

***

Nickie was in a sweet dream. She saw that when mommy closed the door, there was a beautiful angel behind the door surrounded by bright radiant light. The angel came and stood next to her bed. She leaned over and gently touched Nickie's cheek and lifted the scarf out of her hands.

Nickie felt something tug at the scarf and woke up. She was startled to see that the girl who had been sitting with her on the bench was standing by her bed, but the girl was surrounded by light. Nickie blinked at her in disbelief. She then tightly scrunched her eyes shut. When she opened them again, the room was filled with millions of white and blue sparkles. When she blinked again, everything was dark except for the gentle glow of the nightlight and a glimmer of a light in the corner of the ceiling.

The light filled the room, embracing her. It felt warm, like the meadow with the big doggie that was her father. She pulled the blanket over her shoulders and whispered, "Night, Daddy."

Acknowledgments

First and foremost, we want to thank Linda Colón. Anyone who is ever contemplating writing anything should have Linda as an editor. She is brilliant in her ability to teach and to polish the story until it reflects what is truly possible. The primary motto that was genetically ingrained by Linda into us is "show, don't tell." And this simple yet powerful concept is something that we want to share with every potential author, courtesy of the literary wisdom imparted by our extraordinary editor.

We give special thanks to Elmar Reiter and Gabriella Reiter who read and reread every iteration of the manuscript and supplied great feedback and suggestions. Many thanks to Christa Nolte for finding the elements that needed better clarification and spotting the details in the story that were overlooked. Also, thanks to JoAnne Morgan, who sifted through all the fine points many times. And thank you to Patty Martin, who gave valuable insight on how the characters were perceived.

About the Authors

Bernadette Reiter is a leading computer scientist. She is an inventor holding several patents and pioneered the field of object-oriented programming through the development of a new programming language. She has been the recipient of many technical achievement awards for creating breakthrough technologies. Due to her in-depth technical expertise, she consults with Fortune 500 companies and government agencies on the future direction of computing and technology strategies. She has also published numerous articles on the legal issues surrounding software. Bernadette lives in Boulder, Colorado, where she creates advanced software and works with Mr. Pélissié writing books.

Jean-Marie Pélissié, French born, spent the first five years of his life in Morocco, where he was the son of the chief of police. He then moved to the south of France, where he studied acting and directing. In 1964 he joined a world-renowned group of performers called the "Singers of Paris." After touring the U.S., he moved permanently to the United States in 1966 and worked in the film industry with Otto Preminger. Mr. Pélissié is an independent film director and writer. He currently lives in Boulder, Colorado, where he is writing two new scripts to be produced by an independent film company.

Giving a Special Gift to a Child

Dear Reader,

The Secret of Christmas captures the essence of the Christmas spirit through the adventures of a child on a special quest to fulfill a Christmas wish. In today's "hurry up", success driven society it's easy to brush aside the children who need our most urgent attention and love.

While this is a novel for adults, 90% of the royalties from *The Secret of Christmas* are being donated to Childhelp USA. Childhelp USA was founded in 1959, as a non-profit, to meet the physical, emotional, educational, and spiritual needs of abused and neglected children.

Thank you for the support you give to a child by buying and reading this book.

Sincerely – and "for the love a child",

Bernadette Reiter &
Jean-Marie Pélissié

P.S. For more information about Childhelp USA go to www.ChildhelpUSA.org.